Wild WINTER

Cricket Starr   Myla Jackson
Mary Winter   TJ Michaels
Liddy Midnight   Ravyn Wilde

ELLORA'S CAVE
ROMANTICA PUBLISHING

PERFECT HERO
Cricket Starr

Melissa doesn't believe in magic, but when a video game character she creates crawls out of her new monitor she has to wonder if her opinion wasn't a bit too hasty.

Bran is happy to be outside of the computer and wants to stay and make lots of passionate love to his lovely creator. He'll do anything, including setting up a magical Christmas, to prove to Melissa that he is the hero she's always wanted.

POLAR HEAT
Mary Winter

Studying polar bears is Norwegian scientist Aud Myhre's passion. The leader of an Arctic research team, she stays in the frozen north over the holidays to obtain necessary data, with help from her sexy colleague Svein. She didn't count on a storm trapping them in a cave with no means of warmth—except each other. Aud struggles to keep their relationship professional, but there's no fighting their combustible sexual chemistry.

Svein Eide has more insight into the lives of polar bears than anyone knows. To keep Aud safe from the storm, he has two choices. Reveal his shapeshifting abilities and lead her back to camp, or find another way to keep her warm. He knows which he'd prefer. Polar bears don't mate for life...but one taste of Aud's passion could disprove that scientific fact.

FINDING THE LIGHT
Liddy Midnight

Dark Mage Moran is mortally wounded in a battle of magickal wills. Seeking a mage to heal him, he instead stumbles into a small village. Moran's work required celibacy. When he awakens in bed with a naked woman, he isn't certain if this is a fevered dream or she is a Yule gift, a reward from the Goddess.

The widow Enid is the only one with room and time to care for him. No mage, she has only a meager supply of herbs—and body heat. She can't resist the temptation presented by the handsome stranger. Yule is a time of celebration and sex represents the foundation of life.

Moran has lost his magick, but mayhap Enid offers something better.

UNHOLY MAGIC
Ravyn Wilde

Franco has loved Tehya almost since the moment they met. But when work calls him away, he realizes he can't return to her, convinced she'd never survive in his world.

His wolf didn't agree.

Tehya misses Franco, but right now she's got bigger problems. She takes it upon herself to investigate strange vibrations coming from the mountains near her cabin, much to the horror of Franco and her family. After all, she's a mere human—as far as they know.

GIFT WRAP OPTIONAL
TJ Michaels

Melaniece is looking forward to spending a nice quiet holiday at her vacation home up in the mountains. Expecting to enjoy ripping open gifts with her family, she's surprised when they spring the ultimate present on her—Michael Bannon. Could his unexpected appearance have anything to do with the strange vampire dreams she's been having lately?

Michael is determined not to blow a second chance with the woman he should have loved years ago, even if it means revealing his true nature. Is a good guy willing to be very bad to get what he wants? Hell, yes…including drive Melaniece out of her mind. Over and over again.

WITCH'S CURSE
Myla Jackson

As punishment for using magic unwisely, Catherine Wein, ex-witch and totally cursed, is doomed to spend each year in a different woman's life. It's New Year's Eve and at the stroke of midnight she'll make the switch to another host. Catherine's determined to grab for as much happiness as she can with her remaining hours in Kindra Merlot's body.

Enter sexy cop Sam Cade. Dumped by his girlfriend right after Christmas, Sam isn't in the mood to celebrate until he sees the willowy beauty Kindra. Her sensuality and sexual aggressiveness revive his lagging spirits. Is she the one for him or is she another lying, cheating woman like his ex? Will he have more than tonight to find out?

An Ellora's Cave Romantica Publication

www.ellorascave.com

Wild Winter

ISBN 9781419956867
ALL RIGHTS RESERVED.
Perfect Hero Copyright © 2006 Cricket Starr
Polar Heat Copyright © 2006 Mary Winter
Finding the Light Copyright © 2006 Liddy Midnight
Unholy Magic Copyright © 2006 Ravyn Wilde
Gift Wrap Optional Copyright © 2006 TJ Michaels
Witch's Curse Copyright © 2006 Myla Jackson
Cover art by Syneca.

This book printed in the U.S.A. by Jasmine–Jade Enterprises, LLC.

Trade paperback Publication January 2008

WILD WINTER

PERFECT HERO
Cricket Starr
~11~

POLAR HEAT
Mary Winter
~65~

FINDING THE LIGHT
Liddy Midnight
~113~

UNHOLY MAGIC
Ravyn Wilde
~169~

GIFT WRAP OPTIONAL
TJ Michaels
~223~

WITCH'S CURSE
Myla Jackson
~277~

PERFECT HERO
Cricket Starr

Chapter One

℘

Melissa Evans didn't believe in magic. In hard work, good gamesmanship and the power of love, but not magic. So when it happened to her she couldn't believe it even though it started as soon as she walked into her cubicle one morning a week before Christmas.

First she stared in disbelief, then she smiled, and finally broke into delighted laughter. A new monitor graced her desk—a new, shiny, *huge* monitor attached to her computer.

She'd been working with a decrepit fifteen-inch monstrosity since being hired six months ago, trying to ignore the occasional flicker and uneven color balancing. The screen had gotten so bad that she'd gotten special glasses to avoid further eyestrain and even then wound up with headaches most evenings.

Finally she'd had enough. It was hard enough to test games as graphically intensive as Magic World without doing it on a crappy monitor. Over the past four months she'd sent in request after request to the IT department asking for a new one. Ultimately, in desperation and only partially as a joke, she'd written her need onto the "Santa Claus" list pinned to the wall in the breakroom. She'd put it in big letters right below her request for a perfect hero.

One of the administrative assistants had created the list to improve morale during the holiday crunch and to give employees a chance to "ask Santa" for whatever their heart desired. Someone in IT must have seen her entry and finally responded.

Turning it on, she examined the new monitor carefully. The screen was huge, twenty-one inches across and a flat-panel display that was thin enough to not take up her entire desk. The color definition was perfect, and as the character creator screen she was testing appeared she detected not even a hint of flicker. *It was perfect.* One of the tech guys must *really* like her.

For an instant Melissa wondered if IT had gotten any new employees, maybe someone new and good-looking. Perhaps getting her a new monitor was his way of showing his interest. If so, she'd certainly have to look for him and thank him.

Of course he might be like the rest—gobbling candy bars all day, pretending to have an allergy to soap and water and unaware of modern conveniences such as deodorant and toothpaste. It had been her experience that cave trolls hadn't died out—they'd just developed an understanding of hardware and moved into the world of Information Technology. If so she'd have to pass on the man in spite of her gratitude. Melissa might be desperate to get laid, but a girl had to have some standards. She wanted a hero…not a troll.

But speaking of standards, she needed to get to work. Today's task was to see if the latest version of Magic World's character creator software worked properly. The best way to test it would be to make up a new character.

Melissa stared at the screen with its boxes of available statistics and types used to define a character waiting for her input. What should she make this time? A female dwarf magic user? Maybe a lizard troubadour?

No…she still had men on the mind. A warrior was what she wanted. A male fighter? Even better, she'd make him a paladin, a noble soul with knighthood in his heart. Noble, but not a wimp. In fact… Melissa added the thief characteristic to her noble warrior. That would keep him from being too much of a prig and really test his moral compass.

Her character would be a hero who'd sweep a girl off her feet and keep her there for as long as she wanted. He'd be exactly what she wanted in life, the perfect man. The perfect hero.

To be a warrior, she needed to make him a large man...how big? Six foot, six inches she typed into place. Race? She could make him human, but she'd always had a soft spot for guys with pointed ears. An elf then...but wait. It was that human side she loved.

Make him a half-elf with one human parent and the other Elven. Happily she watched as the rest of the statistics began to fill in, the program making some choices for her. The programmers had done a great of keeping the character design balanced to be more realistic, not letting any one characteristic become too overloaded.

He'd be good with a sword, excellent with a bow. She made sure to give him pluses in the use of both types of weapons. She made him a driver, capable of handling vehicles of all sorts. He'd have healing hands. A paladin-thief needed intelligence too. Melissa gave him high ratings in wisdom and charisma.

A set of faces appeared on the screen, allowing her to choose her hero's eye color and hair as well as general overall appearance. This selection was good—the faces were more rounded to look half-human, half-elf, and the ears had a much less prominent point to them. She'd seen enough true-bred elf faces in earlier versions of the software to appreciate the difference. Many of the faces could even pass for human. She picked one of those with blond hair just past the shoulders in length, and gray eyes with a soulful cast.

Her finished man stared at her as she started to fill in the last box on the form. A name—her hero needed a name. Pushing her glasses up on her nose, Melissa stared at her creation. He was beautiful, almost too beautiful to look at. He needed a strong, beautiful name.

Bran. Startled, Melissa glanced around. It was as if someone has whispered the name into her ear, but there was no one in her office. A shiver ran down her spine. It sure sounded like someone had made that suggestion.

Bran. It was a nice name. Her handsome hero looked like a "Bran". She typed it into the last box on the form and hit the "create" button.

The screen blinked and turned black. From the computer box under her desk a high-pitched whirring noise began and the screen displayed a swirling pattern that sped up as she watched, mesmerized at the sight.

Wow, the user interface guys really came up with a cool effect this time!

In the center of the screen a face appeared, her hero's face, but not stiff and lifeless as the original image had been, more realistic instead. It could have been the picture of a real man. His eyes blinked and widened, and Melissa could swear he gazed at her. A smile formed on his lips.

That smile did funny things to her knees and in the pit of her stomach. Funny things to the pit between her legs too. Gack…it really had been too long since she'd gotten laid if the picture of an imaginary character could make her horny.

The face grew to life-size on the screen, then it seemed to push outward. Melissa's jaw dropped as the screen seemed to buckle forward, forming into the shape of a head. Behind the head his neck and broad shoulders formed as well. Jumping from her chair, she backed away.

Hands appeared at the inside edges of the monitor and wrapped around to the outside. With a jerk, they pulled a man's torso through the monitor as if through a window, legs and feet following in its wake.

In moments a six-foot six-inch man had climbed out of her flat-screen monitor and was perched on her desk with his head down, breathing heavily. Under his open hunter's shirt his chest heaved from the apparent effort of climbing into her world.

Lifting his head, his gray eyes met hers and he smiled again, a warm, friendly smile with a strong hint of something else.

"I greet you, fair one. I am Bran, your hero." He reached out a hand to her.

Stumbling backwards, Melissa tripped over the legs of her chair and fell against the file cabinet behind her. Pain blossomed in her head and the world turned fuzzy.

When it stopped whirling there were strong arms holding her far too close to a solid masculine chest. A musically soft voice murmured in her ear, "It's all right. I've got you."

His gentle hand tenderly prodded the wound on her head, and the fingers came away bloody. Holding them under her nose, he shook his head sadly. "You should be more careful, my lady. You could get hurt. Hold still while I heal you."

He replaced his hand over the wound and, closing his gray eyes, began a quiet chant, barely audible. From his fingers on her head warmth flowed and her head stopped hurting. A feeling of wellbeing spread through her.

She moaned a little as the warmth spread to parts of her body not injured and too long ignored. Melissa took a deep breath, filling her lungs with his woodsy fragrance, and the warmth in her privates erupted into flame. The man's smell was incendiary and suddenly she was on fire.

Melissa moaned again, this time with passionate need, and unthinking she sought his lips with hers. At first his response was tentative, exploratory, but then he seemed to gain confidence. In a moment his tongue firmly tasted the depths of her mouth as another moan erupted from her.

Bran leaned back, his gray eyes near silver with molten passion. He licked his lips with relish, obviously still tasting her. "An unusual way to pay for a healing, but nice for the healer."

Putting her hand on her head, she felt no bump or bruise, and her fingers were bloodless when she pulled them away. Melissa blinked up at him. "How did you do that?"

"Magic," Bran said. He pulled her closer and she felt the hard ridge of his erection through the rough cloth of his woodsman's trousers. He nuzzled her neck. "Perhaps there is more of you that needs healing?" he asked suggestively. "I'd be happy to apply a healing touch wherever it's needed."

Oh boy! Melissa pushed against him and extracted herself from his arms. For an instant he seemed inclined to not release her, but chivalry must have exerted itself and he let her go.

Still, there was a decidedly non-heroic look in his eyes as he allowed her to put some distance between them. He looked far more like a tiger eying a piece of meat than a noble paladin.

"What is going on here?" she asked when she found her voice.

Settling back on the desk, Bran shook his head. "I'm not certain. You created me, so I thought you would know."

"I only created you to be a game character, not to come alive."

His mouth turned down and a sad cast came to his eyes. "You aren't happy I'm here? But I'm exactly what you asked for and how you defined me to be…your perfect hero."

"But how did you get here?"

"You asked me to be here and magic allowed the rest."

"Magic?" Melissa shook her head. "I don't believe in magic. Listen, you need to get back into the computer. Maybe if you tried, you could go back into the screen."

The look in the grey eyes turned stubborn. "Why should I go back? I just got here."

Melissa could not help her groan. She had to get him out of here before someone saw him…

"Wow, Melissa! Who's your friend?"

Melissa turned to see Alison in the doorway and cursed under her breath. It would have to be the biggest office gossip in the company who discovered them.

16

The other woman gave Bran a look-over and grinned. "Great costume," she said, although her eyes seemed to be more focused on the manly chest revealed in the opening of his shirt than on the shirt itself.

Melissa stifled a groan. Not only the biggest gossip but the biggest flirt as well. Of course, Alison could carry the flirting part off without a hitch. She had long blonde hair as opposed to Melissa's shoulder-length brown, and a slender figure that men stared at. Only Melissa's bright green eyes compared favorably to Alison's, and her glasses—the ones she needed due to that old crummy monitor—mostly hid those. Overall, Alison was more the kind of girl suited to be seen on the arm of a man like Bran than she was.

He must have thought so too. She watched him get to his feet and take Alison's hand, bending over it to give it a courtly kiss. "I am Bran, fair lady. And you would be?"

Reluctantly Melissa summoned her manners. "This is Alison Banes. Alison, this is Bran..." Her voice trailed off, unsure how to finish.

"I am Bran Elfman, Melissa's hero," he finished for her.

Alison simpered and giggled. "Oh, Melissa, he's perfect. You're bound to win the competition."

"Competition?"

Alison could barely keep her eyes off the man. "Don't be coy... The competition for the new spokesman for Magic World that management wants. Bran would be perfect."

The competition must have been announced some time ago. Melissa got fifteen memos a day and, overworked as she was, barely had time to read any of them.

Alison tore her gaze away from Bran long enough to glance over at Melissa. "The prize for bringing in the winner is a week-long vacation for two to Hawaii. Bran is bound to get the contract."

"A week in Hawaii?" Melissa gasped. Oh that sounded good. She could imagine lying on the beach in the warm sunshine right now. She'd always wanted to go on a tropical vacation, even if it had to be alone.

"You would like that, to go to this place, Hawaii?" Bran spoke softly and she turned to see him watching her. At her nod, he put his hands on his hips and smiled. "A competition where I may act as my Lady Melissa's hero? I'd be honored to attend. Will the skills include the bow, or just swordsmanship?"

Alison giggled. "Probably neither, although I'm sure you'd be great at both. All you have to do is look good. And believe me, you look real good." She put a flirtatious hand on his chest. "If you need help with anything let me know."

Bran captured her fingers and dropped them off him like a stray piece of lint. "I will need no assistance but my lady's," he said firmly. "I am *her* hero, after all."

Surprise showed in Alison's face as she headed back into the corridor. The look she gave Melissa was frankly envious. "Good luck, Melissa, not that you'll need it."

Melissa turned back to him as soon as she was gone. "What do you mean that you are my hero?"

"Just that. Magic brought me into this world for that purpose."

"What if I don't want you to be my hero?"

Disappointment showed in his face. "Then I suppose I'll have to go back. But you asked for a hero and designed me for that purpose. It is only fair that you give me a chance to prove myself to you."

Melissa had no idea what to do. She didn't believe in magic, but somehow Bran was here. She knew he was offering more than to win a trip to Hawaii for her. The way he kissed and the way he watched her now told her he had hot, sensual ideas...ideas she wasn't so sure she had objections to. But did that translate into making him her hero?

Another person came by and stared at Bran for a moment through the cubicle doorway. This was not a conversation to have where anyone could hear them.

Melissa grabbed Bran's arm. "I think you better come with me," she said and headed off to find an empty conference room.

* * * * *

Bran followed his beautiful creator down one long passage of short, fabric-covered walls after another. Clearly this was some kind of maze, if not a particularly sensible one. Why, all a man had to do was stand on one of the many tables to see how it was constructed and find his way through.

There was no need for that as Melissa led the way and seemed to know just how to navigate the labyrinth. It was no trouble to stay right behind her and watch how her tight pants clung to her ample rear end. He wasn't certain he liked pants on a woman...a skirt was far more in keeping with what he felt a lady like her should be wearing. Not to mention that a skirt could be raised more easily for access to her private parts...

Quickly he put that thought behind him. There would be time for playing with Melissa's privates once he was confirmed as her hero. That was why he'd come here from the computer world of games and adventures. As soon as he'd seen Melissa through the magic monitor he'd wanted her favor, and he was going to win it at all costs.

He did like how the pants stretched tight across her bottom, even defining the cleft of her ass. And she had such a lovely ass. Perfect for a man to get his hands on, once he'd figured out how.

He was still pondering how to best get his hands on her ass when she turned into a doorway that led to a small, dark room. As Melissa passed through the door the lights went on, revealing plain white walls, a single table and many chairs.

She closed the door behind him and gestured to one of the chairs.

Bran sat on the table instead. Better to keep to higher ground until he was sure where the enemy was coming from. "Why are we here, my lady? I thought there was a tournament to win."

His creator looked remarkably uncomfortable. "Yes. About that. I thought of a problem. How can I enter you in the contest when you don't really exist?"

He crossed his arms and stared at her. "But I do exist. I'm here right now. You made me as real as I could be."

"But you can't enter a contest. This will be like a job...you'll need papers to work."

"Papers?"

"Some kind of ID, a social security number. Stuff like that!" She looked worried. "You should go back to where you come from before I get caught harboring an illegal alien."

Bran opened his belt pouch where he kept his important belongings. Inside were several small pieces of paper and plastic. He pulled out one and glanced at it. "It has my name on it and some numbers. Five-five-one-four-two..."

Melissa snatched the card from his hand. "That's a social security card. What else do you have in there?"

Bran was already examining the next item. This seemed to be made of smooth plastic and emblazoned again with his name. "It says 'California Driver's License'. There's a picture of me." He frowned at the image. "Do I really look like that?"

After handing it to Melissa, who stared in astonishment, he pulled out a small pamphlet of dark blue.

He opened it. "Another picture of me. This one is better though."

"You have a passport. All you need now is a birth certificate..." Melissa's voice trailed off as he pulled out a many-folded piece of paper.

"Born, Bran, a baby boy, to Evelyn and Thomas Elfman." He peered at the date on the paper. "Hey, next week is my birthday. And there is a year of birth." He rubbed his chin. "I don't feel thirty."

Sorting through the documents, Melissa kept shaking her head. "I don't believe it. They've given you an identity."

"They?"

"Someone. Whoever — whatever — made you come out of that monitor."

"Magic brought me," he said, hedging a little about the truth of his origin, but Melissa just shook her head. He retrieved his papers from her and put them back into his pouch.

Obviously Melissa didn't believe in magic and didn't believe he was here to be her hero. If he didn't succeed in convincing her he'd have to go back.

He liked being in this strange world of fabric mazes and lights that activated when you entered a room. He also liked seeing Melissa so sweetly flustered, and he wanted to make that flustered look due to his making passionate love to her.

"I'm here to be your hero. You need one for this contest, and I think in your life as well. Let me show you that."

She looked uncertain but didn't try to escape as he pulled her into his arms. She fit perfectly between his spread legs along the table edge and he tugged her closer until her belly and breasts lined up against his chest. They pressed softly against him as he slid one hand around her back to secure her. Melissa was going nowhere until he released her.

Not that she seemed to be objecting. Behind the thin, round pieces of glass she wore her green eyes brightened as he leaned towards her. Her lips parted as if she were going to speak. A protest? He better stop it before it started.

Bran covered her mouth with his.

Only Melissa's sharp intake of breath showed her surprise then she seemed to melt into his arms. She tasted sweet and tart, a complex flavor that tantalized him. He deepened the kiss and swept his tongue into her mouth to capture more of that richness. Her mouth was a cavern of taste treasure to plunder and he was just the adventurer to do it.

His cock grew hard, harder even than when he'd first held her. It surged upward and sought more of her softness to press against. Kissing was fun, but he wanted to touch her, explore all of her soft body, check out her crevices, taste and smell her. He wanted to use all the new senses he possessed.

He wanted to see the body he clutched to him. Could her skin possibly be as fair as that of her face? Was it all one color or did she have more of those darling little dark spots that decorated the bridge of her nose? He wanted her sounds too. She made the most enticing noises when his hand stroked across her breast, her nipple hardening under his hand. What would she sound like when he entered her for the first time? Was she silent in bed or did she scream when a man brought her to orgasm?

All these things to discover about this woman and he'd experience them all as soon as he could. But not here—not now. A shadow passed across the window next to the door to the room and he thought he saw someone peek inside.

There was no privacy in this place and he had a contest to win for his fair Melissa. Win the contest and he would be her hero. Bran broke off the kiss and leaned back, studying the look of pleasure and shock on her face. Her eyes held a dreamy expression that faded as she seemed to remember where they were.

A laugh from the hallway outside snapped her attention back. "Oh, we shouldn't have done that."

Bran stroked her cheek with one finger. "Oh, yes we should. And we'll do it again soon. Let me stay, fair one. I will win this competition for you and we will go to Hawaii together."

Melissa stepped closer and tilted her head upward, just out of reach of his lips. "Together?"

"The trip is for two, is it not? No true hero would let his lady go alone." He stood up and headed for the door. "But first I must win it. Let's seek this tournament you want me to win."

For a long moment she hesitated then shrugged. "I guess there's no harm in trying."

Chapter Two

ഔ

It was late evening when Melissa pushed open the door of her apartment. She started to enter, but Bran's hand landed on her shoulder and shoved her behind him.

"I should enter first, in case there is danger to be met."

She nearly groaned aloud. This was at least the tenth time that Bran had pulled this macho nonsense about going in the room first. It had been bad enough at the fast-food restaurant where they'd eaten dinner and the shopping mall, but at her apartment it got ridiculous.

"Thanks, Bran, but I don't think I'm in danger from my refrigerator and it has been weeks since the last time the TV attacked me."

As usual, he ignored her protest, simply doing a brief perusal of the room before turning to the door and, with a flourish, inviting her in. With a sigh Melissa followed, lugging her new monitor under her arm. She hauled it to the desk and set it next to her computer.

When she and Bran had gotten back to her cube she'd discovered a strange multi-legged monster trying to push itself through the monitor. Bran had swatted the creature on the nose with her keyboard and the creature had vanished back into the screen.

"A bumble beast. Not something you want to meet without a sharp sword…or a bludgeon," he'd told her before dropping his improvised weapon. "They have sensitive noses."

Melissa had immediately shut down the computer and called IT. The IT guy discovered that her new monitor didn't have an asset tag and as a result he assumed she'd brought it in herself and insisted she take it home. He'd replaced it with one better than her old one and, while not as big as the magic monitor, it wouldn't let anything else escape from the computer.

It was bad enough hunting bugs inside the software without having to fight them in person.

One thing for sure...she had no intention of turning the magic monitor on again unless she could persuade Bran to return to the computer world he'd come from. Since he didn't seem to have any intention of leaving that wasn't likely to happen soon. He was having far too much fun here.

As Allison had predicted, he'd wowed the coordinators for the contest and was on the short list of people to be called later in the week. Given that he had no place to stay and apparently no money—although she wasn't so sure he didn't have gold or jewels in that belt pouch of his—Melissa had had no choice but to take him home with her.

That had meant dinner out since she'd nothing in the house to feed a six-foot-six half-elf other than bagged salad and a stray carrot or two. Bran had looked horrified when she'd suggested having "leaves and sauce" for dinner and insisted that they find a "tavern" to "slake his hunger and thirst".

While Bran hadn't been all that thrilled with having soda instead of ale, he'd been very pleased with the hamburgers— all three of the super-sized ones he'd eaten, using up most of her cash and forcing her to go the ATM for more. If she didn't want to spend a fortune on fast food Melissa would obviously need to change her food shopping habits.

The next stop had been to purchase new clothes. She'd gotten by with calling his loose-fitting tunic and gathered pants a costume for the contest, but the attention he'd gotten at the restaurant had proved to her that she needed to outfit him differently.

Bran had really enjoyed clothes shopping. The salesgirls had been all over him, helping measure his waist and hips to find the right size jeans. He'd clearly appreciated the attention, but when one of them asked if he might want to see her later and tried to slip him her phone number he'd waved her off.

"Sorry, I already have someone to see." The look he'd given Melissa had held so much heat that she'd been dumbstruck, not even thinking to protest when the quest for a pair of jeans and a few T-shirts had turned into a full shopping spree of a dozen outfits, including a brown suede jacket and a credit card bill that would take a major chunk of next month's paycheck to cover.

At this point she could only hope Bran did get the spokesman job or she'd be paying for his visit for a very long time.

She helped him carry in his shopping bags and for the moment put them into the bedroom. Melissa hadn't gotten so far as deciding where he was going to sleep, but his clothes needed to be somewhere.

Meanwhile Bran settled onto her couch in front of the television. He studied it for a moment. "I don't see a keyboard or mouse. How does this work?"

"It isn't a computer. This is how we get news and entertainment broadcasts."

"But you can do all that with a computer, can't you?"

"Yes, but this is different." Melissa handed him the remote control and showed him how to change the channels. For an imaginary character, Bran was far more familiar with modern technology than she would have expected him to be. Of course that could be because he'd come out of a computer. He refused to say much about where he'd come from other than it was very different.

So he knew about computers but not television. There were gaps in his knowledge.

Meanwhile he'd settled into watching a news program, staring at the screen in fascination.

"Bran, I need to shower and get ready for work tomorrow."

"Fine," he said absentmindedly, his concentration elsewhere. Melissa left him to it.

Bran watched the television in horrified fascination. Murder, war and corruption at high levels of government. This world was as dangerous and violent a place as the one he'd left. The difference was that Melissa lived here, a sweet woman with no defenses at all.

She really did need a champion to watch out for her, and he was just the man for the job.

He looked around but she'd gone to her bedroom and closed the door. Turning off the television, he headed for the sound of running water. It was time to show Melissa one of the reasons she needed him around.

* * * * *

Melissa turned on the shower and left it to let it heat up. She examined her face in the mirror, cleaning off the small amount of makeup she used on workdays before brushing her teeth. Finished, she noticed that the room behind her had fogged up from the shower. She dropped her robe and climbed into the spray.

She didn't hear the bathroom door open over the sound of the water so she had no idea she wasn't alone until the shower door swung out.

"J.R.R.'s glory! You have an indoor waterfall—and it's heated!" Sheer delight was in Bran's voice as Melissa twirled to face him.

"What are you doing in here?"

"Looking for you," he said, as if it were obvious.

"I'm naked, Bran!"

He raked her up and down with his gaze, his smile turning into a lecherous grin. "You certainly are. Very nice. Give me a moment."

Before she could say anything he'd closed the door to the shower, and then she realized he was taking off his clothes as well. Before she could protest he was back in the shower and under the spray, crowding her against the wall.

His grey eyes were near molten as he stared down at her. "Ah, this feels so pleasant. I'm so glad to be living in this time with you."

"Bran, you don't need to share the shower with me. It's so crowded. How do you expect me to get clean?"

She really shouldn't have asked the question. Bran simply grabbed the soap and began moving it slowly down her body, paying special attention to her breasts, her nipples and her ass. Especially, it seemed to her, her ass. He pulled her against his body, her breasts tight against his chest.

"You see how clean you can get with me helping you."

Bran gave another of those mind-bending kisses of his and all thoughts of protesting his presence in the shower with her evaporated. He pressed her against the wall, and then his hand with the soap was between her legs, moving the bar with slow deliberation against her clit. Melissa's cry was swallowed by the sound of the shower and Bran's hungry mouth. His cock was swollen and fully erect, hard against her stomach.

She almost expected him to lift her against the wall and slide inside her, but he didn't. Instead he knelt in the shower, the water cascading over his shoulders. Gently he spread her legs. "Open for me, fair one. Let me touch you."

She did and his hand slipped into the cleft between her legs, spreading her folds. His fingers teased her clit, pressing against it with firm intent. Already receptive after being "cleaned", it grew more sensitive until all she could focus on were the sensations coming from it. Every stroke of his fingers sent flurries of sensation through her. Inside her a fervor grew unlike anything she'd known before.

She couldn't help but widen her stance, giving him even better access. Bran took advantage of that, his fingers now reaching for the opening to her pussy, the palm of his hand chafing gently on her clit. Melissa ground herself against his hand, rubbing until she was close to orgasm. Her hands clutched at his shoulders.

"That's it, my lady." Bran's voice was a soft whisper in her ear. "Give into me now. Give me your pleasure."

One more sharp stroke and she did give up the token resistance, giving into the waves of pleasure rising in her. She cried out, a wail that echoed against the shower stall.

When it was over she collapsed forward. Bran stood and caught her, supporting her with his body until she was able to trust her wobbling legs again.

"What about you?" she whispered. "What should I do for you?"

A surprised and pleased smile took over his face.

"Just let us get dried off, my lady, and you can do anything you want with me. I'm yours to command."

Apparently having decided the house was safe, he actually allowed her to enter the bedroom ahead of him. She spread back the covers from the bed, revealing her sunflower-patterned sheets. She'd bought them because they were bright and cheerful.

Bran smiled. "Pretty. But they are missing something. Ah, I know what it is." He lifted her into his arms and deposited her into the middle of the bed. "They need a sweet little bee to drink their nectar."

Surprised by his playfulness, she laughed. "A bee?"

"That's what the name Melissa means…bee or honey. My sweet little honeybee." He knelt between her legs, spreading them to reveal her soft folds and barely hooded clit to his hungry eyes. "And what beautiful petals my Melissa has."

"I think you are mixing your metaphors, Bran. Bees don't have petals."

"Perhaps." He stroked her nether lips gently. "But these are like petals and I see that they do have honey." Two fingers slipped along the folds, spreading them, and a flood of cream gushed from Melissa's pussy. "Yes. Much honey. Let me taste it."

Bending over, Bran covered her with his mouth, licking and "tasting her honey". Each stroke of his tongue inflamed Melissa further. She cried out at the feel of his mouth on her.

She squirmed beneath him until, with one last, earth-shattering cry, she reached climax. When she opened her eyes Bran had a very pleased look on his face.

He licked his lips. "Very tasty."

"Oh, yeah? Well two can play this game." Melissa sat up and pushed him. Bran went willingly to his back, his cock standing upright from his body, tall and proud. Melissa had a brief thought that it looked like a game joystick, but buried that idea immediately. The metaphors were getting far too dense.

Instead she grabbed hold of his proud cock and delicately licked its purple tip. Bran's smile softened and his gaze intensified. "That feels very good."

"It's supposed to. This should feel even better." Opening her mouth, she took the head of him inside, swirling her tongue over it. Bran muttered something, what she wasn't sure, but it sounded like some kind of oath.

Swearing wasn't something she'd programmed into him and she wondered for a moment how much of him was a result of her creation, or was there something else behind Bran's sudden appearance from the computer. Was he just a simulation or had he existed in some form before? It certainly would explain why he felt so much like a real man to her.

At least there was nothing simulated about the cock she sucked on and like every other man she'd known he loved what she was doing. One thing Melissa knew how to do was give a great blowjob.

He tasted like an ordinary man except better somehow. He smelled better too, and not just because of the shower they'd taken together. He seemed bigger, larger than life.

Next to Bran, the other guys she'd had sex with seemed — flat. Lifeless. One-dimensional.

Funny how an imaginary character brought to life could be more alive than any of her previous lovers. He certainly was better at bringing her to orgasm, like he had earlier. His intent had been to please her, not just himself.

Which was why she was now intent on pleasing him. Melissa simply wanted to hear him groan with pleasure.

He was groaning now, for certain. She sucked hard on his cock and he grabbed her head, holding it gently although she felt the tense strength in his hands. He could easily hold her and direct her motion, but he didn't. Instead his fingers slipped to cradle the back of her head and gently wind their way through her hair.

"Please don't stop," he whispered.

She didn't even pause to answer, just continued to use her mouth on him, letting her hands glide along the shaft where he was too thick and long to fit completely inside her mouth. When she reached lower to cup his balls, she felt them tense and they seemed to grow heavy. His whole body tightened and she knew he was close to coming.

Bran's voice deepened and his breathing was hard and words choppy. "I…I don't know. Shouldn't I be…somewhere else…inside…?"

Melissa pulled back and freed her mouth. Her hands continued to stroke along his cock. "Do you want to try coming this way first?"

"Maybe...I don't know. Oh hell, yes." He thrust up with his hips, putting his cock back into her waiting mouth. Swallowing her amusement, Melissa went back to work, and soon she tasted the first surge of cum from him, warm and earthy on her tongue.

Just a short spurt, but it preceded his turning completely rigid, as if every muscle in his body froze at once. Bran began to growl, a low deep sound, and then he was moving faster, his hands no longer gentle on the back of her head but pushing her to take as much of him as she could. It didn't hurt but she had to open her mouth wider to accommodate him.

"That's it. Yes. Like that. Please." His words grew ever more intent. Finally he arched his back, threw back his head and gave a sharp cry. "Gods —"

Under her hand his cock throbbed and the back of her throat caught his jet of cum as it shot out of him. Where before he'd simply filled her, now she couldn't keep it all within, even swallowing as fast as she could.

His cry petered out and he collapsed back on the bed. Every muscle that had been tense now relaxed and he seemed to soften all over.

Bran released her head and raised his hand to cover his face. Melissa sat up to watch him. He breathed hard, his eyes unfocused and a look of pure astonishment on his face.

"That was...I don't know. Amazing?"

"Amazing is a good word."

"Yes then. Amazing."

Licking her lips, Melissa reveled in his taste. He tasted so good, so different. Then she realized she had his cum over much of her face and grabbed an edge of the sheet to wipe it off.

Bran grabbed her hand and pulled her down into his arms. The expression in his grey eyes was soft as he took the sheet from her and carefully cleaned the outside of her mouth.

Then he kissed her gently and folded her into his side, giving a sigh of true contentment.

Melissa stifled a sigh. It looked like the sex would be over for the night. Bran had climaxed and, like most men, would be happy with that. And she couldn't really complain. After all, she'd already had a couple of orgasms, in the shower and then with his mouth on her.

She'd been looking forward to having his cock inside her but it had been her choice to make him come. This wasn't going to be her last chance to make love with Bran. Since he was going to live with her for the next few days until the contest was decided, there would be lots of other opportunities. Heck, maybe he'd be interested in sex tomorrow morning.

Melissa snuggled in closer to him and fought her disappointment.

Bran gave another contented sigh. "I really enjoyed that, my lady."

"I'm glad."

"Yes. That was really nice." He sat up and moved to crouch over her. Again there was the tiger in his grey eyes, examining her as if she were his favorite cut of meat.

Something poked her in the stomach and Melissa glanced down and saw that his cock was once again fully erect.

Bran grinned down at her. "That was really nice, but if it is all the same with you, let's try fucking for real this time."

Melissa couldn't help teasing a little. "Such adult language from a game character."

He leaned in to kiss her. "Yeah, well, this is going to be pretty adult too."

As his lips met hers, Melissa gave a quick thanks to wherever that monitor had come from. She wasn't quite ready to call it magic but at least temporarily she'd gotten the hero she'd asked for.

Stretching her arms above her head, Melissa surrendered to whatever Bran wanted from her. "Then I think you really should fuck me, Bran."

Chapter Three

Bran couldn't help grinning at her. From the surprise on her face, Melissa must really have thought he'd been done making love. How could that be when he hadn't been inside her yet? Sure he'd loved coming in her mouth, but good as it was he couldn't help wanting to bury himself deep within the folds he'd tasted, delve deep into her depths until he found the opening to her womb and spilled himself there.

He wanted to coat her insides with his cum and leave a little bit of himself inside her, branding her as his for all time. Fortunately he'd confirmed earlier that she used birth control so there was no danger of making her pregnant.

Yet. Later on, they'd see about children, when he'd convinced her all this was real and that he had no intention of ever leaving her side.

He touched the skin on her neck. While they were both made of flesh, hers was so much softer and smoother than his. He was happy to notice that while she was as pale as he'd expected, there were small flecks of color as well. Freckles, that's what they were. Small imperfections in the pigment of her skin.

They looked perfect to him. He wanted to kiss each one but that would take too much time and he really wanted to get inside her. Kissing her freckles could come later. He'd kiss each and every one of them eventually. It would only take thirty or forty years to do it.

Not a problem. He was going to be around at least that long.

But about this fucking stuff. He really should be getting around to that. Melissa lay quiet as he smoothed his hands along her shoulders then down to her waist. Her breasts were just beneath his face, a good handful each. Bran tested that and found they fit his hands perfectly. So soft, and topped with nipples the color of woodland berries. Harder than berries though, and sensitive. She moaned when he pulled one into his mouth, feeling the uneven tip under his tongue.

Her nipple tasted sweet. The moan she made turned into a purr as he sucked on one nipple then the other. Underneath him her hips twitched and then thrust upward, rubbing against his engorged cock.

Her pussy wanted some attention. Bran slid his fingers down to slip inside her and gently stroke the folds of the inner wall. As he slid one fingertip down the inside, the walls contracted, tightening around his digit.

He could imagine how her pussy would feel contracting the same way around his cock and almost lost control right then. He wanted to build up to making love with her but she wasn't letting him. Melissa seemed to need him right now.

Just as he needed her.

"Are you ready?" he asked.

Another thrust of her hips against his hand and another surge of cream from her pussy warmed his finger. "Yes, damn it. Fuck me, Elfman."

Happy to oblige! Bran fitted his cock to her waiting, damp slit and slipped it in. *Gods…*

She was so tight, so hot, and thankfully so wet that he slid partway into that hot tightness with barely any trouble. It felt good. Better than good—amazing, like before but even better. He gave a brief thanks that Melissa hadn't stinted when creating his stamina characteristics. She felt so *amazing* that he knew he wouldn't have lasted this long without the extra marks.

"Bran… You feel incredible," she whispered, echoing his thoughts. "But if you don't finish getting inside me, I may become a desperate woman."

"I like having you desperate for me. But as you insist…" He plunged forward, her tightness encasing him like the too-tight sheath of a sword. But she wasn't too tight, just…perfect.

When he was all the way inside her as far as he could go, he felt the end of her womb, a tight button against the tip of his cock. It caressed the highly sensitive tip and he had to hold still to avoid coming immediately. Taking several deep breaths, he grabbed for control. Once he thought he had it he tried a tentative thrust.

Melissa gave another of those purrs of hers and he couldn't help but smile. He loved it that she seemed to have as little power over the noises she made as he did. He thrust again, and this time followed it with another. Slowly he built into a rhythm they both liked.

Her legs came up beside his hips and then seemed to cross behind his back. It changed the angle and somehow he seemed to be able to plunge deeper into her. The purr she'd started with became a full-fledged set of short cries, each one of which was punctuated by a tightening of her pussy around him. She clenched him to her, both his cock buried deep inside her and his ass wrapped tightly by her legs.

She was heat and sweetness, and Bran couldn't resist dipping his head to kiss her once between thrusts. Melissa lifted her head and captured his mouth with hers, returning his kiss and then some. Her arms went around his neck and then he was kissing and thrusting and not knowing which was better. But kissing interfered with breathing and he was gasping when he pulled his head up.

Cradling her between his arms, he continued to slide into her faster and faster, his cock a mighty sword of flesh plundering her depths. One more, then another. He had to bring her to climax first…

And then she was climaxing, her cries turned to a wail, her eyes bright with crazed delight. "Oh god…"

"Gods..." That was all it took to send him to the brink as well.

"I'm coming." Melissa's voice turned into a sweet-pitched wail.

"Yes. Yes." Bran punctuated his words with two more sharp thrusts as Melissa shuddered beneath him. He finished with a cry as her pussy clenched tight around his now-throbbing cock and milked it to climax. Throbbing and pulsing as the most intense orgasm he'd ever known sped through him, knocking him near senseless. Only the need to keep from crushing the smaller woman beneath him kept him from collapsing completely.

Gods...he'd never felt anything like this before. Flesh to flesh was so much more than he'd expected, and he'd expected a lot. He felt like in a game when he'd taken out the boss monster and found the greatest treasure of all time.

Then he caught sight of the rapturous look on Melissa's face and that feeling grew a hundredfold. Clearly he'd surpassed her expectations as well.

Her words confirmed it. "That was...amazing."

Bran smiled. "Amazing—and magical."

* * * * *

Later, they finished putting away Bran's new clothes in her closet and in a drawer Melissa emptied for him. There was no longer any question as to where he would sleep. For as long as he was staying with her, Bran insisted on sleeping in her bed and she had no intention of fighting it.

Dressed in a pair of sweatpants, Bran gathered her into his arms. For the first time in years Melissa felt warm and safe.

"Happy?" he asked.

"Yes." And she realized she actually was. It had been a while since she'd been this content. She'd been lonely and a little depressed ever since taking a job so far from her family.

Melissa usually spent the holidays with them and by now should have been knee-deep in preparations.

She laughed softly. "This is the strangest Christmas I've ever had."

Bran turned to her. "You celebrate the holiday?"

"Sort of. Last couple of years I haven't put up decorations or a tree and this year there won't be a big gift exchange. My parents went on a month-long trip around the country so I'm not going to see them until after the holidays."

She rested her head on his shoulder. "I'd like to have an old-fashioned Christmas, but it's hard to find the time to buy anything or even think about decorating with the release schedule the way it is." She glanced over at the clock. "Speaking of which, it's getting late and I have to get to work early tomorrow or I'll never catch up and will have to work late all week."

She turned to see Bran watching her with a speculative look on his face. "Are you going to be okay if I leave you here alone tomorrow?"

He smiled and she wondered briefly about the mischievous gleam in his eyes. "I'll be fine. I'm sure I'll find some way to entertain myself. Maybe I'll play on your computer for a while."

"Sure," she told him. After all, how much trouble could he get into there?

Chapter Four

🔊

Bran stared at the computer screen in front of him...not the one he'd climbed out of, which he'd stowed, unplugged, under the desk, but the ordinary one attached to Melissa's home computer. The magic monitor was his way back into the computer world he'd come from and he hoped not to need it ever again.

He fingered the keyboard and mouse. It was much harder working from outside a computer system than inside. For as long as Bran could remember he'd been able to work a system to success in one or another adventure. Even if he'd had a different form in the past, his spirit had remained the same. Not that he disliked this form. On the contrary, he loved the body and face that Melissa had created for him.

Even better was the way she enjoyed what he looked like. When he'd been inside the machine he'd noticed how she'd smiled at him as she'd completed his specs. He'd liked that smile and wanted to find ways to keep it there.

When she'd created her "perfect hero" his spirit had been drawn to her character. He and the other digital people lived for that moment of connection to the real world, when a game player designed a character that matched their spirit, allowing them to slip inside the character and participate in its adventures. They'd stay the same people for the most part but take their strengths and abilities from the game character's statistics.

Fortunately Melissa had given him a wonderful set of stats. This was the best character Bran had ever played—which was a good thing as he intended it to be the last one. This would be the character he would die as, hopefully as a very old man living with his equally old Melissa.

Sometime gaming was dangerous and often he'd been killed in an adventure only to be resurrected later with a better understanding of how to avoid death the next time. This time there would be no extra lives so he'd have to make this one count.

Of course he'd never had the experience of lying in a bed with a woman...that was one adventure not programmed into any game he'd been part of, although there were adult computer games he'd heard of but never managed to encounter—and now never would.

Not that he minded that. Making love with Melissa was far better than a game. Certainly better than dying under the claws of a bumble beast.

Being able to climb into Melissa's world from his made this the best adventure ever. Now all he had to do was succeed in his quest so that he'd gain the greatest treasure a man could find.

The love of a wonderful woman. Melissa's love.

In order to gain this treasure he had to master the weapons of this place...that is, the tools needed. In this case, a keyboard and mouse to use the computer. Fortunately with a little effort and a bit of magic he managed the task and soon was able to begin exploring the internet, where he intended to accomplish his second task of the day...hunting treasure.

He'd come with documents giving him a real world identity but he'd noticed last night that the small gems in his belt pouch weren't used as currency here and he needed to find someone to estimate their value before he spent them. He'd watched as Melissa had gone to a machine set in the side of a building and withdrawn several of those small pieces of paper with the use of a thin flexible card, using them to pay at the fast-food tavern. When he'd asked, Melissa had explained it was an ATM card and it was used to get money. This had resulted in a discussion of banking and how money was stored in accounts linked to the numbers on the card that could be accessed through these machines or even through the Internet.

Later she'd used another card to pay for his new clothes and he'd noticed how she'd winced when the saleswoman had told her the total. Clearly Melissa had limited funds, and he needed his own to finance the campaign he had in mind.

So, just like a game inside the computer, Bran was going on a treasure hunt. He intended to explore the Internet and find money.

So where did one find money on the Internet? There were ways to earn it but those took too long for his purposes. He had a thief's abilities but he couldn't just cheat someone out of it. Melissa had made him too noble for that. But he could steal it… If he could find someone even more of a thief than he was to steal from…

Bran took a peek at Melissa's spam filter and made a list of electronic addresses of those who sought her personal information. A couple he narrowed down further until he was able to discover the true names of those who were running the sites.

He accessed several online banking sites and stuck the names in. Sure enough they had accounts. Using his magic to fake their passwords, he managed to get into the accounts. One had close to thirty thousand dollars in it and had been dormant for almost a year. Not likely to be noticed for a while. From that account Bran did an online transfer to a new, temporary account he'd set up under a false name. Then he did a second transfer to another false account then a third to throw whoever investigated off the money trail.

Finally the money settled into an account he set up in his real name at Melissa's bank. Later today he'd go into the bank itself and get an ATM card so he could withdraw money.

Finished, Bran sat back in his chair and smiled. While he missed using a sword to battle kobolds and other monsters, he had to admit this treasure hunt had been fun...and profitable. He flexed his fingers, wondering how much magic he had left. Not much, he knew, but he didn't mind. What was magic compared to loving a woman?

If he could be her hero he'd give up his magic and much more. Already he was in love with her.

He opened another search engine and typed in "Christmas decorating" to begin the last phase of his campaign. By the time Melissa got home he should have everything ready for a real, old-fashioned Christmas guaranteed to win a fair lady's heart.

* * * * *

When Melissa got home she wasn't even in her apartment before noticing things had changed in her absence. The first thing she saw was a beautiful evergreen wreath decorating the outside of her door. It was made of some kind of fir branches and set with colorful balls and pinecones. She stared at it, remembering her comment to Bran the night before about wanting an old-fashioned Christmas.

Abruptly she wondered if she should have been more careful about what she'd asked for. It looked like she might have gotten it.

Taking a deep breath, she opened the door...and entered Christmas Land.

Melissa stared at what had been her uninspired and simply decorated living room. There was nothing either simple or uninspired left in the room. Bright colors were everywhere, overshadowing the earth-toned carpet and beige walls. She couldn't see her couch for the multitude of bright pillows in holiday prints sitting on top of it.

A brand-new stereo was softly playing an old Christmas album that she'd kept from her childhood, a high-pitched voice singing about wanting some kind of hoop toy. On top of her television she saw a pile of DVDs of popular holiday movies, the price tags still on them.

In one corner sat a brand-new fireplace with an artificial log blazing merrily away. Hanging from the top of the cherrywood hearth were a pair of stockings, one marked "Melissa" and the other "Bran".

In the opposite corner was an undecorated six-foot tree with boxes of bright-colored balls and lights sitting next to it, waiting to be put in place.

Even the air smelled like Christmas. Like pine, cinnamon and other spices, and the scents of roasting beef and fresh baked cookies.

Stunned, Melissa sat on the couch. Bran stuck his head through the kitchen door. "Hi, honey. I didn't hear you come in." He waved a hand cheerily around the room. "Merry Christmas." He ducked back inside the kitchen before she could say anything.

Melissa could only shake her head as she again took everything in. Bran had been a very busy man today, but where had he gotten the money to pay for all this?

Quickly she checked her purse but her one and only credit card was still there. She closed her purse just as Bran came through the door again, a heavy glass mug in his hand. Inside was a thick red liquid that, when he gave it to her, smelled richly of wine and spices.

"Mulled wine," he told her. "I got the recipe off the Internet. Try it."

She took a fortifying sip. It was hot, a little sweet, and tasted heavenly. "It's really good."

Beaming, Bran disappeared back to the kitchen, returning with a mug of his own. "It will be a little while until the meat is done and I've finished making the salad so I'll sit with you now."

She couldn't believe it. "You cook?"

Bran grinned at her. "I can if I want to and I wanted to. So I looked up recipes and bought food. I did use up your salad and carrots though."

Melissa looked at the clear glass mug in her hand, which matched his, both of them decorated with little gold stars. These too were new. She put the mug on the coffee table and waved a hand around the room. "Where did you get all this stuff?"

Bran looked smug. "I bought it. I wanted to give you what you wished for, an old-fashioned Christmas."

"Bran...I didn't mean for you to go out and do something like this."

"Why not? Don't you like what I did?"

"It's not that I don't like it. But it's...too much."

"Too much?" Bran glanced around the place, a puzzled look on his face. "Too many decorations? You don't like the fireplace? I got it because otherwise where else would we put our stockings?"

"The decorations are very nice. And the fireplace..." Melissa did have to admit the presence of the pretty little fire did brighten the place up. "I like it, but something like that is so expensive."

Bran settled back onto the couch. "It wasn't that much. I can afford it."

Now he had her full attention. "Where did you get the money? Did you have it in your pouch?"

"Not my pouch," he said and from the way he tightened his lips she knew he didn't want to tell her more about what he did keep in that small leather bag.

"So where did it come from?"

Bran picked up her mug and handed it back to her. "Drink up and I'll tell you all about it."

By the time the mug was half empty, Melissa was laughing over his self-proclaimed "treasure hunt".

"You stole money from spammers?" When she'd given him the thief characteristic she hadn't thought he'd actually use it. But there was a poetic justice to his method.

Again Bran had a smug look on his face. "I didn't think you'd object."

"Not this time. But I don't think you should make a habit of it."

"No, I won't. But I took enough to cover expenses for a while." He grinned and for a moment Melissa wondered just how long "a while" was.

Bran took Melissa's mug and put it on the table with his. Putting his hands on her shoulders, he pulled her closer. There was an odd look in his eyes. "Do you believe me when I say I love you, Melissa?"

"I don't know. I've only known you a short time. Love doesn't happen that fast."

"It does for me. I've wanted someone like you my entire existence. When I saw you for the first time that was all I needed. Magic brought us together."

Melissa stared at him. "I want to believe you."

He smiled and she saw his grey eyes dance with amusement. "And yet you can't. You don't believe it because you don't believe in magic. But you will."

Inside the kitchen a buzzer went off, and Bran got to his feet. "That means dinner is almost ready. Why don't you bring your wine and we'll talk while I finish up? I want to hear about your day. Your ordinary day. Then we'll eat and when that's done we'll decorate that tree. I have cookies for us to snack on while we do. We must get ready...after all, Christmas is only a few days away."

"It sounds like you have the whole evening planned out."

"I do, my lady." He stopped on the way to the kitchen to wink at her. "Oh, and I should warn you, once the tree is decorated I intend to make very passionate love to you on that couch."

He disappeared into the kitchen and Melissa slowly followed. Dinner smelled great and she had to admit he had a terrific plan.

* * * * *

Later, in the bedroom, he demonstrated just what else he'd found on the Internet that day. They were lying on the bed, Bran lying on top of her as usual. "Did you know there are entire websites devoted to sex information?"

Melissa suppressed a groan. "I hope you ran the spyware detection software afterward."

"Actually, I boosted your protection already. There is some nasty stuff out there."

"So what did you learn?"

"This." He sat up and with one move turned her over onto her knees. "I think they call it 'doggy style'."

His cock pushed deep inside her. From behind the angle was different and he seemed to be even deeper than before. Melissa moaned as his thickness filled her, the tip raking over the front of her vagina, pressing against the g-spot with every push.

Sex with Bran was always an adventure but having him looking for new ways to make love endeared him to her.

His hands held her hips firm as he plunged deep within her. "You have such a great ass, honeybee. Just made for sex."

"Oh please, yes. Like that."

He leaned over and spoke into her ear. "Like what, Melissa? Tell me what you like."

He wanted her to talk? Melissa shoved aside her shyness. "I like you fucking me."

"I like fucking you too. Let's try another position."

He pulled her up and used his hands to fondle her breasts, still pushing into her from behind. His hand found her clit and stroked it gently. After a moment Melissa shook again and felt another orgasm start to run through her.

"I'm coming…"

"Yes, do that for me."

Then she was grabbing his hand and pressing it tighter against her clit, riding his fingers as he drove in from behind.

"That's it," he whispered in her ear. "I love it when you do that."

"God…gods…yes!" she shouted. Melissa let loose with a long, drawn-out scream. As she tightened around him Bran picked up the pace, plunging deeper and deeper inside. He no longer was able to hold her up so she went back to all fours and raised her ass higher, giving him even deeper access.

His hands clutched her hips. "Gods yes. Just let me fuck you."

And then it was his turn to shudder and cry out her name over and over again as he emptied himself into her. The places his fingers clutched her grew sore from how hard his fingers pressed but she didn't mind.

He draped across her back as if he no longer had the strength to hold himself up.

He slid to one side, taking her with him, arms wrapped tight around her breasts, one hand cradling her shoulder. Melissa heard him breathing deeply into her ear. "I love you, Melissa."

"I…" She didn't finish though, not ready to say what he wanted her to. "I'm just not sure what I feel."

Bran sighed and clutched her closer. "Someday you will be, fair one."

Chapter Five

ะา

For the next few days Melissa came home to a similar scene every night. She'd come in exhausted but Bran would have a glass of wine, spiked eggnog or something else waiting for her to sip while she'd told him about her "ordinary day". He'd tell her of his adventures learning how to be a human and they would laugh over the dinner he'd prepared or brought in.

Once the dishes were done they would watch TV or play a video game together—activities Melissa had always done alone, but with Bran there they were more enjoyable. Sometimes they'd go directly to bed and make love. They always made love.

Each day he became more and more a part of her life. Every day she came closer to admitting she was falling in love with him. If only there was more than magic at work here she might have felt safer about expressing herself.

But then Christmas Eve came.

Melissa unlocked the door and went inside. With the company shut down between Christmas and New Year's it seemed like she'd had to do twice as much work all week to make up for it. At least the next week was paid vacation and she'd be able to relax. Maybe she and Bran could go someplace for a brief trip.

The day had been frantic but she had gotten away at lunch for a short shopping trip to find a present for him. Something special...something she was sure he'd like. She wasn't quite up to saying that she would love him always but this much she could do.

The room was darker than usual when she came in. The only light came from the computer monitors sitting on her desk. The TV was off and the little fireplace wasn't burning and there was no light coming from the kitchen. The usual smells and noises of dinner being prepared weren't happening either.

No sound or sign of Bran about the place.

Suddenly worried, Melissa stepped quickly into the room. "Bran? Are you here?"

"Yes." A shadow moved in the direction of the couch. Melissa turned on the lamp on the table nearby and Bran sat blinking in the sudden light. She was so happy to see him that at first she didn't realize he was wearing the clothes he'd come out of the monitor in.

"What are you doing sitting in the dark?"

He looked up at her, his face solemn. "Waiting for you. I wanted…" He took a deep breath. "I wanted to say goodbye."

"Goodbye?" Melissa sat on the chair facing the couch. "I don't understand."

He leaned forward and studied his hands, not letting his gaze meet hers. "I must leave, Melissa."

Now she really didn't understand. "What do you mean leave? Where are you going?"

He indicated the glowing monitors and she realized that the magic one had been placed on the desk as well. While the ordinary monitor showed the start page of Magic World, the second held a whirling pattern not unlike the one it had displayed when he'd crawled out of it.

"I don't have it hooked up to the computer yet. I didn't want to risk anything coming out. But it will only take a moment to do that. Once I'm back inside you should turn off the monitor, disconnect it from your computer and, if possible, destroy it. That way you'll be safe."

She'd known it was too good to be true—that he'd actually stay with her. Girls like her didn't get a man like Bran to keep, even when magic was involved. "I guess I knew you'd leave eventually." A wayward tear escaped her eye and she dashed it away angrily. "I'm surprised you stayed this long."

"I stayed until the decision was made. Now that it has been I have no choice. I can't be your hero anymore so I must go back to where I came from."

It did little good that he sounded as miserable as she felt. Another tear trickled down her cheek and then another and then she was crying for real. Bran was on his knees in front of her, staring up into her face. "You're crying."

Melissa grabbed a handful of tissues from a box on the table, used them to wipe her eyes then blew her nose. "Of course I'm crying. You are leaving me, aren't you?"

"Not because I want to."

"Then why go?"

He shook his head. "Because I have failed."

Melissa's confusion was back. "What do you mean you failed?"

Bran looked so downcast that in spite of her misery Melissa's heart reached out to him. "They called today to tell me the outcome of the spokesman contest. I...I didn't win."

"Oh, that." They'd announced the results at work, and while she'd been disappointed about losing the trip to Hawaii, she was philosophical about it. "I heard that the company president's niece tried out at the last moment and they picked her. Not too surprising, really." In spite of everything she had to chuckle. "They decided a buxom blonde would sell more games to the target market than a man would."

Bran's eyes narrowed. "That's why they picked her over me, because I'm not a buxom blonde?"

"Well, the vast majority of game players are men so, yeah, a buxom blonde is a better choice."

His mouth turned down into a frown and he shook his head. "This is a very strange world."

"No argument here. But what does the contest have to do with your leaving?"

"Because I didn't win. I was your champion and I failed so I can't remain your hero."

Melissa's mouth dropped open. "You are leaving me because you didn't get picked to be the company spokesperson? It was that important to you?"

It was Bran's turn to look confused. "You wanted to go to Hawaii. I thought it was important to you."

She held up her hand. "Hold it! Hawaii would be fun, but we don't need to win a contest to go there. Heck, with the money you, um, *found*, we could buy two tickets and leave tomorrow. What does any of this have to do with us?"

"Us?"

"Us. You and me. Our relationship. Why are you breaking up our relationship?"

Bran waved his hand. "Melissa, I came here to be your hero. Without that we don't have a relationship."

He seemed to fumble for words for a moment. "Where I come from it isn't enough just to be...we have to have a purpose to exist. A duty, you might say. When I came here my duty was clear—to become your hero and win the contest for you. Now that I've failed as your champion I have lost my purpose. I can't remain if I'm not your hero."

"Oh." The odd thing was that she really did understand what he was talking about. In a gaming world you either won or you lost and mostly through your own efforts and luck. "So you don't think you could be my hero outside of the stupid contest?"

"I have tried. But there are difficulties. When I came I had a certain amount of magic. I could heal your head and the next day I used it to hunt for money. Since then there has been less every day to use. I am becoming an ordinary man. I'd hoped that winning the contest would secure my place with you."

After the rollercoaster ride her emotions had taken, Melissa couldn't help bursting into laughter. "Oh, Bran, you are anything but an ordinary man and you don't need magic or to win anything like it to be a hero to me. I've..." Finally she could say it. "I've fallen in love with you."

"You don't mean that," he said but she thought she heard the hope in his voice.

"I can and I do. And I can prove it." Melissa reached into the bag at her feet. "I was going to give you this tomorrow but here..." She thrust the brightly wrapped package at him.

"What's this?"

"Your Christmas present. Open it and see."

He slid the bow off and unwrapped the box. Inside was a gold man's wristwatch. It had cost her half a week's salary but if it proved to him how she felt it was worth it.

"What's this for?"

"To tell the time...and other things. Turn it over. I had it engraved."

He did and read the tiny script on the back. "To my perfect hero with all my love." Sheer joy lit up Bran's face. "You do love me."

"Yes, I do."

Relief shone in his eyes. "Melissa, I love you too. If you let me stay your hero, I promise you will never regret it."

Her perfect hero created from a computer program and a magic monitor. His creation was magic but no more than the feelings she experienced with him. Melissa opened her arms. "You are my perfect hero, Bran, not because of what you do but because I love you."

Triumph filled his face as he crossed the distance between their lips and sealed his promise with a soul-shaking kiss. Then he picked her up and headed for the bedroom. Once he had her in his arms he clutched her tight to his chest. "I thought I'd never do this again with you."

On their way to the bedroom a faint buzzing noise caught their attention and they stopped to see the magic monitor on the desk flash brightly then disappear into a small cloud of sparkling dust that smelled vaguely of gingerbread.

Bran and Melissa stared for a moment then Bran laughed happily. "Well, that's that. I'm glad you love me little honeybee, because you are well and truly stuck with me now."

The finality of it seemed to sink into her. "I guess so. I just hope a year from now you don't change your mind."

"That will never happen," he said. "But I will wait a year if you need to be sure."

Chapter Six

ഇ

Through the open lanai window, the early morning breeze whisked across the bed, bringing the scent of flowers and the sea with it. In the distance he thought he heard "Jingle Bells" being played on a ukulele.

Christmas in paradise. His second Christmas with her in a place she'd always wanted to go, paid for by his signing bonus. Bran had to admit Hawaii was pretty special, but then any place would be right now. She was with him. Bran Elfman pulled his sweetheart closer into the shelter of his arms, nuzzling her neck softly.

He'd been in this world over a year now. In consolation for not giving him the spokesman job, Magic World had offered him a position as a game designer. It seemed he'd impressed them with his intimate knowledge of just how all of their games, and those of most of their competitors, worked.

Since Bran knew how games were built from the inside out, it had been easy to learn to design them from this side of the computer and he was happy to put his knowledge to good use. During the last year he'd turned the job into a high-ranking development career that was as satisfying as any gaming adventure he'd ever experienced.

But it wasn't the new job, the prestige, or the money that made him happy. Nothing meant more to him than the lovely woman asleep in his arms. He leaned forward to nibble on her ear.

Her soft laugh greeted him and his shaft grew hard in response. Perhaps she wasn't so asleep.

"Are you awake, Bran?"

"As always." He ran his hand up from her soft belly to her generous breasts, cupping the nearest. His fingers found the nipple and teased it into erection.

If he had to have one, then so should she.

She moaned at his attention. He turned her to face him, gazing down on her lovely face and the dawning passion it held. His woman, his lady. So beautiful. Since he'd arrived, she'd several times told him that she was plain, that she carried too much weight and that she didn't deserve him.

He saw none of that. She was as she was, perfect for him, and he couldn't understand why she said these things. After a while he'd stopped arguing and had simply taken her in his arms, kissing her into silence. That had proven to be the best way to deal with her insecurities.

He didn't want to tell her that *he* didn't deserve *her*. She might believe it.

The nipple he'd teased was within reach, so he pulled it into his mouth, suckling it slowly. Melissa moaned louder. He used his other hand to take hold of her opposite nipple, drawing it into a point.

Each breast got his attention, one after the other, until her hips writhing beneath him caught his notice. Bran spared one hand to find her hidden treasure, the soft folds that hid her tiny pleasure point and welcoming pussy.

Now her folds were damp and getting damper by the instant. Bran moved to tease her clit with his tongue, giving it the same treatment he'd exerted on her nipple. Immediately Melissa cried out, her body's shuddering telling him how close to full ecstasy she was. He reached inside her with his fingers, found the sensitive spot on the forward wall. With gentle strokes he pressed against it and Melissa reacted as usual, coming instantly.

His mouth flooded with the essence of her pleasure. He swallowed it, pleased that she was so sensitive to his touch.

Again he touched stroked her clit and g-spot, driving her close to ecstasy again.

She trembled under him, but he wasn't going to allow her to climax that way again. This was just to ready her. He intended to drive her to orgasm with his cock, pushing them both into the ultimate pleasure. Rearing above her, Bran slid her legs up to his shoulders then, placing himself at the entrance. Just as she recognized his intentions, he drove home, catching her by surprise.

"Bran!" She shouted his name, a sweet sound, as he pulled back and drove in again. His name became a chant in his ear as he found his rhythm, driving deeper into her with every stroke. Her voice broke off and again he felt the tension rise in her, but this time he allowed her to approach completion.

With her ass raised it was easy for his fingers to find her anus and finger it gently, pushing it like a button, then one squeezed past the tight muscle there. He moved his finger in and out, mimicking the action of his cock in her pussy.

This was a new pleasure they'd found. Her anus was another place she was sensitive to his touch, and stroking a finger into the tight opening drove her fast into even harder orgasms.

Giving her pleasure was what he, as a hero, did best. Melissa shuddered again and again, and he let her climax milk him into his own. In the next instant he shuddered and called out her name, flooding her with his hot cum.

Still linked together, he pulled her up to sit astride him and held her close, feeling her racing heart against his chest. As her breathing calmed he stroked her bare skin, lingering on the soft plumpness of her buttocks.

Outside their lanai a bird sang, probably seeking its mate. As he listened, Bran heard the answering birdcall. Everything had its mate...including him. He couldn't imagine another woman in his life, not ever.

Today was their last day in this tropical paradise. Tomorrow they would again board the horrific flying ship they'd taken to reach this island. Brave he might be but only Melissa's calm presence had kept him from refusing to board the metal bird in the first place. He wasn't looking forward to the return trip, only partly because he'd been terrified by flying.

He didn't want to lose paradise either. If he could get things settled between them, then anywhere they went would be heaven, but even after a year Melissa always seemed able to avoid talking about the future. Even now she expected the magic to end.

"We are mated, you and I." He spoke softly.

Melissa giggled against him, rubbing her cheek on his chest. "We certainly spend enough time in bed."

"I mean more than that. You are my mate. We are mated. We should spend our lives together."

Melissa laughed again but this time sounded wary. "That almost sounds like a marriage proposal. You should be careful how you talk, Bran."

Bran pushed her and leaned over her on the bed. His face must have shown his frustration because her giggles stopped. "We are *mated*, my lady. We love each other. You asked for time to be certain but the time has come."

"But Bran...you've only been here a year."

Always with the excuses. Every time he'd broached the subject of their future she'd found a way to avoid talking about it. He didn't intend to avoid the subject any longer. A warrior fought for what he wanted even in the game of love.

"A year spent discovering one major truth—that we want to be together. All else will work out. You called me your hero, Melissa. Given that how can I be anything but your perfect match? How can you be anything but my perfect mate?"

From under the pillow he produced the ring he'd had set with the smallest of the diamonds that had been in his pouch.

The rest were in a safety deposit box to keep for their future. He'd no idea of their value when he'd first arrived or he wouldn't have had to steal money. Not that he regretted that first treasure hunt…if nothing else its ingenuity had impressed his heroine.

His ring apparently was impressive as well. Melissa's open-mouth stare told him that even the smallest diamond was big enough for the job of binding her to him.

He gazed at her, letting his gravity seep into her soul. This was the moment he'd waited for. "I want to make what's between us permanent. Will you be my wife?"

Her protests silenced, Melissa gazed into his face, reading it as if it were a book. He let her see his determination, his desire to keep her beside him, his love for her. With one hand she traced his jaw, her face uncertain.

"You are serious about this. You want to marry me."

"You know I do."

Melissa nodded slowly. "I guess it's inevitable, after all."

"What is, fair one?"

She smiled at the endearment, his first words to her so long ago. "My saying yes is inevitable. After all, you're my perfect hero. What else could you be than my husband?"

Bran shouted in relief and exultation, the two emotions warring for dominance in him. The game was over and at last he'd won. They'd have their lives to spend finding new and better games to play.

He slipped the ring onto her finger. "I'm glad you finally see it my way."

"Oh, I never had a chance," she told him, still admiring the stone. "I was outmatched by magic, love—and the perfect hero."

The End

Also by Cricket Starr

ℰ꙳

Divine Interventions 1: Violet Among the Roses
Divine Interventions 2: Echo in the Hall
Divine Interventions 3: Nemesis of the Garden
Ellora's Cavemen: Dreams of the Oasis III (*anthology*)
Ellora's Cavemen: Legendary Tails I (*anthology*)
Hollywood After Dark: Fangs for the Memories
Hollywood After Dark: Ghosts of Christmas Past
Holiday Reflections (*anthology*)
Memories to Come
Memories Revised
Rogues *with Liddy Midnight*
The Doll
Two Men and a Lady (*anthology*)

If you are a fan of Cricket's Hollywood After Dark vampire stories, be sure to see the other stories in the series at Cerridwen Press (www.cerridwenpress.com), written under the name Janet Miller.

Hollywood After Dark: All Night Inn
Hollywood After Dark: Tasting Nightwalker Wine

About the Author

❦

Cricket Starr lives in the San Francisco Bay area with her husband of more years than she chooses to count. She loves fantasies, particularly sexual fantasies, and sees her writing as an opportunity to test boundaries. Her driving ambition is to have more fun than anyone should or could have. While published in other venues under her own name, she's found a home for her erotica writing here at Ellora's Cave.

Cricket welcomes comments from readers. You can find her website and email address on her author bio page at www.ellorascave.com.

Tell Us What You Think
We appreciate hearing reader opinions about our books. You can email us at Comments@EllorasCave.com.

POLAR HEAT
Mary Winter

෯

Trademarks Acknowledgement

The author acknowledges the trademarked status and trademark owners of the following wordmarks mentioned in this work of fiction:

Sterno: Candle Corporation of America

Chapter One

ဢ

All Aud Myrhe needed to do was return to camp, analyze her findings and turn the article over to her editor at *Nature*. With the promised payment for the latest on her team's polar bear research, she would secure additional funding for the team. The money was the reason why she and Svein had agreed to stay at camp instead of returning home over the holidays.

Aud fingered the strap on her backpack and took an exploratory step from the mouth of the cave—directly into a cloud of blowing snow. Driving wind howled and ice crystals formed against what little skin she'd left exposed. Overhead, the dark sky—it was always dark near the Arctic Circle in December—promised no hope of light or direction.

So much for heading back to their base camp. They should have tried to beat the storm. But the risk of not returning had been worth it to get the prepartum readings they needed from the hibernating, pregnant polar bear. She ducked back into the cave and turned to give the bad news to her partner, Svein Edie.

Svein puzzled her. Six years older than she, he possessed the qualifications that would have made him the easy choice to lead this mission. But he didn't usurp her authority. Instead, he followed her scientific lead unless he felt strongly about something. Then he stood his ground until he won the point, a stubborn and skillful negotiator. She admired his tenacity when it came to his beliefs. She might want to slug him at times, but she respected him as well.

Aud reassured herself that she had been chosen to lead the mission on the merit of her qualifications, not because

Svein let her. She knew polar bears like the back of her hand. She'd been the one researching them since her childhood. At thirty-two, she also knew her way around the frozen north. Her scientist father had often taken Aud and her two sisters into the Arctic on his research missions. Sure, her father might have been studying orcas, but her gaze had always roamed the shore looking for polar bears.

She knew she was qualified to lead the team, and she prided herself on her professionalism. Still...sexy, intellectual men were her kryptonite—Svein more so than most. All six-foot five-inches of him frustrated her on a sexual level. Just one look at his short-cropped, white-blond hair and icy blue eyes had her pussy weeping. His hard, muscled body looked as if it should be in a body-building magazine. She often heard the clank of weights in the base camp fitness room.

Something about discussing theories with a smart, sexy man soaked her panties. Sitting with Svein back at camp, analyzing the latest scientific news over cups of mediocre coffee, she had often wished she could push her professional barriers aside and fuck him senseless. And from the way she'd caught him looking at her lately, she thought he wanted the same. His gaze reminded her of a polar bear looking at a plump, juicy seal.

Damn! Being stuck in a cave with him would torment her. They'd ranged farther than they'd planned, but at least they'd found some shelter and weren't out in the open. Svein had an uncanny knowledge of the caves around here. This particular one hadn't shown up on any topography maps Aud possessed. She hadn't even known it existed until he had pointed it out to her.

She rounded the corner to find Svein bent over, packing their tools and equipment. Even in head to toe snow gear, the man had a nice ass. Tight, muscled, just the perfect thing for a girl to hang on to—

Wait a minute! She reined in her thoughts. She'd gone twelve months without sex. Her attention had been focused on her mission, her research, her work to help the dying polar bears. Just thinking about the bears reminded her why she'd been living like a monk. Whatever sacrifices she made, if it brought polar bears back from the brink, it was worth it. If she had to rough it in a cave with Svein and his dangerous good looks, so be it.

"We're stuck here until the wind lets up. I'd hoped to get back and start typing up our notes, but I guess not yet." She shrugged. "Could be worse. We have shelter and rations for another day or so."

Svein looked over his shoulder at the leader of their scientific team. He resisted the urge to grin at their predicament. He suspected that although he had no problems being stuck in a cave, especially with someone as smart and beautiful as Aud, she felt differently. He doubted she'd consider it a Christmas present to be trapped here with him, not when academia and a chance to publish their findings sang a siren song luring them back to their base camp. However, if it gave them a chance to pad their research, he doubted she'd be too upset about the delay. It just might take her a while to come around.

He held out his hands in what he hoped was an endearing gesture. "I think we'll manage. I can behave myself."

"I hope so," she said as she slipped off her backpack and set it down. Her smile softened her clipped words.

She straightened, and though she was taller than the average woman, he towered over her. He felt acutely aware of her slim frame. A lock of golden blonde hair tumbled free of her parka hood and his fingers itched to reach out and rub that silken strand, so much so that he nearly pulled off his glove and touched her. He caught a whiff of her natural fragrance, a light floral scent like the warm spring days that came too few and too late in the north. Heat filled his groin and made him hard. He'd watched her, worked with her, and although at times he struggled to keep professional distance between them, his admiration for her grew. God, she was beautiful.

Sure, when the mission had been assembled he'd begrudged her the fact she'd been picked as the leader. He'd counted her youth against her. Yet the more he worked with her, the more he admired her—as a woman *and* a scientist. Glancing back the way she had come, he wondered how long the storm would last.

He focused on the chore of unpacking the bag he'd so carefully packed moments before and pulled out a tripod and a can of Sterno. They'd brought field rations and sleeping bags with them from base camp. Not a lot, but enough to last a couple days in case something happened. Bringing survival equipment for what should have been a day's exploration might have seemed silly to anyone else, but out here a storm could blow up at any time. They lacked driftwood to burn for heat. They'd have to rely on their bodies for that. It wouldn't be a five-star hotel, but they could wait out the storm.

He felt her gaze on him, watching him as he set up camp. "You can come over here, if you want. I won't bite. Not unless you ask me to anyway." He flashed a teasing grin and noticed a flush creeping over her cheeks. He could have attributed the rosy color to windburn, but hoped he was the cause.

If the storm worsened, he *could* shift into his other form and keep them both warm...

No. As much as he wanted to get closer to Aud, he knew he simply couldn't blurt out his special ability.

He listened to the rustle of her snow pants as she sat on the floor of the cave. She held herself distant from him, almost as if she didn't trust him...or herself. He hid a smile as he unrolled his sleeping bag.

"Why don't you join yours to mine?" he suggested. "We can stay warmer that way."

And he could spend time with her curves pressed up against his body, albeit cushioned by several layers. An exercise in torture, but one he'd gladly accept.

She frowned but must have realized the wisdom in his words for she unrolled her bag and moments later they were zipped together. She sat on top of the bags and wrapped her arms around herself.

"So we just sit here and wait." She sounded resigned to the fact, frustrated, and the researcher in him echoed her sentiments. "I need to get back and type up our findings. We need to get them published."

"It'll happen. We just have to wait Mother Nature out for a while, but I think we're more stubborn than this storm," Svein said, offering what support he could. Aud was pretty when she pouted, her lower lip full and ripe, ready for sucking. The need to reassure her, to let her know no matter what happened he'd take care of her, rolled through him. "We'll be just fine, don't worry. And besides, it could be worse."

Aud arched an eyebrow. "You're saying we could be dead?"

"See, we're not." He chuckled in response to her teasing voice and sat next to her. "Seriously, we planned for storms. We're far enough from base that, with the weather, we couldn't possibly reach it today, but as soon as things die down we will."

She shook her head, and then laughed. "I guess you have a point, though we could be back at camp, warm and toasty, and not worrying about what will happen if this storm doesn't let up enough for us to return. I'm anxious to secure that additional funding."

Again he wished he could tell her if things got worse, he'd shift and take her back to headquarters. But of course he couldn't tell her that. Not when there was a very good chance the storm would blow itself out and they'd return safely to camp on their own. He reached across the space separating them and curled his gloved hand around her arm. "We'll get out of here. I promise."

The relieved smile that crossed her lips could have melted a thousand feet of snow, and he'd gladly give his life to make her smile like that again. It lit up her eyes, brought out the rosy tint in her cheeks. Warmth radiated from her body — and suddenly he had to taste her. Professional distance be damned. Staying in the cave gave him an opportunity that might not come around again. If he wanted more than a professional relationship with Aud, and he did, he had to make the first move. Leaning across the space separating them, he kissed her.

Warmth spread from the soft touch of Svein's lips. For so long she'd imagined what it'd be like to kiss this smart and sexy man. Reality made her fantasies pale in comparison. His soft lips sent sparks shooting from her lips to her pussy and all the points in between. He drank from her, coaxed and tasted, until she thought only of her throbbing cunt and how well he'd ease her delicious torment.

She had to remember he was a scientific colleague. She stiffened as she struggled not to succumb further to the pleasure of his kiss. They had to remain professional to work together. Nights spent discussing the latest scientific theories blurred in her memory. The way he seemed to know exactly where to find polar bears, or the way his eyes lit up when they brought down a large male for tagging and samples, filled her thoughts. She struggled to keep the concept of their working relationship firmly in her mind. Then his gloved fingers curled against her cheek, his tongue traced the seal of her lips and her lingering traces of professionalism dissipated.

A tiny whimper of need emerged from her throat. If she'd known it would be this good, she wouldn't have waited so long. In fact, with his tongue making a cautionary dip into her mouth, Aud wondered why she'd even waited at all. She offered no resistance, inviting him to explore deeper. The taste of him exploded in her mouth, rich and decadent like the stash of *Bamsemums* she kept in her desk. The chocolate-covered marshmallow candy was a rare indulgence. Just like Svein's kisses.

She curled her fingers around his broad shoulders as her world spun out of control. If the touch of his lips could arouse her so quickly, then what would full-on body contact do? She shuddered just thinking about it and moaned into his mouth.

The cave fell away. Their current predicament, the storm raging outside, all thoughts of it fled as Svein stroked her arm. He flattened his hand against the front of her parka. Through the layers, he curled his fingers around her breast and she arched into his touch. As if his hand held electricity, its touch zapped through her veins all the way to her aching pussy. Her nipples hardened. Her juices soaked her panties and she wanted more.

The need for air parted them. She stared at him, not quite believing she'd done something so completely uncharacteristic as kiss him. Her breath rasped in her chest and slowly she became aware of his hand still on her breast. Reluctantly, he pulled it away.

"Something tells me neither one of us noticed the cold just then." She pressed her lips together, uncertain how to put some distance between them. She was the leader of this team. She had to remain professional. A line had been crossed and she scrambled to regain control. Except, after feeling Svein's lips against hers, she wasn't so sure control was what she wanted.

"I've been thinking about keeping you warm for quite some time," he said, throwing her a boyish grin. He glanced around the cave. "And it seems like Mother Nature has given me the perfect opportunity to show you how hot I can make you."

Aud's breath caught in her throat. His words enflamed her, because god help her, she wanted to see how hot he could make her too.

She bolted to her feet and backed away. Distance. She needed distance. Right now, with Svein staring at her as if she were the last whole chocolate cookie on a plate of crumbs, and with the memory of his lips against hers too fresh in her mind, she wanted to fuck him until she could concentrate on nothing but his cock pounding deep inside her.

Heat suffused her cheeks. Was it hot in here? Maybe they were finally warming up the cave, though the knowledge of how that happened made her blush deepen. "That's not a good idea," she finally replied, unhappy to hear the wobble in her voice.

"Why not?" Svein rose and followed her. His long strides stalked her across the cave until she stood with her back pressed against the icy wall, the hot bulk of his body in front of her. Even through the parka, heat radiated from him in waves. He braced a hand on the cave beside her head. "Why isn't it a good idea? You know we'd be good together. Hell, I think we'd be explosive."

Aud sucked in a breath at the mental image his words conjured of the two of them, snuggled in their combined sleeping bags, his cock hard and hot and deep inside her. Her voice would echo inside the cave as she came. Her pussy clenched. "No!" she said, sharper than she'd intended. "I don't think this is a good idea."

"I think it's the best damn idea I've had since joining the team." He leaned closer and sniffed. "And I think you agree."

An embarrassed flush crept over her cheeks at his audible inhalation. Her cheeks flamed to think that he could smell her soaked pussy and that he knew he caused it. Aud raised her hands with the intention of pushing him away. Instead, she curled her fingers into the front of his parka. "This isn't—"

"Shh. Don't think. Just feel, Aud. Let your rational mind go, and just feel."

His husky voice permeated her skin, seeped into her pores and flowed through her veins. Behind her sports bra her nipples hardened again, and she curled her fingers tighter into the ripstop nylon of his parka.

Svein covered her lips with his. He pressed her against the wall of the cave, the heat from his body enveloping her. Thrusting his tongue deep into her mouth, he rubbed his hips against hers, letting her know exactly what he wanted.

Aud wrapped her arm around his shoulders, feeling his strength, his bulk. She rubbed against him, each brush against his body growing the ache in her pussy. She sucked on his tongue and drew it deep into her mouth. Svein was a damn good kisser.

His free hand slid over her side to cup her hip and haul her against him. Through the layers she felt the ridge of his cock, and her hand on his chest found the zipper of his parka. She pulled it down, the rasp loud in the cave. Beneath it, he wore a thick woolen sweater. She inhaled deeply, his musky scent filling her nostrils. She nearly pulled off her glove so she could touch him.

Svein released her. For a moment she mourned the loss as she watched him unfasten his bibbed snow pants and drop his gloves to the floor of the cave with a soft swish. He unzipped her parka, his big hands curling into her wool sweater, pulling it up to caress the thin cotton shirt covering her skin. His hands were cold, almost too cold. He curled his fingers against her ribs, his right hand sliding up to cup her breast. Through the thin layers of cloth, his chilly touch puckered her nipple and made it ache.

He unhooked her own bibbed snow pants then pushed them down, along with her pants and underwear. She should have been freezing, but the low-hanging parka shielded her bottom from the cave wall—and with Svein's hand sliding across her drenched folds, she felt anything but cold. The chill of his fingers quickly warmed as he rubbed her clit.

Her hips bucked and she cried out. Heavy breathing echoed in the cave and she reached beneath his clothing, wanting to touch him. Aud spread her legs as wide as she could amid the tangle of her pants as she removed her gloves. She shoved his sweater and the shirt beneath it up and flattened her palms against his chest. Svein pulled away long enough to slide his arms out of the sleeves of his parka, letting it fall to the cave floor. He shoved his pants and long underwear down, revealing his cock encased in formfitting black briefs.

Aud curled her fingers against his turgid length, cupping him through the cloth. Svein growled, the feral sound raising the hair on her arms. And then he moved forward. He stroked his fingers along her labia again and pulled up her shirt with his other hand, just enough to reveal her breasts, and fastened his lips around one nipple, sucking on it through her bra.

Her head fell back. A breathy cry emerged from her throat and her pussy tightened. First one finger, then a second slid into her cunt, stretching her, preparing her. With his thumb brushing across her clit, tiny sparks shot through her veins. The cold now utterly forgotten, she thrust her hips and invited him deeper.

Fingers clenching against his cock, she stroked it through the soft cotton fabric. "Please," she whimpered, and a distant part of her mind realized she was begging Svein to fuck her. It didn't matter, not now. Being trapped in this cave isolated them in their own world. There wasn't a mission, a team or a leader. Just the two of them generating enough heat to melt the Arctic down around them.

He released her nipple. "You want me inside you?"

"Yes! God, yes." She pulled down his briefs, freeing his cock. Aud wrapped her fingers around it and they barely touched. One stroke, two, and then he curled his fingers around her wrist and stilled her hand.

"Much more of that and I'm going to come." He reached behind her, cupping her buttocks and lifting her. Muscles bulged in his arms and for one moment the head of his cock brushed her slick opening. "Last chance," he said, offering her an opportunity to change her mind.

Aud shook her head. "Fuck me, Svein." She pressed her lips to his, telling him with tongue and teeth exactly what she wanted — to be taken, and taken hard.

Chapter Two

ഇ

From the moment he'd seen Aud he'd wanted her. A single thrust of his hips buried him balls-deep inside her. For a moment he waited, suspending her between his hard body and the wall of the cave. His sides should have been cold. They weren't. Not when his inner beast hovered so close to the surface. He wanted to roar, to bellow his joy. Instead, he pulled back so slowly she whimpered with need, before thrusting forward again.

Exquisite pleasure rippled along the length of his cock. It should have been awkward fucking her this way. But with his shifter strength he held her easily, and their cramped position only made her hotter, tighter. If he thrust any farther inside she would taste him in her throat. Her sheath gripping him, so slick, so wet, made him never want to leave her warmth. Aud wrapped her arms around him and buried her face in the crook of his shoulder.

He tried to savor the feel of her hot pussy clenching his cock. He wanted to make it last. Yet, it'd been so long, and he'd fantasized about Aud for months. The tiny flutters of her pussy eroded the edge of his control.

He pulled out slowly, wanting to watch the raw pleasure dance across her face. Then her fingers clenched against his shoulders.

"Svein!" she cried out as he thrust forward again.

As his name echoed in the cave, his control snapped. He thrust with long, hard strokes deep inside her, over and over again. Pressing her against the wall of the cave, one hand still clutching her ass to hold her in place, he reached between their bodies and flicked his fingers over her clit.

Aud screamed. Her pussy contracted around him as she came, her nails digging deep enough into his shoulders to feel them beneath his sweater.

He dipped his head to her breast, suckling her and thrusting through her orgasm. Rolling her nipple between his teeth, he realized he couldn't get enough of this woman. Her taste. Her smell. He wanted to be between her thighs, lapping at her juices and making her come with just his lips and tongue.

He lifted his head and claimed her mouth in a bruising kiss. *Mine!* His animal instincts cried out with the need to claim her and mark her as his own. *Mine.* So close, his balls drawn tight against his body, yet he refused to come. Not yet.

Her cries degenerated into sobbing moans as she reached orgasm once more. She milked his cock, bringing him along with her. He thrust again. His balls ached with the need to come and when he stiffened inside her, he let the pleasure wash through him.

His orgasm slammed into him so hard it felt like the top of his head was going to explode. Jet after jet of his warm seed filled her, rushing from his cock. His harsh breaths mingled with hers, and only then did he feel the sweat drying on his skin and the chill of the Arctic cave.

He knew he should shift to ease the pain of the cold. But not here, not with this woman in his arms.

"Mmm," she murmured against him, offering a tiny snuggle that had his cock hardening once more.

The quickie against the wall wouldn't be enough now that he'd tasted her charms. Outside, he sensed the storm still raged.

"Can you stand?" he asked.

She managed to nod.

His cock slid from her and he lowered her to the ground. As soon as he could, he reached behind him and shrugged into his parka. "Let's get tucked into the sleeping bags. It'll be easier to keep each other warm that way," he said, sliding his ungloved hand along her thigh.

Looking at Svein, Aud wondered where her earlier reservations had gone. Her pussy still tingled and she hated to bend down and pull up her pants, but the air grew frigid without his warm body against hers. She watched him quickly arrange his clothing, only zipping up his parka partway, and then turn toward the sleeping bags. She followed as soon as she'd straightened her own clothes and zipped her parka.

"You did say you would keep me warm," she teased as she sat down on the bags, pulled off her boots and slid inside, snow gear and all.

"I did, didn't I?" He followed suit, and soon had her tucked against his broad chest, his arm wrapped around her.

She snuggled against his warm, male body. She flattened her palm against his stubbled cheek and brushed her lips across his. Trailing her fingers down his arm, she longed for them to be back at the base camp, where she could explore him fully naked and they didn't have to worry about the cold or generating body heat. She opened her mouth to speak and a yawn emerged. Snuggling against him, she intended to rest just for a moment.

Svein watched the woman in his arms sleep. Compared to the no-nonsense team leader he knew, in sleep Aud revealed a softer, more feminine side. Her lips parted slightly, and watching her, his cock hardened. Easily he imagined her pink lips surrounding his cock, sucking, licking, drawing up and down his shaft.

She shivered with cold. Even with both of them in layers of snow gear and inside the sleeping bags, the chilly air pulled the warmth from their bodies. He tucked a corner of the sleeping bag next to her face. Behind them sat their packs and he thought about pulling out the scarf she should have been wearing, except then he couldn't have kissed her pink rosebud mouth.

The need to shift to protect his body from the cold filled him. Maybe a half-shift, just enough to ensure he stayed warm, and in his other form he could keep her warm as well. He lay there and listened to the storm howl until the reason for their being here pushed him into action. He slid his arm from beneath her, gingerly working his way out of the sleeping bag.

Aud didn't stir. Taking a deep breath, he inhaled the searing cold air. Before he could change his mind, or she woke up, he stripped off his clothing. Then, he moved a distance away and concentrated.

In an instant his form shifted. Bulk he didn't have filled out his body, arms and legs changing, until there he stood — nine hundred pounds of polar bear. His white fur and dark skin insulated his body, and he boasted feet with widespread toes that helped him walk on the snow. He padded over to Aud. Careful not to disturb her, he pulled the sleeping bag over her chin and face, trying to keep her shielded from the cold as much as possible. She whimpered, her eyelids fluttering, and for a moment he feared he'd wakened her. Moments later, she settled back to sleep.

He had a Christmas present to deliver. If he could confirm their calculations of the hibernating bear's impending pregnancy and add the information to their previous findings, it'd be a far better present for Aud than the box of chocolates he had back at the base camp. It had been his bear senses that had found the she-bear. In his heart, he thought of her as his gift to Aud. He'd peek at their sleeping mama bear and then return to keep Aud warm until she woke. With any luck, he could help her capture pictures of the newborn cubs. It'd be the perfect ending to their prenatal polar bear research. With a toss of his great head, he strode toward the opening of the cave and the storm beyond.

In that half-aware place between dreams and wakefulness, Aud reached for Svein. Her gloved fingers curled around empty air. She mewled her disappointment then drifted back to her dreams…

The massive male nuzzled at her face and shoulders before grasping a blanket and pulling it over her. She snuggled into it, smelled the hot breath of a predator, and the shiver that darted down her spine was from excitement, not cold. A part of her said she should be scared, yet she wasn't. The beast looked at her, his eyes filled with an intelligence she couldn't deny. Almost like he knew her and wanted to communicate with her. She knew he wouldn't hurt her, and she couldn't be scared of him – not even when she'd witnessed firsthand the power of these large creatures.

Unafraid, she slid from the confines of the sleeping bags. She looked around the cave, wondering where Svein might have gone and how he'd feel when he found out he'd missed this spectacle. Polar bears had been known to eat humans. She offered a meal, if only a small one, for a creature his size, and yet she stood there watching him, and feeling no fear. Only an intense curiosity gripped her. She reached for the bear, her gloved hands sliding through thick, plush fur. Curling her fingers, she gripped a generous handful of the creature's ruff, and had he been a cat he might have purred. Big eyes closed and a heavy, contented sigh issued from the bear's chest.

The rush of warm air against her cheek forced her to release the bear as the reality of what she was doing sank in. The creature looked at her, tossed his head and strode away.

"Don't go," she begged. The bear shook his head again and continued toward the entrance of the cave, into the storm.

Her dream faded, and in her sleep, Aud reached for the beast.

The long walk meant little to him in bear form. His father called it his soul shape. Svein focused on the practical applications of being a polar bear, like his ability to study these majestic creatures on their own terms.

Where other creatures waited out the storm, he forged a path into it, not caring about the sting of wind or snow. His feet acted like snowshoes as he crunched his way toward the other cave where he knew the female polar bear lay deep in hibernation. The need to return to the cave and curl up next to Aud, to keep her safe and warm, nearly had him retracing his steps. Instead, he thought of how she'd feel when he presented the final pieces of their research. The wind howled a little less fiercely as he rounded a massive boulder and the snow caressed more than stung. The storm was starting to blow itself out.

He found the cave, darting in long enough to make sure the mother bear still lay in slumber, her precious cubs yet unborn, though close to emerging into the world. Thankfully, with her hibernating, she wouldn't smell his presence.

He hurried back to where he'd left Aud. Back inside the cave, he shook his fur, drying it, and then returned to the sleeping bags. Mindful that he'd have to change before she woke, he lay down beside Aud, letting his bulk and his fur warm her. She snuggled closer to him, her breath a sigh against his fur, and contented, he rested his muzzle between his front paws.

Let her be warm, let her be safe...and with any luck, for Christmas they'd get to see newborn cubs. Although Aud couldn't know about his secret, he could give her this glimpse into his world. Feeling the steady rise and fall of her breathing next to him, the man inside the bear sighed with relief. When she woke it would be Christmas, a day of giving. He'd give what he was able.

He inched a paw closer to her. *Mine!*

Aud woke feeling warm and toasty in spite of being the only person in the sleeping bags. Opening her eyes, she searched for Svein in the cave. He monitored a pouch of food over a Sterno flame.

"Good morning, sleepyhead," he called.

One glance and Aud decided he awoke far too handsome and cheerful in the mornings. Images of his naked body and his cock buried deep inside her filled her mind. She rolled into a seated position, trying to banish her sexual thoughts.

"What are you cooking?" The aroma of the freeze-dried, prepackaged food made her mouth water with the promise of warm sustenance. She reached for the pocket of her parka and realized she'd slept on her energy bar. Now all she had was an unappetizing squished blob. She pulled her hand away.

"Theoretically it's beef stew, or at least that's what the package said. It's almost ready."

Aud crawled from the sleeping bags then began to unzip them and roll them up. She paused and glanced toward the cave opening, though she couldn't see it. "Has the storm cleared enough to break camp?"

"I think so. We might not have a lot of time with the prospective mama though." He continued to stir breakfast.

Automatically Aud glanced at her watch. Christmas Day. She never expected to spend Christmas in such close quarters with Svein. At least not in a cave. Get out, finish their research and photograph the bear, then get back. That had been the plan, and once back at the base, she would have disappeared into her room and composed the paper they planned to submit. Discreetly watching him, she tidied her ponytail. She finished packing up camp while he cooked. As soon as the food pouch was heated, he handed it to her and opened a second one.

"Eat. You're going to need your strength." He turned his attention back to cooking his own breakfast.

Aud ate straight from the pouch. Although a bit tepid, the food filled her and sent warmth radiating through her limbs. "Thank you," she said between bites.

Svein nodded and stirred his own stew.

No awkward morning-after jitters filled her. Instead, they acted companionable, professional...friendly even. She wondered if they could continue their relationship or if they'd retreat back to being coworkers and nothing more. A heated flush crept over her cheeks and behind her layers of clothing, her nipples pebbled.

"So you really think we should check on the bear before heading back? We probably shouldn't take any more chances," she said, trying unsuccessfully to create a distraction from her lusty — and dangerous — thoughts.

"The storm's died down a lot. We should be fine, and I know how much you want those pictures."

By the time Svein finished his food, Aud had sealed her pouch in a plastic bag to dispose of back at camp and washed her fork. Moments later they were ready to go.

He fastened a rope from his pack to the belt around her waist, securing them together, and led the way out of the cave. His larger size would help create a trail for her to follow.

They moved in silence, hunched over against the biting wind and the flakes of ice in the air. The lantern he held provided enough illumination to make out a trail of bear tracks. All bears should be hibernating this time of year, and she made a mental note to add this to her findings. If bears were coming out of their winter sleep early, a study into this change in their behavioral patterns might provide answers to saving them from extinction. Before she could ponder it further, Svein stopped at the opening to the cave.

Aud nodded, anxious to be out of the elements. Svein strode a little way into the cave and stopped, leaving her just enough room to slip inside. There, pressed against the back wall, barely a foot separating her from where Aud and Svein stood, was a huge female polar bear. Although hibernating, the creature twitched, one mighty paw coming close to them. She hadn't found a cave as deep as theirs, nor as spacious, and her bulk dominated the chamber. A low rumble worked its way from her throat.

Did bears dream during hibernation? Aud always imagining it as a months-long sleep, and suspected they did. From the way this female thrashed and growled, she appeared deep in the throes of a mighty dream.

The female raised her head. Her muzzle swiveled, appeared to be pointing right at them, and the great maw opened and closed with an audible clack of teeth. Shivers darted down Aud's spine. "Svein," she whispered, not quite sure this bear was comfortably in dreamland.

"Look." He pointed to the hindquarters, where a cub struggled to emerge into the world.

The mother slashed the air with her hind paw, so close a breeze washed over them.

Aud stepped back. "That was close—"

Thump! The paw hit the wall, raining ice and pebbles down on them.

"Think you can stay?" Svein glanced uneasily toward the birthing bear.

Aud nodded. "This is what we came for. Start tagging."

She dug the camera out of her bag. There was no way in hell she was going to miss this, and Svein knew it. She raised the camera, checked the angle and started filming.

Chapter Three

ဆာ

Svein grabbed their tags and instruments, his admiration for Aud growing even more. He moved closer to the bear, quickly drawing a blood sample and marking her. She twitched, her front leg slamming into his. He barely managed to keep his balance, but he did. And then the first cub tumbled free of the womb. It lay there scrambling in its sac until it broke, and then a second cub began to appear.

Svein stood transfixed. Bear or not, male or not, watching the miracle of birth coupled with the knowledge that something so small grew up into a hulking creature like him reminded him how insignificant he really was in the world. He glanced at Aud, not surprised to see frozen tears, like diamonds, sparkling on her eyelashes in the light from her head lamp. And then the second cub tumbled free, and in less time than he would have expected, both made their way to the bear's teats, clamped on and began to nurse.

This is it. It's why we do this work. To keep these creatures alive and in the wild.

Time faded away. How long they remained in the cave, taking measurements, dictating notes into a tape recorder and videotaping the new family, he didn't know. Hours must have passed, and he suddenly realized they'd stayed far longer than they should have. He clicked off his tape recorder and stowed his supplies in his pack.

Aud focused on the bears and continued to run the camera. She shivered. Her body shook violently from the chill that must be seeping into her bones. He had to get her back to camp.

He tapped her shoulder and she steadied the camera in her shaking hands. Under her breath he heard her murmuring words, estimating weights, lengths, cursing that they didn't bring more tools and instruments with them.

"We should go," he whispered.

She nodded. He watched her move, noticing her lethargy and the stiffness in her joints. If she tried to walk back to base camp like this, she wouldn't make it. He feared taking her back to their cave, knowing in human form he couldn't generate enough heat to warm her. But in his bear form...

Decision made, he refastened the rope connecting them and they hurried back toward the cave.

He led the way, with Aud close by his side, huddled against him for warmth and protection against the once-more rising wind. He wrapped his arm around her and pulled her closer. He'd never met a more resilient woman. Out in the Arctic, knowing they couldn't make it back to base for a second night and stuck in a cave with rations and freezing her ass off, she never complained.

The cave loomed before them. He ducked inside, feeling Aud's steps quicken beside him. Once inside, she sank to her knees.

"I'm so cold," she said, her teeth chattering audibly. "We shouldn't have stayed with the polar bears for so long. We should have gone back to camp."

"But then we wouldn't have the footage or the information we needed." He unrolled the sleeping bags as he spoke and herded her inside. He followed her, unzipping his parka once he was inside the insulated bags and pulling her against him. Wrapping his arms and the edges of his coat around her, he held her tight and wished warmth back into her limbs.

Her eyelids fluttered closed.

"Stay with me, Aud," Svein ordered. "Damn it, don't go to sleep." The thought of hypothermia's silent death had him shaking her shoulders until she opened her eyes.

"Stop doing that…just want to sleep." She burrowed even closer to him.

"You can't. Not until you're warm." Even as he said the words, she drifted into a cold-induced sleep.

He had no choice. He needed to warm her, fast. He slid from the sleeping bags. Aud whimpered and reached for him.

"Shh, it'll be all right." Once out of the bags, he stripped out of his clothing. With just a thought, he changed. He lowered himself next to her, not liking it when she didn't respond. *Burrow into me. Use me for your warmth.* He projected the commands toward Aud, knowing he had no other means to communicate in this form. As if she understood, she curled against him and he felt the tremors racking her body.

Cold, so cold she felt like a block of ice against his body. He tightened around her, pulling her against his stomach and chest, one large paw gingerly against her back. She snuggled against him, the warm sigh of her breath teasing strands of his fur. He smelled her scent, filled his nostrils with it, and knew that no matter how much he wanted to use other means to warm her, he offered only body heat for now. Sexual heat could, and would, come later.

How long he held her, Svein didn't know. Time passed differently in his bear form than as a man, but eventually, Aud woke.

Her swift gasp alerted him that she no longer slept. "Svein?" she whispered. "Svein, where are you?"

Caught.

To her credit, she didn't scream, not when a male polar bear lay on the sleeping bags close enough to bite her should he wish. He changed quickly back to human form.

"Svein?! *What the fuck?*" Aud scrambled out of the sleeping bag. Wrapping her arms around herself, she stumbled backward. *"You're a polar bear?!"* She backed into the wall and then reached behind her to grab it. "Oh my god! I've been sleeping with a freaking polar bear!"

She sucked in shallow gulps of air and he feared she might hyperventilate.

"It's all right," he said. "Yes, I can change into a polar bear, but I won't hurt you." He knew hedging wouldn't help the situation.

"What do you mean it's all right? You're a polar bear! Oh my god. It's not all right. You're a man, a scientist, not a bear!" Her voice rose with her fear.

He knew this would happen. Frankly, he was surprised she didn't run into the icy darkness. "Aud, stay with me. Breathe," he coaxed, watching her gasp for breath. Slowly, he stepped forward, not wanting to startle her any more. "I can shift into a polar bear. It's how I originally found that den with the pregnant bear. As you can probably imagine, it helps me in my research immensely." He watched fear war with scientific curiosity in her eyes. That was the Aud he knew and loved.

Svein swallowed hard. Yeah...he loved her. He'd claimed her as his own even before they'd made love. He stopped nearly an arm's length from her. "I won't hurt you, Aud. I'd never do anything to harm you."

"I believe you," she breathed. "Dear god, you're a polar bear. One snap of your jaws could break an arm or a leg! But I...I believe you wouldn't hurt me." She exhaled. "I have to see. Please, can I watch you change again?" Aud stepped forward. "All this time and you never said anything." She shook her head, her face suddenly an unreadable mask.

"I couldn't. But you were succumbing to hypothermia. I didn't want to lose you." *I still don't.* He stood there, cautious, half afraid she'd turn from him like the last—and only— woman to whom he revealed his secret. At least she wasn't freaking out anymore.

"I can't believe you're a polar bear." Aud wanted to be mad at him, wanted to scream and yell over all the times they went out in search of bears when all along they had one in their midst. Screaming wouldn't help. Neither would running away. Her dream filled her mind and she wondered now if it had really been a dream at all. The way the bear looked at her with its eyes so full of intelligence, the gut-deep feeling that the bear wouldn't hurt her made her desire to watch Svein shift more acute. She'd always wanted an up-close look at a live and conscious polar bear, not just tranquilized ones. Well, now she could have it. Aud stared at Svein, seeing him in a new light. Looking at him with his pale blue eyes and his hair so blond it was nearly white, she envisioned him as the polar bear. Proud. Reclusive. Dangerous if crossed. "I want to see, please."

She held her breath, afraid he'd refuse to grant the request. She should have been scared. Waking up with a polar bear inches from her hadn't been the experience she'd expected when she and Svein had headed out here. Yet, knowing what he was now, suddenly certain things made so much sense. His uncanny ability to find polar bears or their dens, the way he seemed to think like a bear at times—little facts suddenly clicked together in her mind. And her dream, so vivid and real, hovered over all of it.

She'd wanted—no, *needed*—to spend time with Svein's polar bear form, and she wanted to watch him shift. She had to see it again.

"I'm relieved I can finally show you," he said. He closed his eyes and in an instant his form shimmered. Then he stood there, a very large, male polar bear.

For long moments, Aud simply stared. She'd never seen anything like Svein's transformation before. Then curiosity got the better of her. She walked slowly, hesitantly to him, stopping by his massive shoulder. Reaching out, she stroked him, all the while examining his face, his ears, even looking at his teeth. He withstood it all, standing as still as a statue. She buried her hands deep into his fur. She felt heat, nearly furnace-like in its intensity, and knew without it she probably would have died. She shuddered. "This is amazing. Truly amazing," she whispered, then leaned forward and inhaled his musky scent.

"You're going to have to tell me all about how you do this when we get back to base camp." Aud stepped back from him and met his gaze. "You can understand me, can't you?"

He nodded his head.

"I always thought bears looked keenly intelligent. Now I know why. To think there might be more of you out there. There *are* more, aren't there? And will you introduce me?" She barked short bursts of laughter. "I'm asking questions of a bear. You can't answer me, but you're in there. You hear me. And when you're a man again you're going to answer my questions. To think, I've had sex with a man who can change into a polar bear. No wonder you were so keen on this mission." She closed her mouth, aware she was babbling and that it probably didn't make a bit of difference to Svein. He stared at her as if he had the patience of a saint. Then, he stepped forward and brushed his head against her.

She struggled to remain upright, though she suspected he tried to be very gentle with her. Tamping down her fear, she decided it was her turn to be explored after the way she'd stroked and petted him. It was unnerving having a huge beast rub against her slender frame. If he wanted to, Svein could clamp his jaws around her and inflict considerable damage. Yet, something told her he wouldn't. It could've been the slow, deliberate way he moved, as if working around a skittish animal. Or it could simply be because she knew he was still inside the bear, and Svein the man would never hurt her. She endured his attention, her apprehension slowly melting away. She knew she was witnessing something special, something spectacular…and something she feared she might never see again.

From the touch of her fingers against his fur to the wonder shining in her eyes, Aud accepted his other form. He rubbed against her, half expecting her to flinch away in fear. She didn't. Instead, she stood her ground, reaching out to stroke his thick fur as he rubbed his scent all over her body.

His scent on her body. Just the thought of it had him fighting back a raging hard-on and contemplating switching back so he could fuck her until they both passed out.

When he smelled only himself on her he grunted and stepped back as the human inside the bear made his needs known. He shifted, one moment warm and furry, the next completely naked beside her. He extended a hand, and she followed him down to the sleeping bags.

Twined around him, she pressed her lips against his chest. Her snow pants rustled as she snaked a leg around his hip. His cock hardened with a swift rush of blood. She lay nestled against his body with her eyes closed and her lips parted against his skin. He slid his hand down her back, cupped her ass and pulled her against him.

"Aud," he said, her name a husky plea on his lips.

"Svein." She kissed him, her tiny tongue darting between her lips to swipe across his salty skin. "It's really you." She rained tiny kisses over his chest and his neck, working back up to his lips. She pressed her mouth against his and drank from him.

The need to be inside her hot, wet body drove him. The frigid rocks and ice beneath him screamed at him to move. He helped strip her of her clothing, then slid into the sleeping bags with her.

Cold flesh against warm, Aud shivered as Svein pulled her against his body. He brushed a strand of her blonde hair away from her face. "You don't know what it means to me to have you accept both sides of my nature. I am a bear, yes, but first and foremost, I'm a man." Leaning forward, he claimed her mouth in a deep, soul-stealing kiss as their bodies slid together.

Svein's words sent shivers down Aud's spine. Watching him shift from man to bear and back again aroused not only her scientific curiosity. His cock throbbed against her stomach, and she reached between them to curl her warm hand around it. She stroked him from base to tip, her thumb finding the bead of moisture at the end.

"Right now I need the man," she said when the need for air parted their lips.

"Honey, I'm all man." He cupped her ass, pulling her against his hard length. "And I can't wait until we're back at camp and you can take me in your sweet, pink mouth."

Aud grinned, thinking she'd like the exact same thing. The logistics of their sleeping bags frustrated her. If only they were back at base camp on her bed. Though only a twin, it had more room than these sleeping bags, but she'd make it work. She folded herself as small as possible, bending her legs against the seam at the bottom of their makeshift bedding. She kissed the arrow of hair leading down from his navel, laving the crease where his thigh met his body. The next time they did this, and she didn't doubt there'd be a next time, she'd sprawl him on the bed where she could drink in the sight of his masculine form.

She wondered how much longer they could have worked together without combusting like this, how much longer she might have gone without knowing his secret. Too long. Looking at his cock, her fingers squeezing the base, she inhaled his musky aroma. She licked, just a taste to savor his piquant flavor. Juices flooded from her pussy. Her channel contracted on a cock that wasn't there, and she drew him deeper into her mouth.

His groan echoed in her ears. Fingers speared through her hair, tugging it loose from its ponytail as he held her against his cock. Svein's entire body was rigid, and Aud reached around him and clenched her fingers on his ass. Her only thoughts were of him as she continued to fuck him with her mouth.

He'd risked her possible rejection to save her life. Revealing his true nature probably hadn't been an easy decision to make, and she wanted to pay him back with what she had at this moment—her body, her affection.

Her love?

Aud pulled her mind away from those thoughts. She'd longed for a partner who shared her love of the Arctic and of polar bears. She wanted a lover who understood the demands of her profession. With Svein she might have found him, though a part of her feared their recent intimacy was due only to being caught out in the storm, and once they returned to camp, it would fade away like the northern lights with the approach of dawn.

The head of his cock bumped the back of her throat. She relaxed her muscles, allowing him to slip deeper. With tongue and teeth, she stroked and caressed, nibbled her way along his shaft, until his hips pumped against her mouth. Still she took him deeper. Hollowing her cheeks, she sucked hard. She longed to make him come.

If his groans were any indication, he was close. His balls drew up high and tight against his body. Aud fondled them, rolling each one in her hand before reaching behind them to stroke the sensitive skin.

Svein pleaded with her, his words barely registering. "Stop. I don't want to come without you." He cupped the back of her head, keeping her from going down on him again.

Aud pulled away. She released his cock from her mouth with a soft pop. As much as she wanted to taste him as he came, she wanted him inside her more. Her pussy ached. Her juices soaked her labia just thinking about Svein's cock inside her. She crawled back up the sleeping bag to press against his body, her nipples caressing his chest.

He cupped her breasts, pinching her nipples and palming her flesh until she squirmed against him.

She straddled him, looking down into his eyes. Her breath rasped from between parted lips. Reaching between their bodies, she stroked his cock, wet from her saliva, and positioned herself over it. "Take me. Please."

"Oh yeah," he replied, the husky timbre of his voice sending shivers down her spine. He grabbed her hips and thrust into her welcoming heat.

Exquisite pleasure sparked through her veins. He filled her, stretched her, and when their bodies were flush and his head brushed her cervix, she released a happy sigh.

Svein caressed the lengths of her arms. She shivered, her pussy clenching around him. Looking down at him, his hair nearly as white as the snow surrounding them, his eyes the icy blue of a frozen Nordic lake, she knew no matter what happened, she'd tumbled head over heels in love with him. It scared her. She feared she was putting her professional reputation on the line, yet here with him now, she knew she'd do it all again in a heartbeat. Svein had always been a valuable member of her team. Until now, she hadn't realized how valuable.

Tangling her fingers with his, she leaned into him and began to move. Each inch of him sliding from her was pure torture. She hovered there, wanting to make the moment last, trying to burn the image of him, his body, into her mind so that no matter what happened when the mission ended, she'd have something to keep her warm at night. She couldn't ask for any more.

She sank down on him, moaning as he filled her. Clenching her fingers tightly together with his, she rose and fell on his shaft. Her breasts bounced. In spite of the frigid temperatures, inside the sleeping bags sweat glistened on her skin.

Harder. Deeper. She leaned forward, wanting to take even more of him. Her knees pressed against the ground, the sleeping bags doing little to cushion them. "Please, please," she whimpered, needing release. Her pussy tightened.

Her breath came in shallow pants. A shift of her hips, a swivel on the way down had her moaning with pleasure. Nothing could ever compare to taking him like this in the cave, while the wind howled and raged outside.

And then she couldn't think at all, for a low, keening wail erupted from her throat. Head tilted back, breasts thrust forward, she rode the waves of her release as they rushed through her body with the force of an avalanche. Ripples started at her pussy, milked his cock and then burst through her. Up her spine, down her arms, even to the top of her head, which she thought might come off, ecstasy filled her body. She forced her eyes open and saw Svein.

He smiled at her, his body rigid as she exploded around his cock. And then, with a slow thrust, he filled her.

For as long as she lived, Aud knew she'd never forget this moment.

Chapter Four

❧

Aud amazed him. Right now, with her pussy still convulsing around his penis, he didn't want to think about anything at all except being buried inside her warm, sweet heaven.

He thrust upward, filling her, wrenching another cry of passion from her lips. He pulled her down toward him so she lay draped across his chest. Clasping her ass in his hands, he thrust into her welcoming heat. Over and over again he experienced the silken slide of his cock in her channel. God help him, he never wanted to let her go. He thrust deeper, joining them as intimately as two people could be.

Reaching between them, his fingers found her clit and her cries echoed in the cave as he strummed her to another orgasm. And then, only then, did he allow himself to thrust into her one last time. His cock erupted, shooting streams of come into her body. Her heat bathed him. Their juices mingled and the smell of their lovemaking filled this nostrils.

He listened to her breathing, sensed his own breaths matching hers. Sweat plastered strands of her hair to her forehead, and he knew he'd never seen anything as beautiful as the sight of her sprawled across his body. He rested one hand possessively at the small of her back. She sighed, grinned against his chest and wiggled even closer to him. Inside her, his cock twitched.

"Ready so soon?" she raised her head to stare at him. "I think you have the strength of a bear."

Pride filled him at her words. He slid his hand down the curve of her backside and patted her lightly on the ass. "When it comes to you, I'm always ready."

She looked as if she might say something, then didn't. Had he spoken too soon? Had he said too much? Damn it. After revealing his secret he imagined only good things for them, not a return to the professional relationship they'd had before getting caught in the storm. Except she made no move to leave, and he liked her weight pressing on top of him. He wanted to hold on to her. When they returned to the base camp and the rest of the team came back from their holiday vacations, he intended to make it clear that Aud belonged to him.

She rolled to the side and snuggled against him. "We should put our suits on. We're probably going to notice the cold soon."

Svein wrapped an arm around her. "I'll keep you warm."

"Yeah, you will." And in a few moments, he heard only her deep, even breathing as she drifted off to sleep, leaving him awake with his fears and his hopes.

* * * * *

The next morning brought the long trek back to base camp. In the endless dark of the Arctic winter, Aud struggled to make out landmarks. She saw nothing except a vast expanse of white dotted by boulders and footprints. The emptiness gave her time to think. She feared her abnegated attraction to Svein, combined with their close quarters, sparked their sexual activities, and figured that back at camp they'd have to find a new routine between them. She wondered if it would be one that included an emotional relationship. She paused, allowing him to switch positions with her. They worked together, wasting little time or words.

She stared at the ass of his snow pants in the glare of her head lamp and struggled not to focus on his loose-hipped stride. The thought that warmth and real food lay only a few hours away had her pushing herself, and him.

Lights shone on the horizon. "We're almost there," Svein called. The wind tore his words away.

Shocked, she realized they'd walked the entire distance without talking. Neither mentioned the sex or his amazing shifting ability. She wasn't sure how to take the silence. "Great," she replied in a faux-cheerful voice.

Almost back—back in the warmth, back among lights, back where she could retreat to her own room. She needed time to think. In less than two weeks the rest of the team would be returning from their Christmas holidays and she needed to have the article written, submitted and the additions to their research ready to present. She thought briefly of the presents waiting for her, mostly gifts from her family. She wondered if Svein had any presents other than the small gifts the members of the team had gotten each other.

"So what's the first thing you're going to do?" Svein asked as they crossed the lit courtyard.

Aud strode alongside him. *Find out if you want to continue this relationship. And if not, try to find a way to mend my broken heart.* Out of the corner of her eye, she watched his profile as they stopped at the door and she punched in the security code.

Svein held the door open, looking as if he wanted to press for an answer to his question.

Thankfully, he didn't. She stepped inside then closed her eyes and inhaled. "Warmth. My God, I never thought I'd be warm again." She leaned against the wall and released a sigh. When she opened her eyes, she saw Svein staring her strangely. Then his expression cleared so quickly she thought she might have imagined it. "I mean...*you* kept me warm," she said, "but it's nice to not have to worry about frostbite or hypothermia." She shimmied out of her snow gear until she wore only sweater, pants and thick socks.

As Aud peeled off her layers of clothing, all Svein could think about was getting her naked. Here at base camp they had none of the concerns about warmth or survival. For the next couple of weeks it'd be just the two of them and one research paper. The paper could wait.

He stripped off his parka and snow pants, then tossed his sweater behind him and peeled his pants from his legs. He kicked them off and strode toward her. With everyone gone, they had the place to themselves—and he didn't want to waste a single moment.

"You didn't answer my question." Stopping behind her, he grabbed the hem of her sweater and pulled it over her head. Her undershirt and bra followed then he slid her pants down her long legs. She kicked them off but didn't turn around. She stood there dressed only in her heavy socks.

"If you touch me, then you'll know what I want." She backed into him and rubbed her buttocks against his groin.

"I want to hear you say it." The sweet curve of her ass tormented him. Ignoring it for even sweeter targets, he reached around and cupped her breast. "I think," he whispered against her hair, "that you want me inside you. That now that we don't have to worry about freezing our asses off, you want me to fuck you." He flicked his thumb over her nipple.

Aud bit back a moan. "You think a lot," she whispered. "I want more action." She wiggled her buttocks against him again.

His cock throbbed, balls full and heavy between his legs. His sensitive nose picked up the scent of her drenched folds, and he slid his hand around her hip to rest just above her mons.

"I think you like it when I think." He dipped his fingers down to her honeyed warmth, smiling when he encountered her slick lips. "Spread your legs."

She complied, her hiss of pleasure audible as he stroked her folds. If she thought she could return to being the standoffish leader of the team, she had better think again. He caressed her pussy, loving the way Aud bit back her moans and whimpers of pleasure. He toyed with her nipples, first one then the other. With his nose, he shoved her hair aside and licked a path up the side of her neck.

God, she had him so hot, so hard. And when she thrust her ass at him, legs spread wide, he nearly grabbed her hips and impaled himself in her channel.

"On your knees," he ordered.

She knelt, thrusting that heart-shaped ass in the air and looking over her shoulder with a saucy grin. The pink lips of her pussy parted, giving him a view of her engorged clit.

Svein knelt behind her. He stroked her labia with his knuckles, pressing against her clit. First one finger, than a second slid into her tight channel, and he worked them back and forth. Her moans—husky, needy cries that had his balls tightening—echoed in the room, and when he leaned forward and cupped her breast, he imagined taking her like this, mounting her, fucking her like a bear took its mate.

Aud cried out. Her sheath rippled around his fingers, milking them as she came. "Please," she begged.

Svein slid his fingers from her pussy, ready to give his woman exactly what she wanted.

On all fours, presenting her pussy to him like some animal in heat, Aud struggled to regain her breath after her quick, shattering orgasm. She hadn't answered Svein's question. In truth, she feared what her answer would be, but down here, on the floor, with Svein behind her, she wanted his cock, his body. She dared not hope for his love.

His broad head breached her entrance and she closed her eyes at the sublime pleasure. He seemed to know where to kiss, to caress, two fingers on her clit, his other hand on her breast. His lips blazed a trail down her spine and with a flex of his hips, he buried himself balls-deep inside her.

Her channel tightened around him. For a moment she held him there before he pulled back with exquisite slowness. Thrust and retreat. Thrust and retreat. His cock filled her, stretched her. The friction made her breath catch in her throat.

He palmed her breasts, moving between one and the other. Whispered Norwegian endearments filled the air. He made love to her as if she were something fragile, special, and she swallowed hard as he filled her once more. Curling her fingers against the floor, she wanted to turn around and touch him.

His thrusts quickened. Harder, faster, as if he couldn't get enough of her, and she knew the feeling. He changed his angle, striking her G-spot with every thrust. Oh yeah…just like that until her whimpers degenerated into sobbing moans and then her world shattered apart.

More brilliant than the aurora borealis, her orgasm swept her up in never-ending waves. Higher and higher it tossed her, Svein's pumping rhythm taking her closer to the stars than she'd ever been in her life. Then he stiffened behind her. With a triumphant roar, he came. His hot seed bathed her channel. His fingers clamped on her hips and as she knelt there, head between her arms, she knew she belonged to him. Mated.

Her breath billowed out of her lungs. She struggled to regain her equilibrium as Svein's fingers slowly uncurled from around her hips and he sat back on his heels. He pulled her with him, and together they cuddled on the sprawl of parkas and snow pants on the floor.

"I was hoping for a hot bath," she whispered, when at last she could catch her breath, "but that was good too."

Svein brushed his lips against her temple. "Go, take your bath. I'll get started on putting our notes into the computer. I'll give you thirty minutes."

"If my legs will support me." She leaned against his chest. "Damn, that was good."

"I know."

His masculine chuckle propelled her to her feet, and wiggling her ass at him, she strode into the bathroom.

* * * * *

Svein padded down the hall in his dark navy sweater and matching woolen socks knit by his mother, and a pair of jeans. Not bothering to knock on the bathroom door, he opened it and leaned against the doorjamb.

He stared at her, the blood rushing south at an alarming rate. With her hair piled on her head in a mass of golden strands, buried to her neck in hot water, she looked like a sea goddess come to life. "Your thirty minutes are up."

Aud squeaked with surprise. "What are you doing in here? Surely you haven't input everything into the computer."

What was he doing here when there was plenty of work to be done? He wanted to say that his need for her burned in his veins. That he longed to sink his cock into her without worrying about the ice, the storm, nothing but the bed beneath them and the ways in which he could please her. A part of him wondered if Aud really wanted to hear it. She seemed to have accepted the physical side of their relationship, but the emotional...he didn't know.

"Your time's up. And there's room in the tub for two. Besides, the computer can wait."

Her breath caught in her throat as her gaze caressed him from head to toe, lingering on the bulge behind his fly. "You look toasty."

He burned like gasoline thrown on a Yule log. "I'm heating up," he said, his gaze deliberately resting on the mounds of her breasts. "You need someone to wash your back." He reached for the hem of his sweater and pulled it over his head. To hell with the subtle approach.

"I could be persuaded." She leaned forward, her golden hair coming lose and spilling over her shoulders.

Svein bit back a groan. He knelt beside the tub and slid his fingers through the warm water. "You better be willing to share." He drank in the sight of the vulnerable curve of her neck, down along the straight line of her back to where it disappeared below the water. Oh, to follow that curve down to her buttocks, to taste the dimples there at the base of her spine...

She turned to face him, her lips inches from his. "Is all this going to change when the team returns?" Her soft voice wrapped tendrils around his heart. "I mean, our attraction has been simmering for a long time. It was inevitable we give in to it, but I want something more than a quick poke in a cave." A pained grin twisted the corner of her lips.

He sent a silent prayer of thanks that she thought the same way as he and resisted the urge to laugh aloud. "Ever since the moment I met you, I couldn't walk away," Svein replied. "I'm sure the other members of our team can adjust."

He leaned forward and pressed his lips to hers. A gentle touch, one meant to soothe, but the instant his lips touched hers, an almost bestial hunger roared to life inside him. He slid his fingers into the mass of her hair and held her steady as he plundered her mouth. Sliding his tongue along the seam of her lips, he urged Aud to part them. She swayed toward him. His tongue swept inside the hot, moist cavern of her mouth.

Svein groaned. He reached down and unfastened his jeans, unable to take the steady pounding of his cock behind denim and cotton. Then he reached into the warm water to cup her breast. Her nipple pressed into his palm and he wanted to be buried deep inside her, right here, right now.

"Svein," she breathed, parting the kiss long enough to breathe. "You're serious aren't you?"

She struggled to contain the bubble of hope rising within her. She loved him. He might not have said the words, but then again, neither had she.

Svein nodded, rising to his feet and sliding jeans and briefs down before kicking them off, along with his socks. Her gaze roamed the length of his long, muscled legs, pausing at his thick erection. He straightened, and she noticed that it nearly touched his navel. Her mouth, and her pussy, watered. Her muscles clenched. She wanted him inside her, right now. She nearly rose to her knees so she could lean forward and suck his beautiful shaft into her mouth.

"I've never been more serious about anything in my life. I've told you my secret. You know the animal that lives just beneath my flesh." Water sloshed over the sides of the tub as Svein stepped in and then lowered himself behind her.

She waited, taut with anticipation.

"You're mine. I'm not going anywhere, so you better get used to sharing your bed with a polar bear." He stretched out his legs on either side of her then reached for the soap and washcloth that sat on the edge of the tub. He worked up a generous lather and started to wash her back.

Aud closed her eyes. His hands on her back felt heavenly, yet she still feared it wouldn't last. "Polar bears don't mate for life." She struggled to mask the pain in her voice.

The washcloth dropped into the tub with a soft splash. Reaching around her, he cupped the mounds of her breasts in his hands. His breath teased her ear. "You're my golden angel," he said. "I love you. I have for a long time. I admire your strength and your will. It might be too soon, but I hope you can find room in your heart for me." He brushed his thumb across the valley between her breasts.

"Oh, Svein! I already love you." She needed to see his face, needed to see the truth there. She rose on her knees, turning to face him before straddling his legs. She reached between them and circled her fingers around his shaft.

Hot and hard, silk over steel. She stroked him from base to tip. Her hand stilled against his flesh, and she leaned back on her heels to stare at him for a long moment. Love shone from his blue eyes.

Reaching up, he caressed her neck before rubbing strands of her hair between his fingers.

She gave a tiny moan of pleasure. She squeezed the cock in her hand gently. How long had she worked with him and never realized the depth of his feelings? She hated to even contemplate it. Had they not been caught in the storm, she doubted she'd have found out. They had lots of lost time to make up. She positioned her pussy over his cock. "I love you, Svein." With those words, she held his cock until the head slipped inside her, then released it and impaled herself on his shaft.

Spending Christmas with Svein in a cave, and then the second day of Christmas with him here, might not have been how she originally planned to spend her holidays, but it was certainly more fun than spending them hiding in her room working on papers and research. She grinned. "You know, this might be my best holiday ever."

"I know it's mine." Svein surged into her. "Polar bears might not mate for life, but this one does." He punctuated his sentence with another thrust.

Aud pressed her lips to his. With his cock in her body, his tongue plunging into her mouth, she never wanted to let him go. The long, slow slide of his cock into her slick channel filled her. She wound her arms around his neck, her breasts pressing against his chest. Aud clung to him.

Her eyelids fluttered closed. This was exactly what she wanted, what she needed. Svein loved her. And she loved him. A man to share her research, her bed, her passion for the bears and for the science. She never imagined she'd find someone who fit her so perfectly.

Svein palmed her ass. Water sloshed around them. The need for air parted them and she tilted her head back. Svein kissed a trail of fire along her jaw, her throat, his love nips sending heat straight to her pussy. The chill in the air beaded her nipples into diamond-hard points, and heat from Svein's hand seared her as he palmed her sensitive flesh.

Aud cupped the back of his head, watching as he kissed a path to her breast. His white hair against her skin, the heat from his mouth, the water around them, it swamped her senses. She watched transfixed as he pulled her nipple into his mouth and sucked.

"Oh yeah!" She tilted her hips to send his cock deeper inside her. Doubting him seemed foolish now, and as he pinched and sucked her nipples, simply *thinking* seemed foolish. His talented hands and cock drove rational thought from her mind.

Aud curled her fingers into his muscled shoulders. Solid, secure, the hand on her ass lifted her even as he used it for leverage as he fucked her. Fingers slid into the cleft of her buttocks, swirling around her puckered hole. Teasing. Tormenting.

Her breath came hard and fast as her pussy clenched down on his cock. With every thrust Svein demonstrated the depth of his need for her. And when he pulled his lips from her breast to tilt his head back against the tile wall, Aud watched, spellbound by the rapt pleasure on his face. His deep moans echoed off the walls.

Her pussy tightened around his shaft. One more thrust, two, and her orgasm burst through her. She cried out, fingers digging into his skin. Her breath caught in her throat as she rode the riptide of her release.

"Yeah, baby. Just like that!"

Distantly she registered Svein's voice urging her on. Her own cries drowned out his words as he surged into her once more. Before she had a chance to catch her breath, she spiraled toward another release.

Svein slid the finger at her anus past the tight ring of muscle, to the first knuckle.

Oh damn! She'd never felt anything as wanton as the slender penetration of his finger. With his cock stuffing her full and his finger in her ass, Aud wanted to ride him all day and all night long. She bet he had the stamina of a bear, and she longed to give him a workout.

She leaned forward, her lips inches from his. "Fuck me, Svein." She licked his lips then kissed him, turning into the aggressor. Her tongue dove into his mouth before pulling his own into her mouth to suck on it. In her mind, she imagined the thick penetration of his cock in her mouth, wrapping her lips around his girth and drawing him deep into her throat.

The finger in her ass slid a little deeper. Svein lowered himself in the water trying to get a deeper angle—and then he had it, his cock brushing against her G-spot with each thrust.

She couldn't last much longer. Wrapping an arm around his shoulders, she pressed him to her. Stroke after stroke he took her, the desire inside her coiling tighter and tighter.

Svein swallowed her whimpers, his finger sliding in and out of her anus. Just like his cock, it filled her, stretched her just enough to be on the pleasurable side of pain. Her orgasm rose like a bubble, rising for the surface. Aud released his lips, her head titling back as she screamed. Her body convulsed around him, wave after wave of pleasure slamming into her body. Water sloshed violently over the edge of the tub.

Svein clenched her hip and thrust once more. His cock surged forward, growing even larger inside her, and then his hot seed filled her. Svein shouted his release, her name on his lips.

Aud sank into him. Her breath gasped in and out of her lungs. The water around them grew slightly tepid but she barely noticed. She focused on Svein, his cock still half hard inside her body, his forehead pressed against hers, their breaths mingling. Against her chest, his heart pounded. His finger slipped slowly out of her.

She leaned back and grinned at him. "I have an idea for our next paper," she said between panting breaths.

"Oh?" Svein arched his eyebrow.

"The mating habits of polar bears." She grinned at him, ready to step from the tub, lead him to the bedroom and begin round three. "We better get a head start before the team returns."

She kissed him and knew they'd get to their other paper eventually. Right now, far more scientific work needed to be done. Svein slid his fingers along the crease of her ass, the gentle pressure driving coherent thoughts from her mind.

She had no doubt the mating habits of the polar bear would prove to be a fascinating study.

Also by Mary Winter

Au Naturel

Bjorn's Mate

Ellora's Cavemen: Dreams of the Oasis III (*anthology*)

Ghost Redeemed

Ghost Touch

Once Upon a Prince (*anthology*)

Pleasure Quest (*anthology*)

Prodigal Son

Revealing Photos

Riding Partner

Snowbound

Treaty of Seduction

Water Lust

About the Author

Mary Winter began writing when she was 16, using it as an excuse to skip gym class. She currently lives in Iowa with her pets and dreams of writing full-time. Ghost Touch is her first published novel, and her advice to anyone is: "Persistence pays off. Don't ever give up on your dreams!"

Mary welcomes comments from readers. You can find her website and email address on her author bio page at www.ellorascave.com.

Tell Us What You Think

We appreciate hearing reader opinions about our books. You can email us at Comments@EllorasCave.com.

FINDING THE LIGHT
Liddy Midnight

ഇ

Prologue

ଉ

"You know nothing of female magick, Moran!" Beatrice sneered. "You mage hunters are all alike, seeking to destroy what you do not understand." As graceful as a cat, she strode back and forth on the crushed stones before her manor. She was the most powerful mage he had faced. The spell that gave her beauty never wavered—she maintained the illusion even while she cast a series of crackling balls of black fire at him in a blur.

Moran stood his ground, holding a large bowl-shaped shield of magick before him. Her attack spattered on the surface and dripped onto the ground. Burned patches marred the snow around each of them. 'Twas not her first attempt to kill him; she struck first, and he had answered her blow for blow.

He squinted into the sun. "I understand that the darkness has overtaken your will." Knowing that she was determined to destroy him, he still tried to reason with her. "You were once like me, a servant of the light."

"Never like you," she laughed derisively. "You forget that Her consort must die each year, feeding the earth with his blood, while the Goddess is eternal. As a woman, I am made in Her image and thus *I* am eternal!"

Without even a pause to gather her strength, she shoved both hands toward him. A blazing wall of Power swept across the snow-covered yard.

He met it with his shield, grunting beneath the onslaught. The wall collapsed over him and he barely managed to expand the bowl to cover him in time to avoid being consumed.

Moran's breath came in gasps as he watched the remnants seep into the earth. Were he a Shaper, he could gather and use those shreds against his foe, but his Power sprang from within him. As such, he had limits.

Goddess, but Beatrice was strong. One more attack like that and he was finished.

Unless he came up with a more powerful response. He reached deep inside, to the place that held his magick, and found there was no more Power in him.

At least none he could use. Locked away behind a door he dared not touch, darkness seethed. He felt it every minute of every day, testing the bonds he'd placed around it, seeking a way to escape, to sink into his soul.

If he were to die, he might as well loose that night-black threat on Beatrice before he went. Such a foul mage should have been no match for the magick he drew on, that of the Goddess. Possibly melding the darkness he carried with Her Power would forge a weapon that could pierce Beatrice's shields.

The decision was made in less than an instant. He tore open the door and darkness poured forth. Exerting all his strength and discipline, he bent it to his will. Forging together both light and dark, he imbued the massive force with a need to prevail over dark magick at any cost. He formed a spear of energy and hurled it at Beatrice.

A missile of gray, equal parts shining white and matte black, flew across the clearing. His weapon expanded as it reached its victim, throwing out a glittering net of darkness that wrapped around the female mage.

Moran had one glimpse of Beatrice's true face, distorted by terror, before the net contracted. Bits of her flesh bulged through tiny spaces in the tightening mesh before the entire mess burst into flame.

His weapon found more than just one target. Spinning shards of netting flashed past Beatrice to envelop her remaining servants, along with the tools and objects she had invested with evil. Shutters burst asunder, allowing the slivers access to the rooms inside. From within the manor house came cries of anguish and the sizzle of burning flesh. The structure itself burst into flames.

He steeled himself against pity. These were not innocent wretches caught in an unintended backlash. They were Beatrice's willing accomplices. He knew she recruited mortals with an evil bent, for they were easier to control.

A tiny piece of gray magick remained, whirling in the air without a target. Satisfied that every bit of her foul legacy had been destroyed, Moran smiled grimly. That smile changed to horror as he realized the only dark magick left lived within him. He had wrested the darkness from its prison, but there was more. Through the years of battling the shadows, a significant portion had become inevitably woven into the fabric of his being.

Loosing the darkness in his soul had won the battle with Beatrice, but at the cost of his life. He had little time to trace a warding spell before it struck.

Moran pushed himself to move onward, placing one foot in front of the other, and again. Agony lanced through his chest with each breath.

Somehow he had survived the attack of his own weapon, but he was sorely wounded. The combination of light and dark magick he used to defeat Beatrice crawled beneath his skin, seeking to destroy the part of him that was the very darkness he had made his life's work to defeat.

In this, he had failed. Aye, he had prevailed in the battle, but at what cost? He had, in that desperate act, overcome a powerful black mage, but also destroyed one of the few warriors who served the Goddess.

He had no idea how long he'd forced himself to follow the snowy track. 'Twas long enough for the fever to rise and bathe him in heat. Tossing back the hood of his cloak to bare his head to the chill wind provided a little relief. Occasionally the breeze would dislodge a clump of snow from the branches above to land on his head, where it melted and trickled down his face. He imagined it steamed in the frigid air.

His breath gusted white when he gingerly exhaled and grimaced. As the force he had sent against Beatrice worked to eradicate the darkness, he was losing his strength. Too much of him *was* the darkness. With each cough, he feared seeing blood on his hand.

At some point since the storm died, a wagon had come this way. Where there was a wagon, there would be people.

As if his thought summoned them, two small boys tumbled into sight before him like dice from a cup. They ceased fighting and quickly gained their feet, staring at him with wide eyes.

"Sir, are you ill?" one asked.

Were they a vision, brought on by the fever?

He blinked, looked beyond them, and realized he had come upon a village. Part of him noted that their snow-pocked garments were shabby but clean. Their anxious faces were healthy, not lean and pinched by hunger. Possibly he would find aid here.

The lads ran off. Possibly not.

Ahead of him, a handful of cottages lined a narrow street. Not much of a village. More of a settled crossroads. Just where was he? Behind, he'd left death and justice burning, cleansing a foul nest. Ahead lay...what? To survive, he required a skilled mage. He would find no such help in this tiny place.

Another step tore a gasp from his throat. The intake of breath escalated the agony in his chest. He coughed, unable to stop despite the wrenching pain.

He was barely aware of the boys' return, with several men and someone who glowed like the sun. A woman. Nay, no woman burned with so bright a light. The Goddess. She

116

caught him when his strength failed, cushioning his fall to the road.

This was the end. He would not die as he feared, alone, far from those he fought to protect. His last task was finished. Her cool, loving embrace surprised him, for he never expected to be forgiven his sins. He welcomed the cessation of pain as complete darkness descended.

At the last, he knew he had come home.

Chapter One

Enid stared down into the handsome face of the man in her arms. His body radiated too much heat and his skin was pale, his brow furrowed with pain. Young Piers and Ruddy had the right of it; he was indeed close to death. While she watched, the rise and fall of his chest paused. He moaned and resumed breathing.

"He's a goner," Alice said, adding, "Merry Yule."

Enid ignored the sarcasm. Usually she found Alice's sharp wit amusing, but today it grated on her. She handed the stranger over to the men and rose to head back toward the clustered cottages with her friend. "He might live. Burning with fever, though. I should have enough willow bark to see him through the night."

Alice sniffed. "If not, yell out the door. I'll send one of the girls over. You won't be joining us for supper." Without waiting for a response, she continued, "I'll fill a bowl."

"Many thanks. I'll be too busy tending him to cook."

"Mayhap he'll live, and settle here." Alice cast her a sidelong glance. "He is handsome, and you need a man."

Enid sighed. 'Twas the second year since her husband Daven had died. Time to think of marrying again, and her friend kept trying. There were few eligible men about. Having one literally fall into her lap was more than Alice could resist.

Tonight the rest of the village would be feasting and celebrating the end of one year and the beginning of the next. She had dreaded sitting again by herself at the loud, crowded table. Now she would labor to help a stranger instead of dwelling on happier times. An opportunity to avoid those sad thoughts was welcome. For that, she was grateful to both the ill man and the Goddess who delivered him to her care.

"Take him to my cottage," she directed Ruddy's da. With luck, he'd survive the journey. If not, well, the risk that he would perish was still high. There were limits to her knowledge and abilities.

Should he die, she'd lay him out and help her neighbors see to his burial. She was no gifted mage to work wonders, even if today was Yule, a holy time of miracles.

Despite Alice's speculation, she sensed the Goddess had handed her a challenge this year, not a gift. There were others in the village just as skilled with herbs and healing, but only she lived alone.

"Hurry," she snapped at the boys. "Piers, bring more wood. Ruddy, fetch a bucket from the well. Full, mind you, no half-measures."

"I'll send a boy for leeches," Alice offered.

"Nay, 'tis not what he needs." Enid hesitated to bleed him, for that would sap his strength far more than the pain and fever. "I'll give him hot drinks and warmth."

Alice laughed and grinned. "'Tis only one sure way to warm a man, you know. And tonight, 'tis tradition to fuck like rabbits."

Enid had to smile in return. "I think he's beyond fucking, but I'll keep that in mind."

Alice snickered, called out, "I'll send supper for you both—you'll need to keep up your strength," and waved as she turned down the alley to her back door.

Enid put her friend's teasing aside and contemplated the tasks that lay before her. He would need to replenish his body's fluids. Hot broth, simmered all morning for her noon meal, would ease his breathing. If he could swallow it. She'd make a hot herb poultice as well, and tuck it against his chest.

What ailed him? He'd had a coughing fit as they reached him that flushed his pale skin with fever. He looked to be young—not much older than she was—and strong but anyone, of any age, could succumb to a lung complaint.

He might have broken bones. Mayhap he had been set upon while traveling. Such would account for his painful cough, but shattered ribs often penetrated a lung. She winced at the thought and prayed that was not the case. Such an injury was beyond her ability to treat.

Their village was unworthy of that title, made up of no more than a score of families. They didn't even have a smithy. For most needs, they had to travel. Even the proper towns nearby didn't boast a mage.

She threw open the door to her small cottage and crossed to stir up the fire. Cold air swirled in behind her, lifting her hair and rising up the chimney in a sheaf of sparks.

The men carried the stranger in and laid him on her bed. As soon as they were free of their burden, they backed out, nodding and whispering hope for his swift recovery. By their glances and perfunctory words, they did not expect him to survive. She knew they would hasten from her cottage to the carpenter and have him begin a casket.

She gathered her meager supplies and turned to examine her patient. She should have asked the men to help her remove his clothing. His heavy cloak proved difficult to work out from under his limp form.

The quality of his garments was obvious as soon as she touched them. The woven wool was soft and thick, dyed in deep colors and tailored by an expert hand. The subtle plaid was marked as much by a cunning twill as by the changes in hue. At the folds of his elbows, the linen shirt remained clean, gleaming white. A man of means, then, to be clad in such fine cloth.

He filled her bed completely, his head on her pillow and his ankles on the foot. Although it had taken three grown men to carry him, she hadn't expected him to be so large. And so male. The scent of him, musk and smoky maleness, surrounded her.

How handsome he was, even ill and in pain! His features made her ache to stroke that jaw, to kiss his firm lips. She shook herself from those thoughts. Daven, nearly two years in his grave, had had similar coloring, but not the strong character this man's face and form showed. There was little resemblance to draw her attention.

Despite his being unconscious, the man's presence filled her one-room home. She couldn't believe he might die. His presence was too strong, too vital.

She sat beside him and began to wash his shaven cheeks, removing a layer of grime and — was that soot? She had smelled no smoke outside, but now the sharp odor rose from his wet garments. He had been in a large fire. Or fought one. Might that be what had injured him?

His clothes bore signs of a blaze. Holes from small cinders pocked his cloak and speckled the sleeves beneath. She picked up one of his large hands and turned it over. A network of fresh, angry burns overlaid the calluses and old scars. A man who worked, then, not an idle lord. She had to smile at that, for idle lords were so scarce she'd only heard rumors of men who had hands as soft as a weaver's and no chores to occupy their time.

There were no homes for many miles in the direction he'd come. How far had he walked, growing ever weaker?

For the first time, she wondered if others might be in distress. When she was finished making him as comfortable as she could, she'd send some of the men to see.

Piers burst in, lugging an armload of firewood and followed by Ruddy bearing a full bucket of water. They jerked the door shut, cutting off the wind for the moment it took Piers to dump the logs near the hearth. Water slopped over the brim of the bucket as Ruddy set it down. She barely had time to ask them to have the men retrace the stranger's path before they left in another chill blast.

Enid huffed in frustration. She shouldn't have to deal with this on her own. Aye, she now lived alone, but there were other women who knew just as much as she did about herbs and illness. Why could they not help her care for this man, here in her home? But tomorrow was Yule and they had families to feed.

Once free of his heavy outer garments, her patient lay still and pale on her bed. Heat poured off him in waves. She debated the wisdom of feeding him broth and decided to attempt to get him to swallow. When he'd last eaten, she couldn't guess.

She stirred powdered willow bark into the broth. If making him drink proved to be a struggle, she'd only have to do it once to get both into him. Willow would work to lower the fever and help dull whatever pained him. The rich stock would give him strength.

He drank without much coaxing on her part, a little dribbling out the corner of his mouth. She held him, supporting him with her shoulder and steadying the mug with her other hand. He swallowed and guzzled, quickly emptying the large cup. She took it and seized the opportunity to wrestle him out of the rest of his clothing. After a short struggle, she fetched a small knife and slit some of the seams. Repairing them would occupy her hands while she watched over him through the night. 'Twas work of but a few minutes to pull the pieces out from under him.

With a sigh, he subsided onto the sheet. For a horrible moment she thought he'd stopped breathing, but nay, his chest rose and fell in a slow, steady rhythm.

She couldn't resist touching him, running her hands over his bruised ribs and across his taut belly. A slight snore issued from his open mouth. Reassured that he was unaware of his surroundings or her presence, she peeked beneath his braes and caught her breath.

Oh, my. His cock was larger than she expected, even at rest. Her fingers itched to touch him, to be sure her eyes didn't deceive her. An empty ache invaded her belly. It had been so long since she'd made love with Daven. So very long.

A knock at the door sounded. With a guilty start, Enid turned away to open the door. Darkness filled the lane. The longest night of the year was taking hold. Alice's eldest daughter handed her a heavy bowl. A cloth protected its heaped contents from the chill. Savory aromas gusted in on the wind.

"Mam said you'll not be joining us. There's enough for you and him." She jerked her chin toward the still form on Enid's bed. With a saucy wink, she left.

Enid had not thrown the latch on the door. Had the girl arrived but a moment earlier and not knocked, Enid would have been mightily embarrassed. After a glance under the towel at heaped slices of roasted meat, dumplings and a few root vegetables topped with a loaf of fresh bread, she set the bowl aside. That would serve for later, once 'twas clear if the man would live or die. She prepared broth for herself and sopped it up with a heel of old bread, keeping one eye on the large man in her bed.

The strings of his braes were knotted and she had to sit close while she worked them loose. The fever heat rolling off him warmed her past comfort. Or was it her awareness of him as a man? By the time she untangled the knot, sweat trickled between her breasts and heat pooled in her womb.

Shifting his weight to remove his last garment brought her too close. Each breath was filled with his scent. Each breath increased the ache in her belly.

When she pulled his braes down over his hips, the sight took her breath away. Handling him had brought her face within a hand's span of his cock. 'Twould be but a small motion to take him in her mouth…what would he taste like?

She chastised herself for thinking such thoughts. The man was dying. He needed healing care, not the mooning lust of a lonely widow. With brisk motions, she freed his legs and tucked the blankets back around his naked form.

She distracted herself by straightening the cottage and found herself handling his garments. The linen shirt was nearly dry. She rubbed at the soot on the sleeves and neck. This garment needed a good scrubbing in the stream as well as mending, but would suffice for him should he live.

His braes were twisted and wrinkled. The cloak was still damp but in good shape, made to face the wind and snow and dry without harm. She spread them out near the hearth and tried to keep her mind off the way his scent lingered, mingled with the odor of smoke.

Try as she might, her home was too small to ignore him for long. Every time she moved, she caught sight of him from the corner of her eye. Every time he moved, she became aware of him all over again.

A small bit of embroidery inside his cloak snagged her attention. Sewn in matching thread, almost invisible, the roughness beneath her fingertip was the only way she noticed it. A rune. She ran her hand down the fabric and found more, a line of magickal signs that rimmed the entire garment. How curious. Her father had once had such a cloak, and her father was a mage. Was her guest a mage or a priest?

Moving the chair closer, she settled in to watch him and mend his shirt.

He appeared at rest. His face was more handsome than she had thought before she washed him clean. Dark hair, trimmed not long ago, framed his cheeks in loose waves. From the lines etched around his eyes and the grooves in his brow, he didn't look like a man who had much pleasure in his life. Despite that, or mayhap because of it, she'd like to see him laugh.

The cloth warmed and dried, filling the cottage with his scent as she plied her needle and thread. For the first time in weeks, she felt keenly the fact that she spent much of her time alone.

She had no one to share a feast, to celebrate the holy day. And no one to make love with. The greatest gift of the Goddess was life, and she had always considered sex on the high holy days to be an essential part of worship. Most especially this holy day. From now on, nights would cease to grow longer and, as the cycle of the year turned, the length of the days would increase, making way for spring and summer to follow.

Her imagination roamed. Mayhap Alice's flight of fancy was right. The Goddess would grant her a miracle and the stranger would recover overnight. What a marvelous gift that would be! And she could imagine so many ways to celebrate with him. She smiled in the firelight. He wouldn't have to struggle back into his damp clothing, either.

Chapter Two

Hours later, she awoke with a start. The fire had burned down and she shivered in the cooling air. Hastening to build up the fire, she rubbed her arms. This would do her patient no good. Once the flames rose up around the logs, she crossed to lay a hand on his forehead and judge the state of his fever.

At her touch, he bolted upright and stared ahead with unseeing eyes. One of the warm stones rolled onto the floor with a thump. When she tucked it back close to his feet, he shuddered and cried out. She murmured comforting nonsense and coaxed him to lie back. He thrashed about, casting off the blankets.

Sweat streamed off his brow. His dark hair was plastered to his scalp, highlighting features etched with pain. His teeth clattered together with his violent trembling.

She had no more stones hot from the hearth to add to his bed. Every blanket and cloak she owned was piled atop him and still he shivered. There was naught else in the cottage to help warm him—except her body.

Not stopping to think, seeking only to ease his fevered state, Enid stripped in the chill and slipped in behind him. She wrapped her arms around his waist and pulled him close. Warming him would require as much skin-to-skin contact as she could achieve.

His flesh was clammy. Cold he might be, but his thighs were lean and strong. His buttocks were tight and high, nestled into her as though made to fit there against her belly. Under her hand, the planes of his abdomen were taut and muscular.

All the tension went out of him in a sigh. He relaxed.

Surrounded by his scent, very conscious of his warming flesh against her, Enid kept watch over him until she slept.

* * * * *

Moran awakened to warmth. The heat surrounding him was comforting, not blistering. He was out of the fire. That left him—where? He dimly remembered defeating his foe, and that the victory had taken every ounce of his strength. He'd even been forced to release the darkness in his soul, using every shred of Power he had to win the magickal battle. His successful effort had turned on him at the last, seeking to destroy him. He had become a Dark Mage himself.

And the shining woman of his vision had forgiven him. That moment grew and became clear in his mind, when the Goddess—for surely the glowing woman could be no other?— had taken him into Her arms and eased his pain.

He sighed deeply and the agony returned. He was not completely healed, then. No matter. He had survived worse injuries.

The draining of his Power was the most disturbing. Even now, when he reached inside himself for it, he found no response. No answering surge of Power tingled through him, not even a trickle. All he felt was a growing sexual urge.

His cock hardened. He became aware of softness pressed against him. Feminine softness.

His cock throbbed and he opened his eyes.

She was cradled in his arms, her warm ass snugged up against him holding his cock in a warm embrace. Tousled golden hair, lighter than honey, clung to his chin and obscured her face. Her left breast filled his hand.

For all he knew, this was a dream, and her body a reward for his service and constancy.

Great Goddess, what a gift!

His training and practice as a mage required celibacy to control his Power. Did this mean he was no longer bound by those strictures? The Goddess had led him here and placed him in this bed with a warm and no doubt willing woman. Who was he to gainsay Her wishes?

He cupped the woman's plump breast, exploring the texture of her soft skin. A bounty of flesh filled his palm to perfection, as if made just for him. His finger brushed against her tight nipple and she drew in a quick breath, wriggling against him. His cock nestled between the cheeks of her ass, but that was not what he wanted. He wanted, nay, he needed to possess this woman, to pour his seed into her fertile womb.

That need threatened the foundation of his life. He had never encountered such a craving. He had desired women, aye, and wished to fuck, but never had this deep-seated longing to create life compelled him. Young voices from a distance, many of them running together, filled his head. The prospect of a child and that child's children, a long line of his flesh and blood stretching into the future, called to him.

What if this was no dream? Possibly he was too ill to survive his injuries, and this was Her way of ensuring him a measure of immortality. Days ago, even hours ago, such would have been unimaginable. To a man sworn to celibacy for the sake of his battle against the darkness, this was a high reward.

The woman in his embrace moved her head and her sweet-smelling hair tickled his face. Unfamiliar emotion swept through him. With her, he had a chance to connect with one of those he was sworn to protect. With her, he had a chance to touch the Goddess.

An intriguing idea. He had mistaken her for the Goddess upon his arrival in this place. Perhaps he had not lost all his Power and saw her for what she was, the embodiment of the Goddess. He smiled into her silky locks and breathed in the heady fragrance. Lavender. A relaxing herb.

When she shifted her hips and ground against him, nothing about him relaxed. His hand tightened on her breast, wringing a soft moan from her. His cock throbbed with eagerness.

His choices were few. The odds of surviving his injuries were slim. He was either dreaming or he wasn't. If he wasn't, he could not turn down this Goddess-given chance to sow his seed for the future.

That She had also provided an opportunity for him to explore the pleasures of the flesh, so long denied, was not lost on him. She must hold his work in high regard to reward him so handsomely. He resolved not to fail Her in this as he had in his struggle against the shadows he carried.

He told himself he was trapped by the weight of the woman who would bear his children, refusing to acknowledge the truth. He was loath to release the wonderful softness of her breast. He slipped his other hand across the slight swell of her belly to delve into the curls between her thighs. A rush of moisture met his questing fingers. As he slid a finger into her slick cunt, she tilted her hips into his hand.

His finger sank into hot flesh that parted beneath his touch to draw him deeper. He explored her nested folds that hid woman's wonders and mysteries. Creamy juices coated his hand. He wondered what they tasted like, and if he'd be granted the opportunity to learn all there was to know about lovemaking and slaking a woman's hunger. In the back of his mind, he uttered a prayer that he might be worthy.

The motion of his arm moved the covers that blanketed them in a cocoon of warmth, releasing a breeze filled with the heady scent of her sex. Full-bodied, like rich wine or potent ale. Promising delight and a different kind of oblivion—with no headache come morning.

She shuddered at his touch, arching her back, pushing her breast into his hand. She was softness and goose down, curved and sinuous against his firm muscles. Her hair shifted across his chest and his breath hitched as lightning sensations rippled through him. Sweet Goddess, if her nipples were half as sensitive as his, 'twas no wonder she squirmed and gasped in pleasure each time he brushed one.

He thumbed the tightly pearled peak within his reach, and grinned as a rush of liquid bathed his other hand. She moaned and pressed her legs together. One trapped finger encountered something firm hidden within her swollen folds. 'Twas too tempting and he fought the pressure of her thighs to swirl her juices around it. She whimpered and pulled away from his hand.

Her movement brought the back of her wet slit into contact with his balls. He could stand no more. Urgency drove him to claim her. With a simple motion of his hips, he pulled back to rest the head of his cock at her entrance.

One word passed her lips in a soft plea. "Aye."

He knew what to do, having witnessed couplings in his travels. He knew she should be wet and ready to receive him, and she was. He knew that one swift thrust would seat his cock fully within her.

Moran plunged into her wet heat. She pushed back against him and gasped. For an instant, her softness molded around his shaft. The sensation was akin to drawing on a well-worn and comfortable glove—until her muscles tightened, trapping him in an iron grip. Shock drove the breath from his lungs in a groan. To his amazement, his cock grew harder and swelled against the pressure.

He had not known ecstasy would flood him as he fought to withdraw and thrust deep again. He had not known how he would lose himself in the sensations, the scents and the sounds of their joining. Sweet Goddess, to think that this was what he had been missing!

'Twas no wonder mages were sworn to celibacy. Had he known such ecstasy existed in fucking, he would never have had the discipline required to complete his studies and claim his full Power.

The pop and crackle of the hearth was lost beneath her breathless cries and the soft slap of flesh against flesh as he filled her cunt over and over. His breath came in shallow, ragged pants, as much from the scintillating sensations pouring through him as exertion and his weakened body. Despite the toll this took on him, he would not—or could not—stop.

She met him push for thrust, grinding the cheeks of her ass against his hips and pulling him ever deeper, until the sensitive head of his cock rasped across something deep within her cunt. At that touch, she arched her back and keened a wordless cry. She pulsed around him, driving his pleasure impossibly higher.

Another perfume mingled with the lavender of her hair. The earthy essence of woman, spiced with his own musky arousal, filled his head. He nuzzled her neck, finding sensitive flesh behind her ear to kiss and nip. She tipped her head and whimpered.

Time stilled as they gave and took pleasure. He became aware that his hands cupped her breasts, holding her close and playing with the hardened peaks of her nipples. With each tug, she jerked and shuddered around him, coaxing him to fuck her faster and harder.

The possessiveness he felt for this woman mixed with his desire and grew. She was his. He knew it in his bones, in his soul.

"Sweet Goddess!"

The cry was torn from both of them as she clenched around him, clasping him in an internal embrace that ripped something loose inside him. That release triggered the release of his seed, and he spurted again and again, filling her womb while the most marvelous sensations he'd ever felt coursed along his skin and settled into his heart. 'Twas brighter than lightning, more powerful than a tornado. Even after he was drained dry, he continued thrusting while she gasped and shuddered, until he imagined his very soul had followed his seed into her keeping.

Enid rested in the stranger's arms and floated on a cloud of wellbeing, thanking the Goddess for sending him to her door. How could she call him a stranger now, after the incredible pleasure they shared? He had given her a holy celebration worthy of Yule. She had thought his fucking would never end. To be so energetic in the wake of his illness was truly a miracle.

Oh, Goddess, his illness! She tried to pull away, to look at him, but he held her close.

"Nay, lie here. I am still cold." He cleared his throat and coughed.

Enid waited as he hunched against the pain. She gripped his arms and tried to support his weight while he coughed. So, despite the strength he had just showed in fucking her, he was not completely well.

Finally, the fit subsided and he breathed more easily. "I am Moran. Will you tell me where I am, and how I came to be here?"

That was not what she'd expected. For some reason, mayhap her fanciful ideas of him being a Yule gift, she thought he might utter words of love.

While searching for coherent answers to his practical questions, it struck her that they'd fucked, but never kissed. How odd. They hadn't known each other's names, but she could very well bear his child come Samhain. The implications of what they'd shared made her suddenly shy and unsure.

She tensed as she answered him. "I am Enid. This is my cottage. You came from the west, stumbling through the snow. You were alone and gravely ill."

"I am always alone." The bald statement made her ache in shared loneliness. She, too, was always alone. "So, I came east. An odd choice." His voice trailed off in thought.

She held her breath a moment before she dared speak. "You seem much stronger now." 'Twas true of her, as well. She felt as though their fucking had left her with greater vitality, beyond her normal vigor. Never one to lounge about, preferring to keep busy, Enid now felt as though she could sweep the house and chop wood for hours. Or fuck like a rabbit, as Alice had said. She stifled the urge to giggle.

"You have taken good care of me." He tightened his grip on her breast. "Thank you. For your care of me, and for the use of your body. I have never felt such ecstasy." He pressed a kiss to the back of her neck. "You are my first lover, little one."

She blushed so furiously, she wondered he didn't comment on the heat rising from her. "That cannot be! You knew just how to give me more pleasure than I believed possible."

"I thought the same of you." His cock hardened and leapt against her ass, ready for another round of the exquisite delights he'd shown her.

With her renewed strength, she was more than ready to give him access to her cunt again. She didn't think that term "using her" was accurate, for how could he use her if she was just as eager as he? But his illness must make him vulnerable to overexertion. If she killed him, how could she live with herself?

"I have lived my life under vows to serve the Goddess, forbidden to indulge in sexual pleasure."

He was a priest, then. An odd one, to be sure, if he served the Goddess chastely. "Oh, I am sorry! I made you break your vow!"

He chuckled, a husky sound that warmed her heart. She wished she could see him smile, but he still held her firmly tucked against his chest. "Do not fret, little one. My vows no longer bind me."

"Where do you come from? What injured you?"

133

She'd pushed too far. He stilled and said, "Enough questions for now. I am tired."

Chapter Three

၆၁

A cry woke Enid. In the dim light of the banked fire, she found Moran hunched over, groaning in agony.

Hastening to light a candle—the wick took far too long to catch fire from a glowing coal—she flew back to his side. As she approached, she felt heat radiating off him from several feet away. He held one hand tight against his chest and struggled against a cough.

"Moran! What happened?"

He made no answer. When he opened his eyes, they were glazed. A trickle of blood ran from his mouth. Her heart plummeted. Her worst fears had come to pass. He was doomed to die. Tonight, and soon.

She sighed and helped him back onto the bed.

He waved aside her offer of more broth or water. She handed him a rag to mop up the blood that covered his hands when next he coughed.

At least it would be a quick death. She had tended Daven through a long decline and knew what a blessing a swift passing was.

The crack at the bottom of the shutter showed no light outside, so dawn was hours away. How long had she slept? She had no idea, nor did she know how long they had spent fucking in the night. She still tingled all over when she thought about that glorious Yule celebration.

So much for her dreams of having Moran overcome his illness and to be persuaded to stay.

The Goddess had a peculiar way of showing Her favor.

Mayhap this was Her gift to Moran. For the first time, Enid considered what this night meant to him. He claimed to have never made love to any woman, but he'd known exactly what to do. She had only lain with her husband before awakening to Moran's caresses, and Daven's fumblings on their first time together had been nothing like the wondrous skill Moran possessed.

She could well be Moran's reward for lifelong service to the Goddess. Unless she was a test for him—and since he had not resisted the temptation of her body, he must die. Nay, she could not think that. The Goddess was beneficent.

Speculation made her head ache as much as her heart did.

How had she come to care so for Moran? Was she deluding herself into believing she was falling in love, simply because she was tired of being alone? 'Twas possible. She'd always been given to dreaming of better times and a better life. For the first time, she wondered if she wasted her time in such thoughts.

He had stumbled into her life only hours before and spent much of the time since then unconscious. They knew little of each other.

Nay, that was a lie. She knew him as well as she would ever know anyone. Somehow, in the dark hours of this night, she had looked into his soul, and he into hers. There was no other way to account for what she felt. He had become a part of her, as Daven never had been.

And now he was dying, struggling for each breath, fighting the urge to cough. 'Twas as if she watched him fade before her eyes. A dark mist crept over his skin. She blinked and it disappeared.

Enid sat beside him and held his hand. When he relaxed, she mopped the sweat from his brow and the blood from his chin. Through it all, she held a tight rein on her emotions. 'Twas the only way she could keep from drowning him in her tears.

* * * * *

Try as she might to control her grief, sobs escaped her tight throat as she filled a shining copper basin with warm water. She might as well finish preparing him for burial. Filled as she was with that unusual vigor, she was unlikely to return to sleep.

'Twas not a good omen, to begin the new year with a burial. The old year had died, aye, but a birth was more suitable for the day after Yule.

A teardrop fell into the water, sending ripples across the surface to the rim of the bowl. The sight evoked a childhood memory.

What was the rhyme her mother chanted over water before she washed an injury—or a body, when she was about to prepare the dead for their final rest?

An old blessing, one her mother, and her mother's mother and *her* mother before her, had said. Enid hadn't thought of it in years. Without children to comfort, she'd had no need. Daven would have teased her without mercy, if ever he'd heard her chant something over a bowl of washing water.

May the Goddess, through my hand,
Ease your pain and help you mend.

May this water wash away
All the sins you bear today.

May this water evil ban;
Safety, virtue here command.

May this water pain dispel;
To every care you bid farewell.

May this water flesh restore;
Become whole and clean once more.

May the Goddess, through my hand,
Ease your pain and help you mend.

Each word reverberated inside her. She spoke as though she meant them, even as her mother had, before she bathed Enid's scrapes and cuts. A tingle ran down her fingers to vibrate the bowl. The rippling pattern now went the other way, from the rim to the center.

Enid stared as though the water had turned into wood. Never had she seen — or heard of — such a response. A shiver ran through her body and she almost dropped the bowl.

Her emotions were getting the better of her. She was overwrought. The man she had thought she rescued had first given her unimaginable pleasure and then died. What she imagined she saw was doubtless a reaction to that.

She knelt beside Moran's body on the hearth, wet a rag and began to wash him. She started at his feet. The soles, like his hands, were marked with signs of hard use. She rubbed the calluses with the cloth, wondering what kind of work he might have done, to gain the wealth indicated by his garments.

Were she to linger over every inch of him, she would not finish by Ostara.

Setting aside her curiosity, Enid traced the muscles of his leg, dipping and wringing the cloth as she needed. She paused when she reached his hip.

She could not bring herself to wash his cock. Was it wrong of her to wish him to sleep in his grave with a remembrance of their shared love? Such a thought made his death bearable. He had, at the last, experienced the most intimate of human pleasures. She should concentrate on that and ignore the pain of his death.

His hands fit into the basin, and she carefully worked the soot from the lines in his wrists. She picked up the basin again and frowned. The cloth had disappeared. She groped in the water and found it easily, but the water was far dirtier than it should have been.

Moran was obviously a man who bathed regularly. Where his clothing had shielded him from the soot and ash, his skin had been clean. Aye, and she had wiped his hands, face and neck clean earlier, while he was sweating with the fever.

There was no explanation for the filthy water or the black scum floating in the bowl.

She pitched it out the door and refilled the basin. Again, she recited the blessing. Again, she retraced the areas she'd washed and continued up his arms to his face. She examined the cloth as she worked—but it remained as light in color as when it began.

Again, the water darkened and a nasty-looking film accumulated on the surface.

Once more, she pitched it out into the night. Once more, she went through the ritual and this time, bathed him again, starting with his toes.

By the time she reached his hips, the water was only tinted with dirt. She washed his arms once more, and the water barely changed at all.

Holding his head up, she let his long hair fall into the water and massaged his scalp with her fingers. The water rapidly turned dark and scummy.

A fourth and then a fifth time, she emptied and refilled the basin. Each time, she blessed the water before she touched him with the cloth. She could see absolutely nothing that would account for the debris in the wash water.

In the ninth bowl, the water remained clear. She had washed every inch of him repeatedly. As might be expected, much of the filth came from his head, which had not been shielded from the soot and fire. What puzzled her was the repeated washing required to clean him from the waist up, particularly his upper chest and head. That skin had been covered by his garments.

She washed his face again, just to be certain she had done everything she could. Her fingers traced his lips. They had chatted a bit, and they had shared intense intimacy, but they had never kissed.

Without volition, she dipped her head and touched his lips with hers.

His mouth was warm beneath hers, and she lingered, tasting him. Her hearty broth remained on his lips, with a bitter hint of willow. Such a shame, that a man so strong and kind should die so young. She pulled a hairsbreadth away and sighed.

In that moment, something loosened deep inside her and flowed out with her breath.

He sucked it in.

"Sweet Goddess!" She stumbled back and fell to the floor. Eyes wide, she stared at his chest. Aye, he had drawn in a breath. As she watched, he gave a small, gurgling cough and inhaled again.

His eyelids fluttered and he stirred. Although his eyes did not open, he reached unerringly to grasp her hand. An unintelligible sound passed his lips. She leaned closer and made out his soft words. "Thank you, My Lady of Light."

Silently, Enid shut her eyes and added her thanks to the Goddess. 'Twas too soon to tell if this awakening was a reprieve or a true miracle, but she could not help but be delighted that Moran had regained his senses.

Nay, after more than an hour, he had returned from death.

He squeezed her hand. She looked and found him gazing up at her with wonder and adoration in his eyes.

"You glow like the moon, Lady."

His reverent words left no doubt in her mind that he had confused her with the Goddess. She shook her head. "You are mistaken. I am but a normal woman."

"Nay, you are far more." His smile lit up his whole face. His gray eyes were clear and intelligent.

She palmed his forehead and found no trace of the fever. Oh, Goddess, he had a devastating smile.

"You have given me life." He paused and his gaze turned inward. "And my magick has returned! Never label yourself normal, most beautiful and precious woman." He lifted her hand and pressed a kiss on her knuckles.

He called her precious, and beautiful—and the import of his words struck her. He was no priest, but a mage! Embarrassment heated her cheeks.

She blurted out, "You are a mage!"

When she looked up, he met her gaze calmly. "Aye."

"You should have been able to heal yourself. How did you come to be so ill?"

Chapter Four

Moran thought frantically to come up with words that didn't hurt him to say. A mage's strength lay as much in what others expected as what he could do. Often, a fight could be avoided by a strong reputation. His reputation was all he had at the moment. The tingle of Power coursed along his skin, but when he touched the source within him, he found only a weak trickle.

Yet he had shared much with this woman. She had taken him in. She had cared for him. She had shared her body, given generously of pleasure. For all of that, he owed her the truth.

"I drained too much Power in a battle."

Her eyes widened. "Can you do that? I thought mages were invincible."

"Nay." He couldn't prevent the quirk of his lips. She might take it as a sign of smugness and that bothered him. To the contrary, losing his Power had humbled him. "We can all be defeated. That's what I do, track down those who abuse their Power and destroy them."

The woman—Enid, if his memory could be trusted—sat down heavily in the single chair. He noticed now that the cottage was furnished with no more than the basics for one person. A small table. One chair. One wide pallet near the large hearth. There was no husband then, and no child in this woman's life. Her lot must be hard, as a widow alone in this remote cluster of dwellings.

"No one values you? Have you no mate, no family?"

Her blush deepened. "Nay, I live alone since my man died. My father is a mage of some small skill. Our lord sent him away on business two years ago, and my mother chose to go with him."

Moran nodded. "That explains your abilities."

Enid shook her head. "I did not inherit his abilities. I wish I had, but I have not even a trace of magick within me. I have been tested and found wanting."

He rubbed his thumb across the back of her hand in a caress. "I would argue that. There are many different forms of magick. The most powerful mages, warrior servants of the Goddess, are forbidden to indulge in sex. In some way, that is the base of our Power. Or so I was taught, and so I swore celibacy."

She made a small sound of distress.

He placed a finger on her lips. "Do not fret, little one. My Power is mostly gone. Should the Goddess grant its return, I may become celibate once more. Although I am sore tempted to trade that Power for one such as you."

A small smile played about her mouth. "I believe I would have the better part of that bargain."

He touched her hair, smoothing it back from her face. Did she truly not know her worth? "Never underestimate the power of a woman. You wield far more than you know. You can take my breath away with but a glance."

"Honeyed words," she protested, but happiness glowed in her voice. She rubbed her cheek against his palm. Goddess, but her skin was soft. He frowned in confusion. What if he were forced to make that choice? Could he trade his life's work for carnal pleasure? There was no question what his answer must be. He pulled away.

"No mage I have ever encountered, dark or light, man or woman, has been able to restore life."

"I did nothing!" she protested. "I but recited a charm my mother used, when she would wash away my hurts as a child." But she told him the particular words she had said over the water, and how it had become unwontedly black as she bathed him. "Could that have been the illness that plagued you, that somehow I cleansed more than your skin during the ritual washing?"

"I cannot say what happened, but that is possible. At least as possible as my dead body quickening under your kiss. Nay, whatever you may believe, you have been an instrument of the Goddess this night. When the need arises to do Her work, She does not choose those without some tie to Her through magick." He paused and lay back against the pillow. "Possibly She led me east, knowing that you were here."

Alone, waiting for him. Was he led to her for a reason other than his healing? The possessiveness that sprang to life during their midnight fucking still pulsed within him.

He watched her as she spoke of her life, her friends in the village, how they occupied their time during the winter season. Anything to keep her from thinking of her dead husband. Seeing sorrow creep into her eyes made his heart clench.

He wanted to wipe that from her, to protect her from disappointment. He might not have the Power he once did, but he could envision a future here, with Enid—as a mortal. Such had never entered his mind. He'd always thought he'd die without his mage's abilities, but this slight blonde woman had given him reason to live.

She might not accept him, but there was something he could do to ease her life whether she did or no. Rising to his feet for the first time, he found his pouch, neatly wrapped in his belt. His dagger accompanied it. 'Twas proof she was honest, but he'd expected no less. Unwrapping the bundle, he sought the heavy object at the bottom.

He drew a smaller pouch from within his larger one. It clinked as he tossed it on the pallet beside her.

"Here. I owe you compensation for my care."

Finding the Light

Enid stared at him. He paid no attention to his nakedness but she could not keep her eyes off his muscular form. With difficulty, she focused on his words. "What?"

"You healed my battle wounds. It is just that you should have this."

She opened the pouch and spilled out a colorful stream of coins. He wagered it was more than the whole village had ever seen. "What of you?"

He shrugged. "I have no need for wealth."

Understanding lit her face. "Thank you. I shall spend it wisely, I promise."

He could not help but smile at her solemn declaration. "As you will. It is yours to do with as you wish."

"Thank you. For this, and for the Yule celebration."

"Nay, I must thank you for that. Or we must both thank the Goddess for bringing us together. I have never felt such pleasure." He strove to explain his past in terms she could understand. She must, before he could secure his future. "I have been on quest after quest, pulled to fulfill my life's work. When the Calling is upon me, all else falls aside."

"I have heard of mages who work for no man. If such is your lot, then you must regain your strength and continue on your way." Speaking the truth weighed down her spirits. She might have him for only a short time more.

"Aye. I may have found my next Calling." He pulled her up from the pallet and gathered her against him. "The magick within me is a mere spark of what it was. In the days to come, I will see if it grows. From the feel of it, that will not happen."

"But you are a mage. Does Power not always live within you? How can you lose it?"

"Once I was powerful beyond most mages, which is why I fought for the Goddess. But over time, the darkness began to consume me. Those who labor to rid the world of the threat posed by mages who have surrendered to the darkness must

145

walk in the shadows, and they take on some of the dangerous qualities of those they hunt. My life was a constant war with myself, as well as the evil mages I destroyed, to hold the darkness at bay and keep my eyes riveted on the light."

"What happened to you, that made you so ill and drained?"

"I sought a truly powerful evil mage. We sparred for months. Her minions tested my strength, chipping away at my defenses. I realized she toyed with me, as a cat with a mouse. I determined that she had led me astray, while she herself never moved from her lair. I tracked her by her magick, and came upon her in her manor stronghold. It lay west of here.

"During my drawn-out battle with her proxies, she had grown in Power. When cornered, she proved to be even stronger than I feared. I had no choice but to use every weapon I had or be destroyed. This required I free the darkness in my soul and mold it to my will.

"Darkness is dangerous and potent Power. With its aid, I defeated her. As you may know, all uses of magick come at a cost. I paid with my life."

"But how did you come back from death?"

"That I wish I could answer. When I spent my seed, something happened to me. Too many emotions I have never felt rose within me, cascading through my heart and mind. I knew an outpouring of ecstasy, intense and unprecedented. At the time, having nothing with which to compare it, I simply was grateful to the Goddess for granting me a moment of bliss. Now, I wonder if that was more than the seed of my body. Possibly the seed of my magick was planted within you. Your heritage would indicate 'twas fertile ground, where it took root and bloomed."

"And I returned it to you in a kiss."

"Aye, but it is not what it once was. Carefully tended and trained, the magick I knew had a long history of strong growth. What I find now is a different sort, more diffuse and misty. Less of a weapon."

"Will you not be able to defeat the evil mages now? Have I cost you your livelihood, your reason for living?"

"Nay, my sweet, never think that. You have given me life. Without you, I would be cold and dead. Through you, the Goddess has given me a new life."

She dared to voice softly, "I thought you might be a Yule gift from Her."

His head jerked up, eyes sharp upon her. "'Tis Yule?"

"Aye, 'tis Yule. Had you forgotten the season?" How could a mage lose track of holy days?

"When I am on a quest, I do not mark the passage of time. I did not realize when you mentioned Yule celebration that today was Yule. You are *my* Yule gift, my love." Moran swept her up into a kiss.

The same tingle invaded her that she had felt when he was dead, but nothing shifted from her to him. Instead, something beautiful blossomed deep inside her.

"Do you not need to eat, to regain your strength?"

His bright gaze met hers and she held her breath. "Might I have water?"

"Oh, forgive me, I did not think of your health." She scrambled from the bed and caught up her linen gown.

He winked. "You might as well leave it off. 'Twill save me the trouble of removing it again."

The cold air prickled her skin into goosebumps. Enid hid a small smile as she fastened the laces. Daven had never played such games, and she found she liked Moran's gentle teasing. She hastened to dip a ladleful from the bucket by the hearth. "You seem so much stronger."

"Aye, but right now, my love, I need you more than food." He drained the ladle in a gulp and grinned at her, the first time she'd seen him completely carefree. "I need to celebrate life and thank the Goddess, and the best way I can imagine that is with you. If you'll let me."

He pulled her back to sit beside him and rested his hand on the gentle swell of her belly. "I have no home, no family. My former life is lost to me and I must make a new one." Tipping her chin up, he looked directly into her eyes. "I would build one here with you, if you will have me."

His face wavered as tears obscured her vision. "I can think of nothing I'd like better. But what will you do for your livelihood?"

"I can teach you to use the Power you have gained, however strong it proves to be. I will find some way to be useful to this village. My back is strong. Surely there are times another pair of hands will be useful? I want to give you babies, children to fill a larger house and give us both gray hair. I will love you. I do love you." He stroked her cheek with his thumb, wiping away a tear. "But know that if you agree, you will be stuck with me for life. Can you tolerate facing me across the supper table each evening and awakening in my arms every morning?"

She cocked her head and a smile slid onto her lips. "I believe that I must have a sample before I make such a momentous decision. Last night, pleasure was given me without a face or a name attached. Mayhap it could have been any man."

He growled and clasped her against him, rubbing the bulge of his erection against her belly. "Any man, you say? Nay. You belong to me, and I to you. The Goddess brought us together and blessed our joining. Would you go against Her wishes?"

"I think you must prove to me that you are what you claim. If you can truly awaken magick in me, then I am yours."

"Oh, my sweet, that I can and will do." He shifted her off him, sliding to his knees beside her pallet. "One thing I must do as soon as possible is give you a proper bed. I cannot worship your body without the correct altar."

"I think I will like living with you." She helped him remove her gown. Seeing such ardor in his face, she found she could not be embarrassed. He almost devoured her with his gaze. The ties fell away and he pulled the halves of her bodice apart, baring her breasts. She could not afford a servant, so like all the women in the village, her laces were in the front. How convenient for him. Nay, for them both.

He merely looked upon her for a while, while his smile grew. When he met her eyes, his burned with desire. "You are perfect." When she would have voiced a protest, he set one finger on her lips. "To me. For me. Do not argue. 'Tis true. You are perfect in every way." He leaned forward and gently kissed a nipple. A shot of excitement arrowed from his mouth to her belly. She gasped when he licked where he had kissed and let out a slow breath. The contrast of cold and heat tightened the nub into a hard peak. He ran his hand down from her shoulder to cup the weight of her other breast, running his thumb across that nipple in a soft caress.

Her breath hissed in as shivers rocked her. "Sweet Goddess!"

"Aye. As sweet as you." He drew her nipple completely into his mouth and she arched against his kiss. His fingers worked her other breast, kneading and pinching and sending her spiraling into pleasure. A keening cry was torn from her throat when he scraped his teeth across the sensitive flesh.

His tongue soothed the tiny hurt. He drew back. "You are wearing too many clothes," he complained. "Will you help me?"

"Aye," she managed to push the syllable out of her trembling lungs. Breathing had become difficult to remember how to do.

Moran pushed the gown from her shoulders and down her hips. He lifted her legs and whipped the crumpled garment off the bed. She had no idea where he dropped it and cared even less, for he was parting her legs and stroking his warm hands along her inner thighs.

"Pay close attention." He lifted one of her feet and set it on his shoulder.

Enid braced herself on her elbows to see what he was doing. Her eyes widened as he repeated the action with her other foot. Her cunt was totally open to his view. Her hips strove to close on their own.

"Nay, leave be. You are beautiful and I would see the most precious part of you. This," he placed one palm on her curls, "is where all life begins. 'Tis where I would begin our life together. I can think of no better way to worship the Goddess than to pay homage to her greatest blessing, that of childbirth."

He surprised her by lowering his head and laying his cheek against her thigh. "Ah, the scent of you fills me with peace, woman. But I would have more." With both hands, he parted the curls and touched the swollen flesh within. "You are so wet. I can almost see my child here, emerging from your womb."

He lifted a glistening finger to his mouth and ran his tongue across the tip. He closed his eyes on a sigh. "Your taste is divine." An impish look crept into his eyes and he winked. "I would drink from that most sacred of springs."

Before she divined his meaning, he dipped his head and lapped up her juices. His tongue pushed into her as he licked, much like a small and flexible cock. When he reached the apex of the folds, he swirled the tip around her clit and she jerked. Her elbows no longer would support her and she fell back, to clutch at the covers and writhe against the hold he had on her hips. Little moans escaped her. He hummed against her slick folds and glittering pleasure rose within her. His tongue continued its exploration, seeking out every fold and delving deep into her cunt. He suckled at her clit and pleasure peaked in a shower of stars that sizzled everywhere they fell upon her skin.

"Did you feel any magick?" He climbed into the bedding beside her.

Enid roused herself and blinked up at him. "Aye, 'twas magick indeed, but not what I expected."

"There are many kinds of magick. Let me try another." He straddled her with his arms, settling his hips above hers. Wetness glistened on his lips and he licked them, relishing the taste. "Your delicious cunt is wet and more than ready for my cock." His mouth curved into a smug smile. "You must take worshipping the Goddess very seriously, possibly as seriously as I do. I am most fortunate to have found such a pious woman. I can see I will have to devote considerable time and effort to matching your devotion."

With a very long stroke, he entered her, stretching and filling her passage to its limit. Tight from her recent orgasm, she felt each inch of his slow penetration. His eyes closed and his breath became fast and shallow. "'Tis so hard not to thrust into you, like a bull rutting in a field. You feel so right."

Mayhap was because he had never had another woman, but Enid wasn't sure. In his arms, she fit better and felt more at home than she ever had in Daven's. She had enjoyed marital relations with her husband but she believed she would find sheer bliss with Moran.

Lodged deep inside her, Moran paused. A spasm shook her.

"Look within. See if you can find the source of magick," he directed. "'Twill be a shining spark, glowing with the Goddess' light."

Enid closed her eyes and tried to separate out the varying sensations she was experiencing. 'Twas not easy, with his cock filling her and his breath warm on her forehead.

"I feel a heat within my womb, and your cock stretching my cunt. I feel so blessed, but I can't find any magick." Tears sprang into her eyes.

"Nay, love, do not weep. All is well. You have lived your life so far believing that you could never own magick. It may take time to find the path to it." He lowered on his elbows until his chest brushed her breasts. His hands came up to frame her face. "We will learn together. I know little about female magick, which is one reason my final battle cost me so much."

Moran pressed a kiss on her nose. "Ofttimes revelations come when we least expect them. Relax, and enjoy being with me."

She sniffled and smiled. "I think I can do that."

"I hope so. I have years of celibacy to make up for — and a healthy curiosity." He withdrew in another long, slow stroke before sliding back into her. "You must tell me which you prefer, slow or swift."

Her smile grew. "I will require many examples before I can decide."

He matched her expression with a grin. "Aye, my lady, I believe we are well suited."

Four more slow pumps, and his hips gave way to a series of quick thrusts. She raised her legs and locked her ankles over his back. The changed angle drove him deeper and she sighed at the increased sensation.

"Aye, love, that is good," Moran panted as he continued plunging into her cunt. Her hips rose to meet him, tilting and allowing his hard length to reach something that made her yelp with delight.

"But that is even better," she declared. Her eyes widened as he hit the sensitive spot again and again, until she thought she might die of pleasure. She remembered to breathe and the feeling subsided — but only until he lowered his head to draw a nipple into his mouth.

She lost control as joy swept through her. A well of ecstatic desire, nay, two wells of desire poured sparkling delight into her. She filled up from her toes. Tingles marked the cresting pleasure that came from his mouth and his cock, until she could hold no more and her passion burst forth like a fountain.

She clenched around his cock again and again, wringing a cry from him that shook the rafters. His seed poured forth in a hot stream, filling her womb as his climax pulsed through them both.

He collapsed atop her and rolled to the side. "Next time, we will try slow and steady," he panted.

"Unless we don't like it," she reminded him.

"Aye. Unless *you* don't like it. I shall like it any way at all, so long as I am deep inside your sweet body."

Chapter Five

ക

Alice prattled on about the Yule celebration she'd missed, but Enid didn't correct her. She wasn't ready to share her happiness, so she nodded and lowered the bucket into the well.

Another voice snagged her attention.

The well lay behind the small tavern, sheltered to the north by a high wall along the road. The wind carried the sounds of a conversation to where she stood. Two men's voices, one strange and one now familiar. Alice fell silent and they both listened.

"Moran, your presence is little more than a glowworm, where before you burned like a signal fire. I had not expected to find you so diminished," the stranger rumbled in a deep timbre. "'Tis a great loss. You were the best of us. None can fill your boots."

"You flatter me, Stefan. One will step forward, I am certain." Moran's confidence rang in the words.

Enid smiled in satisfaction. He would be missed, but wasn't irreplaceable.

"I'm sorry you have chosen this."

"Do you think I would turn my back on what has been my life's work, knowing how important it is? Never believe this was my choice."

The sadness and regret in Moran's voice tore at Enid's heart. Hearing it, she knew she had no choice. She would have to let him go. She would help him regain his Power and send him on his way. No matter what it cost her.

She turned and met Alice's horrified expression. For once, her friend was struck silent. The pain in Enid's heart overflowed, filling her eyes with tears. Blindly, she groped for the bucket, brushed aside Alice's outstretched hand and somehow stumbled home.

"'Tis sad to see you laid so low," Stefan continued. "I pity you, Moran."

"Do not. I have served the Goddess my whole life, and we both know Her actions are often incomprehensible. I am well content to walk the path She has shown me."

Stefan cocked his head as if listening. For a moment, the two of them stood in silence but for the groaning of the pump rope and an occasional birdcall. "'Tis another Calling. I must bid you farewell." He took up the reins. "If you can, ward this place. Many among our enemies would seek you out, especially those with old scores to settle." Stefan hauled himself up into the saddle, turning the bay. "In general, our kind does not survive to be turned out to pasture when our work is done."

"Aye, I am aware of that, and grateful for the reminder."

Stefan lifted a hand in farewell and rode east, without looking back.

Moran watched him go with a light heart. He had spoken the truth. He felt at peace and sensed he would find happiness with Enid.

He tucked a pouch of coins into his belt. Stefan had also received the Call to fight Beatrice but arrived too late. The battle was over by the time he arrived, so he gathered everything of value left in the ruins. Moran had insisted Stefan keep half, for a mage on the road had need of wealth. Far more than he had now, in a tiny village. Even with a woman he planned to wed, his needs would be modest.

As he hoped, the trickle of magick he felt bubbling beneath his skin was sufficient to establish wards around the entire cluster of houses. No need to endanger those who helped him. He set the spell to alert him should anyone with Power approach the area, and turned for home.

Home. That had a lovely, warm sound to it.

Home. Where Enid waited, with her soft skin and fragrant hair. His woman.

The coins jingled in the purse as he walked. Ah, he remembered now. Before he saw Stefan, he had left the cottage on an errand and not completed it.

Enid waited for Moran, pacing. Alice's supper from the night before steamed in a pan by the fire, filling the air with mouth-watering aromas. She'd dried her tears and come to terms with losing Moran. He would not see her blubbering like a child.

What had made her think that she might be blessed with happiness? A pox on Alice for putting that notion into her head. Loneliness had been her companion for too long. She'd lost first her parents and then Daven.

'Twas the way of the world. People lived, they moved on, and they died. Moran had taken the opposite course, dying first and then living. Mayhap that had fooled her into believing he might remain with her.

He would leave. She believed the emotion in his voice when he spoke to his friend more readily than his words to her. Promises made in bed were always suspect, as Alice told her daughters.

No mage would turn his back on the immense Power Moran had wielded. Especially not for life in a tiny, poor settlement, sharing a hovel with the likes of her.

How had he wormed his way into her heart so quickly? After only a few hours with him, she could no longer imagine living alone. She'd rediscover it soon enough.

The latch lifted and Moran stepped inside, accompanied by a gust of cold air. "It smells like we'll have more snow." He stamped his feet to dislodge clumps of mud.

She could only stare. His long dark hair, a little damp, curled around his shoulders in slight waves. Oh, she prayed she carried his child, or would before he left. She would love to have a daughter with his hair. Her knees gave way and she sank into the chair.

His mouth, once set in grim lines, now curved up at the corners as he crossed to kneel before her. How devastating their son would be, with such a smile.

"I have news for you," he began.

She forestalled him with a finger across his lips. "Not yet. I would eat first."

"But 'tis—"

She cut him off, clapping her hand over his mouth. "I heard you speak with your friend. I know what you're going to say."

"I didn't mention it to him." He grinned. "You're wrong. You can't possibly know."

"And you find humor in this?" She leapt to her feet, not bothering to hide her dismay and hurt at his amusement. Facing him, she planted one fist on her hip and pointed to the door. "Go. Now."

His grin fled. He stared at her, open-mouthed, like a fish. "What?"

"Did you think to coax your way into my bed, have me play at being your wife until your magick returned? Abandoning me and whatever child I might carry? I will not be used and cast aside in such a manner."

He made no move toward the door. Indeed, he remained on his knees, before the empty chair. His mouth worked soundlessly. A muscle beside his left eye twitched.

In the face of his obvious confusion, she began to feel a bit foolish.

Mayhap she had been hasty—and wrong. She had been home long enough to heat supper, cry her eyes out and punch down the bread before he arrived. Much could have happened in that time.

Hope welled up, mingled with embarrassment—she felt more foolish every minute he stared at her in disbelief. Oh, sweet Goddess, had she ruined any chance she had for happiness with him?

"So." Not quite knowing what to do but determined to salvage at least her equilibrium, she smoothed her skirt. "Well." Seating herself before him, she swallowed the lump in her throat, stilled the trembling of her hands and took a deep breath. "Mayhap I jumped to conclusions and we should start over." Despite her outward composure, her pulse thumped like a galloping horse. "What were you going to tell me?"

He shook his head as if to clear it. "I have no idea what you thought, but I agree. Let us begin again." He took her hands in his. "Stefan followed me here, with a purse gathered from the ruins of Beatrice's manor. This gives us plenty, far more than we need."

Her heart leapt at his use of the word "us" and hope blossomed. His warm fingers tightened around hers.

"I visited a few of our neighbors and introduced myself. I will have a better Yule gift for you in a fortnight but I found a small one for you now. We will make do until the other is ready."

Pleasure flushed her cheeks and she burst out, "You are staying!"

"Of course, my sweet. If you'll have me. 'Tis your decision. I have made mine—I wish to remain with you." Moran dropped her hands to cup her face between his palms.

"I want you, too." Her fears tumbled out on a rush of words. "I thought you did not want to be here, that you missed your old life."

Adoration shone in his eyes. "How could I leave my Lady of Light? You are the best gift the Goddess could ever give me." With his thumb, he brushed away a tear on her cheek. "Why do you weep?"

"'Tis from joy, not pain." She smiled through her tears, but couldn't stop the flow.

"Ah. I see you have a lot of joy." He chuckled. "So do I." With a swift movement, he rose, pulled her up after him and swung her around. He set her down but didn't let go, his hard cock pressing against her.

"And do you weep?" She reached down and palmed his erection, rubbing slowly, until he growled deep in his throat.

"Aye. Keep that up and I shall do more than weep."

"I'm counting on it."

He backed her against the small table. Pushing between her thighs, he thrust his hips forward until the bulk of her skirt shifted to the sides. She parted her legs willingly, reveling in the sensation of his hard cock parting her cunt lips, teasing her through the thin layers of wool and linen barring the way.

Moran paused, his mouth hovering an inch above hers. His scent surrounded her, potent and masculine. "Never doubt that you are my one and only love." His lips met hers, and he proved that claim—with a searing kiss and his mastery of a different kind of power, one that weakened her knees and tightened her nipples. Shivers danced across her skin.

Had not the table supported her, she would have fallen. Instead, she lay back, wrapping her legs around him. He pressed into her harder and she tilted her hips to rub his hard shaft just where she wanted.

With a groan, he bent over her. His teeth found a nipple through the layers of her clothing, bit gently and tugged.

Streaks of fire sizzled from her breast to her womb and back again. Her breath caught in her throat. "Aye, like that," came her breathy encouragement.

'Twas all he needed. He gently tortured her with his mouth until she whimpered and tried to push him away. The tender assault on her breasts continued, joined by his hands, which found their way beneath her hem to caress her thighs before rising higher, to part and delve into her soft curls. He thrust several fingers deep into her cunt, stroking the sides of her channel, touching places she hadn't known existed. She fisted her hands in his hair to anchor herself. The maelstrom of sensations sparked by his teeth and touch threatened to overwhelm her.

"You are so beautiful." He raised his head.

She could fall into those dark eyes and drown. She dragged his mouth to hers and kissed him, staking her claim just as he had moments earlier. Moving her hips, she guided his touch but it wasn't enough. She wanted him filling her. A need grew, for him to possess her fully.

He pulled his mouth from hers. His eyes were glazed with desire. She began to understand the power she possessed. Not the same as his, but power nonetheless.

His breath was hot on her cheek. "I want to sink my cock into your wet heat, lovely Enid. I want to ride you until you scream and squeeze my seed from me with your tight, sweet cunt."

'Twas the same image that filled her mind. "Oh, aye, please do," she breathed.

They each wielded their own kind of power. His low, husky whisper alone sent her halfway to completion.

"You pleasure me as no other has, as no other can," she whispered.

Moran fumbled with her garments, finally hitching her skirt above her waist. She tore at his laces impatiently. Would his cock never be free of its confinement?

He stood long enough to shed his braes. Catching her gaze and holding it with his, he stroked his hands down her thighs. The tip of his cock nudged her curls. Taking his cock in his hand, he circled the tip around her clit. Once, then again.

She closed her eyes and whimpered. "More!"

He circled once more, and rubbed the tip down her cleft, parting her plump lips. She jerked her hips, urging him into her. He increased the pressure, slowly, too slowly, First the engorged head of his cock passed inside, stretching and filling her a little bit at a time. Glittering promises of ecstasy shimmered through her, making the hair on her arms rise. She thought he would never finish as he slowly pressed home. She beat on his lower back with her heels, encouraging him to hurry.

"Nay, I promised you slow, sweet Enid. Do you not like this?"

She could only gasp in answer.

He chuckled and began to pull out just as slowly. "I think you like it too much. You have no idea how much I like this, seeing your inner pink lips separated around my cock, pulling outward in a pouting kiss, as if your cunt is loath to let me withdraw. Do you want me to fill you again?"

"Aye." Her breath came shallow and quick. "If you will."

"Have no doubt, my love." He unlaced her bodice and guided her hands to her breasts. "Touch yourself, for me."

She stared at him. Touch herself?

"Aye, you must know what feels best. Give yourself pleasure, while I do the same. Touch yourself for me," he repeated.

Warily, eyeing him for any sign he was jesting, she began to massage her breasts. Her finger rubbed over her nipple and a streak of delight shot through her.

He nodded and smiled at her gasp of pleasure. He reached back to grasp her ankles and lifted her feet to his shoulders. "You have no need to hurry me. I am as eager as you."

With a jerk of his hips, he thrust his cock deep into her, filling her completely. His balls slapped against her ass. He withdrew and thrust again. She tightened her muscles, grasping him firmly. Each thrust sent her closer to the edge of that precipice.

"I can see every part of you, as we are joined in that most intimate and holy of unions. You have no idea how beautiful you are at this moment. Offering yourself, pleasuring yourself, accepting my worship, you are the embodiment of the Goddess. I love you, Enid. I pledge my life to you."

She tossed her head back and forth, moaning his name.

Her climax began with shivers that squeezed his cock like a fist. As he continued to plunge into her tightening channel, the force of her climax brought stars before her eyes. The celestial vision spread in waves of joy, tingling down her spine and curling her toes. She cried out as the wave crested, sending her senses reeling. Her spasming cunt milked the last of his seed from him as he collapsed atop her.

"You wished to know all the reasons to let me stay. 'Twill require least a fortnight, possibly more, to show you every one." He gently kissed her brow.

"I look forward to learning all of those reasons."

"I will fill your days and nights with them. But before that, my first Yule gift to you." He pulled up his braes and crossed to the door. Stepping outside, he returned with a snow-covered chair.

He thumped it on the doorjamb and a shower of snow fell way, revealing the seat.

'Twas a mate to the one she had.

"A home needs two chairs," he declared. "And there will be more, for our sons and daughters, should the Goddess bless us further."

He placed the chair at the table. "We will need a larger place to eat, too. But that's all in the future. Our future. Provided you keep me."

His eyes promised many, many reasons to let him stay.

The End

Also by Liddy Midnight

ℬ

Ellora's Cavemen: Dreams of the Oasis I (*anthology*)
Fire and Ice
In Moonlight (*anthology*)
Rogues *with Cricket Starr*
Small Magick
Transformations (*anthology*)

By Liddy Midnight writing as Annalise
Equinox II (*anthology*)
Venus Rising

About the Author

ॐ

Liddy Midnight lives, loves, works and writes in the woods of eastern Pennsylvania, surrounded by lush greenery and wildlife. Although raccoons, possums, skunks and the occasional fox eat the cat food on her back porch, she's no more than half an hour from some of the finest shopping in the country. Situated in this best of all possible worlds, how could she write anything other than romance?

Liddy welcomes comments from readers. You can find her website and email address on her author bio page at www.ellorascave.com.

Tell Us What You Think

We appreciate hearing reader opinions about our books. You can email us at Comments@EllorasCave.com.

UNHOLY MAGIC
Ravyn Wilde

ॐ

Dedication

❧

This book is dedicated to Mindy. A marvelous individual who came up with the perfect drink!

Trademarks Acknowledgement

❧

The author acknowledges the trademarked status and trademark owners of the following wordmarks mentioned in this work of fiction:

Boones Farm: E. & J. Gallo Winery Corporation

De Kuyper: Johs. De Kuyper & Zoon B.V.

Sno-Cat: Tucker and Sons

Taser: Taser International, Inc.

Zip Ty: The Zippertubing Company

Chapter One

ℬ

An airplane was *not* a good place to let his werewolf have the upper hand. The howl of his sexually frustrated wolf echoed in his mind, leaving him unable to focus. Harder and harder to control, the animal wanted his mate. If Franco didn't appease him, the wolf would take matters into his own hands. Er…paws.

Mentally caging his perturbed inner being, Franco repositioned his large frame in the seat and pulled back his long blue-black hair, quickly binding it at his nape. Staring blindly out the window, he saw Tehya's big brown eyes alight with sexual need, instead of clouds and blue sky.

Tehya. Her Native American name meant *precious*.

He'd left her six long months ago to track a rogue paranormal creature able to shift into a Tyrannosaurus Rex. Pauly'd been causing havoc—killing humans, torturing anything he could get his hands on. Franco found the T-Rex in Denver nosing around his sister, Marissa. After a very brief contest of wills, Franco took Pauly to Europe. There, the homicidal creature would stand trial and await his sentence. The organization Franco worked for would make sure of it.

Franco didn't decide guilt or punishment. He was the brawn, the muscle. The enforcer.

After leaving Europe he'd drifted. Tehya's life would be in danger if he gave in to the urge to take her as his mate. So he couldn't go back to her.

His wolf didn't agree. He wanted his mate.

The beast stayed hyperalert to anything reminding him of the woman they'd left behind. A scent reminiscent of Tehya's spicy-sweet skin was enough to cause the wolf to pull Franco in a direction he didn't want to go. He'd battled to keep the wolf from howling in disgust each time the teasing trail led them to a dead end.

Today had been the last straw. A glimpse of long, dark hair falling to an ass that looked like Tehya's had him reaching out to touch. Franco rubbed his aching jaw — mistaken identity could be painful. This time the dark-haired *man* turned around and punched him. Franco could've ended up in jail for sexual harassment. Not that the wolf cared.

He knew his world couldn't commingle with Tehya's. Taking a human mate meant concealing not only the fact he was a werewolf, but also his job, which included dangers she could only imagine in her worst nightmares.

Since he couldn't share his secrets with her, he'd have to lie to the woman he loved. *Not* a good start for a relationship. Any way he looked at it, he was screwed.

Franco had met Tehya at the beginning of summer. Driving from San Francisco to Denver, intent on visiting his sister, he'd stopped overnight in Salt Lake City.

Bumping into her on the street in front of his hotel, he'd been immediately captivated by the Native American beauty. Enchanted by the long, dark brown hair brushing the bottom of her ass, he'd looked into chocolate brown eyes…found himself held by their secrets.

Mentally reaching out to see if his interest was returned, he was surprised to find her mind closed to him. He couldn't even read her surface thoughts.

From childhood, one of his strongest powers had been mind reading. Yet somehow Tehya erected a shield he couldn't penetrate. After spending a few hours with her, he decided the shields weren't something she built purposefully. She was naturally protected.

Intrigued by his inability to truly *know* what she thought or felt, he convinced her to have coffee with him. The ensuing conversation was a blur, as he focused on how she smiled or touched his hand when she wanted to make a point. Franco found himself delaying his trip to Denver indefinitely in order to follow Tehya into the mountains. To see a place she referred to as "magical".

They'd spent several weeks holed up in those mountains. Occasionally stepping outside at sunrise or sunset to watch moose, deer and elk feed on the sweet meadow grass and drink from the Bear River. Most of their time together had been spent exploring—finding new ways to give each other pleasure. After long days and nights of making love, they would fall asleep wrapped in each other's arms.

Sometimes late at night, Franco had snuck out of bed to let his wolf reign supreme. Anyone catching a glimpse of a black timber wolf in the meadow would assume he'd wandered down from Yellowstone.

They had the area to themselves for most of those weeks. The owners of the other four cabins nearby came up occasionally to spend a day or so, interrupting their privacy. Tehya had wondered vaguely if her neighbors left so quickly because chopping enough wood to keep warm during the cold summer nights wasn't their idea of a vacation.

Franco knew the neighbors' short stays had more to do with listening to a wolf howling at their doors during the night.

Tehya had been right about the magic—both in the setting and the connection between them. When they'd first arrived, they'd gone for a walk in Christmas Meadows. With pine trees on three sides and an Aspen grove on the fourth, all surrounding a multicolored carpet of wild flowers, it was definitely a magical place. His wolf senses had told him they were completely alone. Intent on stealing at least one kiss, he'd turned to her, placed his hands on her shoulders, gently pulled her to him. Gazing into sweet chocolate eyes, he'd kissed her—and lost his sanity.

The kiss wasn't a mere touch of lips, but an exchange of souls. He should have turned around and ran down the mountain. Instead, the moment their mouths fused, lightning raced over his skin. The bolt slammed into his heart, with an echo of pleasure-pain in his groin. He'd drawn back a scant few inches to gulp in air.

Many times he'd tried to dissolve the vivid picture of what came next. Unfortunately the relentless loop of that erotic afternoon played with astonishing detail in his head.

Constantly.

As if it were yesterday, he saw Tehya's startled look at the sheer magnitude of their desire for one another. For a few moments the image in his mind was a blur. They'd fallen on each other. Stripping off clothing and throwing shredded pieces in a scattered pile on the long grass.

The mental movie slowed down at this point, adding the benefit of phantom sensation. Much like an amputee who felt a missing limb, his skin still tingled with the remembered touch of her body against his. The echoing sensations happened so often he'd given them a name. *Spirit-touch.* It was crazy, but he could almost believe their spirits kept reliving that afternoon.

Every time the mental movie played, he lost a little more of his soul. Unable to stop the trip down memory lane, he closed his eyes, shuddering in reaction to the vivid memories.

The first touch of warm skin made him moan in anticipation. Skimming his hand over her soft flesh, cupping her heavy breasts in his palms, he leaned over to worship her dark coffee-colored nipples with teeth and tongue. He licked and suckled her for long moments, reveling in her strident responses to his touch, the spicy-sweet taste of her flesh.

Shifting to recapture her lips, to drink in her moans of erotic rapture, he slowly traced one hand down her lush body. Teasing over the little pooch of her stomach, his fingers feathered over soft curls damp with arousal. Parting her vaginal folds, he slipped over the slick clit, finding her drenched with need.

Without pausing to think he lowered himself over her, panting with a desire so fierce it caught him by surprise. He wanted to feast on her hot flesh. Settling between her legs, he pushed her heels up, spread her knees wide, let the sun kiss what he was about to devour.

"Hold on, baby," he crooned. Leaning down, he licked her slit from back to front, at first slowly gliding his tongue then rapidly lapping her sweet juices. His eyes roamed up her body while he tormented her, the sight of her head tossing from side to side in pleasure causing him to growl into her flesh. She whimpered, her hands clutching the long meadow grasses at her hips. She shifted, pressing up to offer more. Happy to appease her, he plunged his tongue into her passage. Retreated.

She was so sweet. He rejoiced in her keening demands for more.

Feeling her body tense in preparation for explosion, he surged over her. Using one hand to guide his throbbing cock to her entrance, he slowly forced his way into her tight, hot sheath.

Thrusting his hips, he sank deep. Teeth clamped together to keep from howling in delight, he started a slow pounding rhythm that kept them poised on the brink of sanity. Franco wanted her desperate for release. She wrapped long legs around him, meeting each movement of his hips. Thrust for thrust. He felt his balls slap her ass. With one hand clutching his shoulder, she reached her other hand around her hip, leaning into him so she could reach those small globes. Cradling them in her palm, she used her talented hand to massage him.

Throwing back his head, he'd howled like a madman. Or one **very** *aroused werewolf.*

His mind linked with hers. He felt her unbridled reaction to his wildness. Felt the other half of his soul reach out, lock into place.

Feeling the wolf rise to the surface, he glanced down. The vision of Tehya spread naked before him, eyes tightly closed in rapture, assured him she hadn't seen his own eyes glowing with the internal fire of his wolf. He felt the shift of molecules under his skin, signifying a change was near. Forcing the beast into submission with his last thread of control, he quickly pulled out of her clenching heat.

Franco knew he couldn't sever or deny the connection with his wolf. He flipped Tehya onto her stomach, helped her to her knees and gently pushed her head down. Smoothing one hand between her legs, he found her core, slipped his fingers over slick flesh.

Sliding his cock slowly between her swollen labia, he followed her crease with his shaft — then stopped with his huge cock resting hot and hard against her clit. Tehya wiggled her ass in protest. "Franco. Don't stop!"

Reaching around her, he cupped her mons, playing with her clit while he pressed her back against him for a sharp moment of torment. It was too much.

Jerking back, he positioned the head of his shaft at the entrance of her blood-engorged pussy and surged forward. Thank god and goddess Tehya was too wrapped up in her body's pleasure to notice the growled sounds of satisfaction coming from his throat.

Digging his cock in and out of her clenching heat, both hands guiding her hips to fevered motion, he felt the wolf inside struggle to stake his claim. This time Franco gave in. Bending over her, he raked sharp teeth against the tender flesh where shoulder met neck, drawing a small amount of blood. With the wolf overriding him, his saliva would ensure the mark would never completely heal. Leaving a visible and sensual brand on his mate.

As the wolf staked his claim, his cock expanded beyond normal human limits in a partial change in form. The increase in length and thickness caused Tehya to sob in shocked stimulation.

"Am I hurting you?" He stilled. Waited for her answer.

She moaned, shaking her head. Pressed her ass against his groin. "Please!" she cried.

Again he slid one hand around to the front of her body, tugged her hardened nipples. Riding the wild bucking of her ass, he moved his hand down to work her clit, simultaneously licking the blood from her shoulder.

The taste of her made him crazy. He leaned back, once more bracing his hands on her hips...pushing her forward, tugging her back. Relentlessly pounding his flesh into her clenching pussy. Neck muscles tightening, he threw his head back, gritting his teeth in an effort to maintain control.

Slipping a finger between her stunning ass cheeks, he pressed lightly against her anus, felt the little rosette resist. Then slowly give. Tehya screamed. He felt her orgasm slam through her body. Felt her clenching muscles milk his cock. Finally gave in to the luxury of the first of many releases, spurting deep within her womb.

It was hours before he finished with her. After carrying his mate back to the cabin, he fucked her in the hot tub, on the floor in front of the fireplace, on the stairs leading to the loft. When they'd finally made it to the pillow-soft embrace of the bed, he still hadn't had enough. Wolf and man were united in their hunger for the woman.

Coming back from the erotic recollection, Franco was shocked to find himself still seated in the airplane seat, the memory so vivid he'd believed himself to be in the mountains with Tehya. Silently cursing, he focused his breathing and pulled his tray down, trying desperately to hide his arousal from the eyes of the man next to him. He'd already been down this road once today.

Returning to his thoughts, he realized he hadn't initially regretted the fact he'd mated with Tehya—until he'd been forced to leave her.

A phone call from his boss was a harsh reminder that Tehya was human and would be at risk in his world.

Nothing had changed since he'd left six months ago—*except* the realization that no matter how hard he tried, he couldn't live without her. To live *with* her, he needed to come up with a plan.

One option would be giving up his beast.

She was mortal. Compared to his, her life would be short. As a Druid-mage, he could pick another incarnation, give up his beast and take a temporary leave of absence from his duties at Controlling Creatures of Myth.

If he did, people would die. Working for CCOM was more than a job. It was a responsibility. The world's only preternatural police force, CCOM was tasked with containing law-breaking supernatural creatures. Or those otherworldly megalomaniacs who wanted to rule mankind. Franco shook his head. It amazed him how often nonhuman species thought they should dominate the world.

If he gave up his wolf to live with his Indian maiden, his other choices weren't any better. Vampire—no sun, limited diet. Not a real choice. Dragon—forget it. Centuries ago the dragon's strength and fierce fighting skills had been a benefit, but not in today's world. If humans saw the wolf, they assumed he was just a big dog. A dragon would be a little harder to explain.

He could revert to his original form. Give up everything but his Druid-mage powers for the length of Tehya's life. But the magic didn't fascinate him like it did his brother, Ricardo. Franco didn't like spending time in a laboratory or bent over moldy books, studying his race's powers. He'd still have to explain his frequent absences to his mate, unable to share even the call of magic with her.

He was jealous of his siblings' newfound happiness. Both Ricardo and their sister, Marissa, had found supernatural mates. They were disgustingly content with their lives. Franco knew he was in for centuries of pain when Tehya's very brief human lifespan ended.

So. Without a plan or believable excuse for his six-month absence, he was landing in Salt Lake City. Going to his mate meant he would miss the first of what he suspected would be many Winter Solstices with his family. Throughout the centuries, any relatives living above water got together for a week in December. It would be more than a little difficult to hide his family's quirks from a human wife.

He planned on telling Tehya he was an orphan.

Franco winced, hearing his mother's screech of outrage in his mind. He didn't think he imagined it. Too far away to speak with her telepathically, he knew she'd still sensed his decision. As soon as Mom could make her way to the cave where his parents kept their cell phones, he'd be getting a call.

He might have to give up his family for his mortal wife's lifetime, but he could *never* leave CCOM. Never let humans deal with the truly demented paranormal creatures even other CCOM employees couldn't handle.

They'd be nothing more than fodder. Left to face creatures like Pauly, who thought being a were-Tyrannosaurus Rex gave him a license to kill.

He supposed he could invent some type of traveling salesman gig.

Franco sighed, preparing to leave the plane. He would be starting this relationship with myriad deceptions. Not something he wanted to do, but the other option meant living without Tehya.

Both wolf and man agreed *that* wasn't acceptable.

Chapter Two

&)

Tehya knew coming back to the cabin was a mistake. Even with the Christmas tree in the corner reminder her of the upcoming holidays, she couldn't forget lying on the sheepskin rug with Franco poised above her, olive-toned skin gleaming in the firelight, his curling black mass of hair brushed against broad shoulders. The deep blush wine-colored nipples felt smooth under her fingers as she plucked the nubs in time with the shift of his hips. If she let herself, she could even feel the sensation of him pumping his thick cock in and out of her body. The wild look in his moss-green eyes pierced her soul when he'd bent down to kiss her senseless.

She clenched her teeth, her body throbbing in response to remembered passion. Raising her hand, she covered the marks he'd left on her neck with his teeth. Whenever she thought about Franco, the light scratches would pulsate, sending desire escalating through her body. He'd made those marks the first time they'd made love. Every time her marks ached, she felt the phantom sensation of his hand pressing into her back, guiding her to her knees.

Closing her eyes she swayed against the wall. Her legs buckled under the phantom sensations. She held herself up with sheer will. Damn it! The impression of his cock nudging her blood-engorged pussy felt real. This was crazy—endlessly reliving the sensations of making love to a man who'd left her six long months ago.

If she closed her eyes, Tehya could hear her whimpering cries echoing through the meadow, excitement rising at the dark sensuality of Franco's possession. Feel his soft breath tickling the back of her neck, the scrape of his sharp teeth over her shoulder. When he bit down, his cock had seemed to somehow grow longer. Thicker. Having seen his body in the bright sunlight, she would have said that was impossible.

Once he'd started pumping his cock in and out of her spasming channel, she'd scrambled to find something to hold on to. Franco braced his body by planting one hand beside her head. Eyes closed in mental anguish, she could still see her fingers wrapped around his arm, digging into the corded tendons.

She'd spread her legs for him, forced her butt back against the thick curl of pubic hair at his groin. Impaling herself over and over on his shaft, she reveled in the total immersion of her mind and body with Franco's soul.

It should have frightened her, but at the time she hadn't questioned their actions, or the strange connection she'd experienced when they'd made love that first afternoon. Only afterward had everything started to make sense.

Franco wasn't entirely human.

Her body exhausted after the marathon of sex, she'd opened her eyes to gaze mindlessly at the trampled flowers beneath her. She'd wanted nothing more than to sleep. Instead, he'd carried her back to the cabin and started over again.

He'd been insatiable.

In mounting irritation over her inability to forget the damn man, Tehya repeatedly thumped her head against the cold, front room window. Staring blindly at the wild winter beauty before her, a tear trickled down one cheek. How long would it hurt, missing Franco? How many months until this stabbing pain in her heart deadened to a dull throb?

The visceral memory of him pressed against her back as they'd lain tangled in the sheets kept her from sleeping in the loft bed. If she stepped outside on the back deck, in the steam rising from the hot tub she saw a ghostly version of herself straddling his lap, riding him hard.

No matter what she did, the memories remained vivid. The soft touches and breathy moans should have faded to nothing more than whispers by now.

No. The winter snow and change of scenery hadn't altered the memory of what happened here last summer.

As a last-ditch effort to save her sanity, Tehya had counted on the isolated cabin's rejuvenating solace. The cabin, perched high in the Uintah Mountains between Utah and Wyoming and overlooking Christmas Meadows, usually revived her. With so much snow, the road was closed to traffic this time of year. The other four cabins in the meadow were typically used between May and November.

Only Tehya's family would brave the whisper-quiet land to savor the solitude of the winter months, the breathtaking vistas where the world appeared as it had before civilization. Untouched. Uninhabited.

In pain.

It took a few minutes for her to realize the pain she felt wasn't solely her own.

Mother Earth's throbbing anguish fed her heartbreak.

Frowning, she quickly threw on her red insulated snowmobile suit and stepped outside. When she'd arrived at the cabin, she'd spent the first day shoveling several feet of snow off the second-story porch. She'd also cleared a path to the shed where the snowmobile was kept. Towering walls of snow on either side of the narrow path created a white, roofless tunnel. Tehya walked down the stairs extending from the porch, used her booted foot to sweep away the few inches of new snow that had fallen last night.

Knowing she would be unable to dig her fingers into the frozen soil, she stooped down to place her hand on the ground. Hoped the connection would be clear enough for her to figure out what was wrong.

The blast of sadness emanating from Mother Earth sent a shudder through her. In a wordless language, Earth's spirit spoke to her of unholy magic. Of being used for evil purposes. She could feel an *otherness*—a hint of the strange aura she'd seen around Franco. Tehya dismissed that thought. Franco wasn't evil. He had secrets—but then, so did she.

Obviously.

In her mind the frozen ground screamed of the horrors it was being used for.

Raising her hand, she shook off the ache of Mother Earth's desperate call for help. Looking toward the mountain a few miles away, she knew someone needed to investigate. Since she was the only one around, this meant Tehya would be the one taking the look-see.

Immediately she thought of calling Franco, guessing he would know what to do. Just as quickly she dismissed the thought. She wouldn't use this as a reason to contact him.

Six months ago he'd received a phone call from a man he said was his boss.

She'd heard snatches of the conversation. Enough to know he'd left her to risk his life. She heard him ask, *"How many has he killed?"* and *"Do we know what his weaknesses are?"* The strangest part of the one-sided conversation had been a particular bit of murmured disbelief.

"A T-Rex? Are you kidding me? Shit!"

Then he'd taken the phone into another room.

Before he left, he'd kissed her lovingly, real regret showing in his eyes when he said he loved her. There'd been no promise of return. She'd refused to press for one.

Well, that had been last summer. While Tehya wanted to believe she'd read his emotions correctly, it would be her luck finding a man who felt he needed to shield her, just as her family did.

Precious Tehya, unable to deal with harsh realities, needed to be protected from the big, bad world. She'd been excluded. Sheltered.

She was so tired of being treated like a fragile flower she wanted to scream.

The only member of the close-knit Ute family not privy to their deepest secrets, Tehya, in response to their lack of trust, had guarded her own secrets very carefully. Her reaction to Franco's otherness had been the same. Even though she'd wanted to, she hadn't been able to confide in him. She'd waited for him to trust her.

Silently she'd watched the wolf play in the meadow, hardening her resolve.

No one knew Mother Earth spoke to her. Or that she carried within her spirit a totem animal, given to her during a dream. By keeping their powers from her, her family and Franco forced her to play human.

It was high time she shucked the protective shell placed around her. *Without* acting like one of those heroines from a bad horror movie—she wasn't TSTL.

No. Instead of being Too Stupid To Live, she would be smart.

She'd send an email to her Uncle Jason.

As her laptop booted up she checked her snowshoes, changed into a lighter colored snowmobile suit so she wouldn't be easily spotted, and loaded a backpack with supplies. Sitting at the computer, she thought about what she should say.

Ultimately, she told her uncle she'd gone to investigate strange noises coming from one of the surrounding mountains. Not exactly a lie. Just before she ended the message, she promised to call him within twelve hours.

By then it would be dark. She'd either be home—or need help.

* * * * *

Franco looked at the barricade in the road and swore. Access to the cabin was closed for the season. He debated backtracking to Evanston and trying to rent a snowmobile. No. It would take several hours. He'd call his wolf, switch back at the cabin and tell Tehya...something. Franco sighed. The lies would start today.

After hiding the rental car in the trees, Franco got out, stretching his hands over his head while looking around. Satisfied he was alone, he simply thought...*wolf*.

The space surrounding him began to flicker. His jeans slowly dissolved into his body, fur sprouting in its place. Franco allowed the beast to rise. His bones started to pull apart, knitting back together in an entirely different way.

Happy to be free, at first the wolf took time to play. Chasing a rabbit. Running down a deer. Finally tired of the games, he eagerly set out to find his mate, covering the miles at a fast pace.

Reaching the cabin, he realized quickly that Tehya wasn't here. From her lingering scent he could tell she'd only been gone a few hours. His wolf stilled while Franco used his Druid senses, trying to get a feel for where she might have gone. He'd used this same magic in the rental car at the airport, psychically tracing her to Christmas Meadows. This otherworldly tracking ability was one of the reasons he was good at his job.

He felt her not far from the cabin, a little higher in the mountains. He started to relax—until he realized he sensed more than just her location.

Tehya was nervous. Scared. He couldn't sense what made her feel this way, but he knew he needed to get to her. Now. He dove off the porch, hitting the snow on all fours, immediately picking up her trail.

Chapter Three

ᔕ

Tehya climbed the frozen mountain until she reached the bottom of a sheer cliff. Beneath her snowshoes sat several yards of icy white snow, a ton of dirt—and something that didn't make sense. Taking off one of her gloves, she reached out to touch the side of the mountain. Closed her eyes to concentrate on the visions Mother Earth sent to her.

An unnatural cavern. Mixed pain coming from not only the ground itself, but from several beings locked inside.

Looking around her, she decided standing in the open was just dumb. She moved a few yards to the left, into a small grove of spindly pine trees. At this altitude the trees didn't get enough oxygen to grow thick and strong.

Now what do I do?

The only thing she *could* do. Gather information. She'd be taking a risk—of being seen, of alerting those within to the fact someone knew they existed. All her life she'd been shuttled away from these kinds of risks. If she went inside the mountain, there would be no pretending to be human.

She'd be coming out of the supernatural closet.

Taking a deep breath, Tehya said a silent chant and reached for her magic.

Mother Earth had evolved into a sentient being for Tehya. Most of Tehya's powers came from the connection they shared. Using this bond, she could manipulate the Earth's structure in small ways. To get into the cavern she asked Mother Earth to silently create a small passage for her. Then she called on her spirit totem, asking for help with her eyesight and hearing.

In small increments, dirt and rock shifted in front of her. She stuffed her snowshoes into a tree, hiding them on one of the thicker branches. On hands and knees, she slowly crawled into the emerging tunnel, continuing down the passage until emerging on the other side. Finally able to scoot out on a rock and look over the edge.

Her jaw dropped.

Tehya couldn't believe what she saw in the cavern below. Cages. Lots of big cages lining the walls, with two small rooms set up like labs on the far end and two smaller offices right underneath her. Where the cages had bars across the tops, the rooms were open, the walls extending four or five feet above the heads of the guards stationed in some of them. From her vantage point she could see into every room.

She listened to the steady drip of water onto one of the rocks above her. Afraid to move, Tehya kept perfectly still, not wanting to draw the attention of any of the dozen black-uniformed men she counted below. They were all armed. Rifles slung over their shoulders, knives strapped to their legs and Tasers clipped to their belts.

The fear and hatred emanating from the men locked in the enclosures resonated within the mountain. Besides the gut-wrenching emotions, she sensed an otherness surrounding all the captive beings. The uniformed guards were harder to read. Human? Some of them. A psychic taint surrounded the guards, similar to the one she sensed on the earthen walls surrounding her. Within their embrace, she felt the scorch of black magic that built the cavern. It played over her skin like an angry, biting insect. Her totem animal didn't like this place, wanted her to run. Tehya fought to stay in place.

It irritated her. Knowing the men were something other than human, yet unable to tell what they were. She'd been foolish to avoid discussing her powers with her family. She might have gotten some training. In this situation someone's life could depend on her. If something happened, the best Tehya could manage would be to make the roof cave in.

Bad idea.

The setup below looked like some mad scientist's lab. Made her wonder what the men in the cages were being subjected to—and why. Speculation drove her crazy. Why go to all this trouble? What were they trying to accomplish? Who the hell *were* "they"?

While her mind raced, her hands quietly dug into her pack for the objects she needed to begin cataloguing the scene below. Drawing a basic diagram in her notebook, she marked the occupied cells and exits from the room. She surreptitiously snapped pictures—without a flash, of course—noting the guards' movements. There didn't seem to be any schedule to the comings and goings.

When several guards dragged a man out of a cage and into one of the labs, she watched helplessly as they strapped him onto a gurney before surrounding the table, blocking her view.

Suddenly the man screamed. Tehya began crying silently. The sounds of pain and guttural anguish coming from below made her clench her fists in anger. She actually had to hang on to one of the rocks to keep from leaping over the edge in an attempt to rescue the poor man.

I can't. I can't! If I get caught, no one will ever find out about this place. Get information and get out. Get to Uncle Jason. Come back and save them. Tehya kept repeating the litany in her head. Not going down into that lab was one of the hardest things she'd ever done.

She had to do *something*. She'd seen everything she could from this vantage point. Now she needed to get into one of the small office rooms below to check the computers and filing cabinets. Where she wasn't adept at using her otherworldly skills, she was an expert at extracting information from supposedly secure machines. As a professional security software designer, Tehya spent a lot of time poking holes in her competition. On the very small chance she couldn't assess information on the computers, maybe she'd find something in the file cabinets.

She didn't want Uncle Jason to have to come back here for information. She wanted to get everything they needed to annihilate whoever created this place.

Touching the dirt wall beside her, she thought about where she wanted to go then waited patiently as Mother Earth slowly created a second tunnel. She descended, crawling quietly on all fours, and hesitated when she reached the room, looking into its shadowy depths. The only light came from the computer monitor. *Perfect.* The machine had been left on.

The normalcy of the computer equipment in this bizarre environment didn't escape her notice. Now she needed to figure out how to access the secrets she hoped it kept. Standing silently, she crossed to the computer, within moments locating password-protected files. Stealthily opening drawers and looking under the paraphernalia on the desk, Tehya knew most people kept their passwords close. Given enough time she could hack into anything, but she'd rather do it the easy way.

She lucked out when she lifted up the edge of the desk calendar, finding everything she needed written on a little sticky note. Shaking her head at people's stupidity, she quickly typed in *Gemini1*, smiling with satisfaction when the file opened.

* * * * *

Franco followed Tehya's scent to a tunnel hidden in the trees outside a nearby mountain. Gathering his magic, he shifted. In true were-form, his fur morphed into the clothing he'd been wearing before he changed into a wolf. Crouching down, he crawled a few feet down the passage.

Then came to a horrified stop.

He felt dark magic bite into his skin like vicious fire ants. Whatever the source, it started pulling his magic, draining his energy in alarming waves of pain. He tried erecting a shield, knowing the only way to stem the flow might be to change back into his wolf. Narrowing his eyes, he fought against the sudden compulsion to change.

And lost.

In centuries of life he'd never met anyone whose magic was strong enough to combat his own strength of will, except for his brother Ricardo's. The magic crackling like wild lightning within the small tunnel forced him to bring his wolf to the surface. Locked inside the black fur, Franco fumed. No matter. He would find Tehya and chase her out of here. Then he'd come back and kick some black-magic butt.

At the end of the tunnel, the scene in the cavern made the wolf's hair stand on end. Franco couldn't believe what he saw. The entire place looked like something out of *Frankenstein*.

A vampire lay stretched out on a steel table, electrodes and needles attached to his body. It didn't look like he'd submitted to the treatment willingly. His face was bleeding, his body bruised. If that wasn't enough evidence of reluctant participation, the silver cables binding him to the table were a strong hint.

Franco tried to sense his mate. Off to his right was a second tunnel. Catching a lingering scent at its entrance, he sighed. Of course she'd gone down to the cave floor.

Holy, shit! Tehya sat back in the chair, rubbing her eyes. These people were crazy! She finished duplicating a few files on to a blank disc she'd brought with her, thinking about what she'd read. Without understanding the medical jargon, she didn't have a clear picture of what was going on. Words like, "terminated due to inability to control" and, "subject resists indoctrination—suggest extreme retraining", didn't make her feel all warm and fuzzy.

Tehya heard a sound in the tunnel across from her and froze.

Fuck! Someone had discovered the tunnel. She ducked under the desk, curling around herself. There'd been little light in the office. Under the desk it was completely dark. She said a little prayer of thanks that she'd put the computer screen back on the page it'd been on when she arrived.

Who was she kidding? Like they hadn't already discovered the big hole in the wall?

Clasping her arms around her knees, she stayed rock still, holding her breath and listening for any sound.

She heard nothing.

A few moments later a big, black, furry nose ruffled the hair on her head.

"Nice doggy—or should I say wolfie?" she whispered, waiting for the wolf to make the first move. Then she noticed the moss-green eyes.

"*Franco?*" she hissed in disbelief.

Her sense of relief quickly changed to irritation. The wolf licked her face and she swatted him away. "Stop that, you mangy beast, you scared the crap out of me. We've got to go." Without wasting time or trying to hide her actions from Franco, she touched the wall and asked Mother Earth to get them out of there by the quickest route possible.

As soon as they emerged outside, Franco changed back to human form. Glad to be out of the mountain, away from the insistent bite of magic pulling at his mind. Aside from vampires, he'd sensed a couple were-creatures in the cages. A few of the guards had magic skills but none of them were powerful enough to force his change. Someone else had done that. Any being with that kind of power might eventually notice the cavern held visitors. They were lucky it hadn't already noticed them.

He pulled Tehya away from the mountain, intent on putting distance between *it* and them.

She struggled against him. Planted her feet firmly, placed her hands on her hips and demanded, "What are you doing here?"

Though his wolf would have sensed anyone around, Franco still didn't like standing close to the mountain. It was too open here, too dangerous for his mate.

He clamped a hand over her mouth and wrapped his other arm around her shoulder to pull her into the trees.

When he released her, she spun around to glare at him, stomping her foot in the snow.

He grinned and the action made her mad.

"Arrogant, selfish, asshole of a wolf!"

That reminded him. "How did you know I was the wolf?"

She rolled her eyes. "As if I wouldn't notice you sneaking out of bed to get furry every night we were together!"

"You watched me?" She hadn't said anything. Why hadn't he felt her? Did her mental shields somehow keep him from sensing her? Or had the wolf, recognizing his mate, failed to warn him?

"You think you're so smart. Well, you aren't the only one with an inner beast!" Throwing the small backpack to the ground, she stripped off her insulated snowsuit, letting it drop at her feet. Knowing she'd be toasty warm inside the suit, she'd only worn a thong underneath.

Distracted by the spellbinding sight of coffee-tipped breasts bouncing before him and the small slice of fabric hiding the dark thatch of hair between her legs, he paid no attention to her comment.

Tehya slipped out of the thong and raised her hands over her head, chanting in an unfamiliar language. The sound raised chills along his spine. He blinked and looked down into the chocolate eyes of his mate…

Peering up at him from the form of a brown-pelted wolf with red-tipped fur.

"Tehya!" Voice rising on a note of surprise, he took a step toward her. Yelping, she turned and snagged her backpack in her jaws, then fled through the trees. Looking back over her furry shoulder, her eyes dared him to chase her.

He wasted precious moments hiding her snowsuit under a log then changed into his beast to race after her, intent on following her very intriguing flash of tail into the rapidly approaching night.

Her musky-sweet scent was a trail he could follow with his eyes closed. It called to him. Beckoned. Urged the wolf to claim what was his.

A few miles from the cabin he caught her, tumbling her into the snow and sending her backpack flying. He clamped his jaws around her exposed neck, growling low in his throat. He mentally staked his claim. *"Mine!"*

Tehya relaxed in submission. *"Yes."*

The whispered word thrilled Franco. They could communicate telepathically! He tried to shift, wanting to hold Tehya in his arms. To show her how much he'd missed her with loving kisses. The wolf had other ideas. He'd denied the beast his mate for far too long.

Evidently the mental bond worked well. She sensed his turmoil, responding with a telepathic hug of acceptance. *"It's okay."*

Twice her size, the black timber wolf released her, lowered his muzzle to lick a path down the soft tan fur of her underbelly to breathe in her scent. Her alpha bitch panted encouragement, wiggling on her back to keep his attention.

A deep growl from Franco's throat, followed by his lowered head nudging into her side, got her to roll to her feet.

Raking his teeth over the faint marks on her fur—evidence of his claim on her—he straddled her back and mounted her. Keeping his mind locked with hers, he shared both the man's love and the beast's pressing need.

He found her swollen opening on the first thrust. Drove deep as she dropped her head on her paws and arched into him. Grunting, he buried his cock deep inside, riding the she-wolf beneath him with a fierce pleasure. He raised his head, howling in rapture as the clenching heat of her channel milked his shaft. The sensations were different than making love in human form. More primal. He let his beast take over.

Clamping his teeth on her shoulder to hold her beneath him, the wolf pumped his haunches, digging his engorged cock in and out of her slick passage. Over and over he thrust against her, felt her body stiffen as the knot on the head of his wolf penis swelled. It kept their bodies locked together for long moments. They shuddered from their mutual orgasms, convulsing repeatedly in sensual overload.

"*Mine,*" he growled in her head again, and she howled her acceptance. The mental bond wasn't fully formed. Franco heard what Tehya projected to him, but he couldn't read her thoughts, as she seemed able to do with him. Her shields were strong. She'd need to learn to share more than her body.

When the knot relaxed he withdrew from her tight sheath. After snatching her backpack up in his jaws and herding her toward a nearby cave, he switched to human form, watching intently as Tehya transformed. With a wave of his hand, he used magic to start a fire by the entrance and cover the floor with soft rugs. Adding a fur blanket for warmth. Finally, he pulled her down beside him, enveloping her in his arms.

Damn! He'd missed her. Missed watching the light dance in her eyes when her passion built.

But she was already asleep. He lay back on the rugs, content to hold her.

Tehya must have dozed. Worn out after several sleepless nights, a stressful trek into the mountain and wolf sex. Wow! She looked at the burning candles in the cave and frowned.

Where had those come from? Then she remembered Franco waving his hands when they first entered, the blankets and fire appearing out of nowhere. Evidently Franco had more secrets than she'd realized. It was past time they had a talk.

"I can smell water." Franco's voice interrupted her thoughts.

"Umm. There's a hotpot at the back of the cave." At his look of confusion she explained, "Yellowstone's only a couple hundred miles away. This area has all kinds of geothermal activity. A hotpot is a pool of water, deep enough to sit in. This one has been used for years. It's safe. You wouldn't believe how many people just step into any pool of water without first checking the temperature. Not with their hands, but a thermometer. Some hotpots will boil the skin off your bones in seconds. Want to go sit in it and talk?"

"You make it sound so appealing, how could I resist," Franco replied sarcastically. Scooping her up in his arms, he carried her to the back of the cave. She gave him credit for only hesitating slightly before stepping into the water. He positioned her on his lap, strong arms encircling her torso. His hard, muscular body enfolded her gently. She sighed. Laid her head back on his shoulder.

She thought they might take this time to discuss things. Franco had other plans.

He licked the never-fading marks on the side of her neck. That soft glide of tongue made her nerves snap to attention. If she'd thought she was tired and satisfied, she now realized just how wrong she'd been.

The soft, exploring tip of his tongue circling her ear forced a moan from her lips. She squirmed in his lap. This time *she* had plans. Pulling away from the shelter of his arms, she stood in the water and turned to face him.

"Let me." She bent forward to lick one of his nipples and felt him shudder. "Sit up on the edge," she murmured against his skin.

As he left the water and her hands started to play over his chest, she watched his cock stretch, growing in girth and length. Tehya couldn't wait to get her hands on all that lovely flesh. Overwhelmed by Franco's appetites, it seemed as if she'd always been a submissive participant in their lovemaking.

She decided she would start at the top. Her fingers sifted through the wild mane of black hair, fingernails scraping over his scalp.

Franco closed his eyes, stretching into her touch. "Ah, Tehya...that feels wonderful."

Smiling in satisfaction, after a few minutes she moved her hands down to his face, skimming the pads of her fingers over each feature, memorizing every detail of his chiseled appearance. She'd missed seeing this face beside hers on the pillow every morning.

Tehya traced the line of his lips with her tongue, gently slipping into a deep kiss when he opened to her. "Ummm." Now it was her turn to moan. Her hands continued their journey, testing strong muscles, provoking shudders from his body with each stroke.

When she pulled away, Tehya watched as one bead of water ran down Franco's body. Starting just above his left nipple, it ran slowly over the ridges of his abdomen, to the flat plane of his stomach, catching in the dark curly hair of his groin. The cock springing from the hair jerked in reaction to her light touch.

She pressed a finger over the small hole, spreading the slick pre-come over the head of his shaft. Bending over him, she drew air and the dark musky scent of his arousal into her lungs. Swiping her tongue around the swollen purple crown, she tasted his salty-sweet essence. She slipped her lips over the tip—pressing them together to ensure he felt himself breaching her mouth. She hummed in delight, his thick cock a velvet treat.

Damn, but she loved doing this. For herself. For him.

She wanted more. Moving her hand up to Franco's chest, she pushed. "Lie back."

She didn't blink when a pallet of blankets appeared beneath him. He helped her out of the water then reclined, while she sat facing him. Intent on the hard shaft directly in front of her—the glistening, dark plum tip oozing fluid every time she swiped a finger over it—she didn't argue when Franco reached between her legs to stroke her soft folds. She felt the rasp of his fingers as he played with her flesh in rhythmic duplication of her strokes.

For long moments they teased each other. Guttural moans and gasping breaths filled the small cavern with sounds of their passion.

Once more she bent to take Franco's cock into her mouth, and he went completely still.

Franco's entire being focused on his cock, the combined pleasure of her sucking mouth and the circling pressure of her hand sliding up and down his shaft. If he didn't shake her rhythm, he wouldn't last another minute.

His fingers found her pussy again, the wet heat a siren call. With his hands he urged down to her side, shifting slowly to his own, careful not to dislodge Tehya from her frenzied ministrations on his cock. With her long legs stretched in front of him, he twisted his body to maneuver his head between them and lapped her tempting flesh.

That did it. She gasped, releasing him for a second to concentrate on her own pleasure. Franco placed his arm around her hips, rolling her on top to settle her pink flesh over his mouth. Moving her body to accommodate the new position, she sucked his shaft back into her mouth. Bobbed her head on his cock while he buried his face between her legs.

Tehya groaned, vibrating the cock in her mouth and setting off Franco's deep growl, which in turn resonated to her core. Tehya spread her legs farther apart and relaxed into the intimate position. It was difficult not to lose herself in the pleasurable motions of tongue and teeth. She struggled to focus on the mass of flesh in her mouth, wanting to return the pleasure.

The soft puff of his breath against her heated core made her clamp her thighs against the sides of his head. The fiery wet slide of this tongue made shivers race up and down her spine. When his lips encircled her clit, he suckled hard and shook his head. She had a vision of being his personal chew toy.

Increasing her efforts, she used one hand to gently cup his ball sac. *Squeeze.*

"Tehya, stop!" Franco's voice was strangled. He tried to move her away. When she wouldn't budge, instead growling a warning, he eagerly went back to eating her pussy.

Within scant seconds, Franco moaned into her flesh. The hot gush of his seed filled her mouth and she drank him in. Swamped by an orgasmic tidal wave, she slipped her mouth from him with a wet pop. Threw her head back to scream through her release. When she realized her hand was wrapped around his recovering erection, she wished he'd bury more than just his tongue in the moist heat between her thighs.

He immediately inserted his thick finger inside her and swirled, causing a smaller burst of lightning within her core. Not what she wanted.

"Damn you, Franco. Fuck me!"

He didn't need to be told twice. Untangling their bodies, he pushed Tehya to her back. Moving over her, he set the crown of his cock over her clit. Used his hand to rub the tip over her swollen nub, dipping into her cream. The honeyed lubrication helped ease his way into her flesh and he felt her stretch around him.

The feel of her vaginal muscles clamping around his shaft was exquisite torture. Grabbing her hips, he lifted her for leverage. Eagerly she spread her legs for him—begging with her body. And her voice.

"Franco!" Her demand became a cry of delight as he pulled out, surged forward.

He set the pace. Slow. Deliberate. Fierce. With every forward thrust he ground his pubic bone into her clit until she shattered beneath him, screaming through her orgasm.

Bending down he nuzzled her ear. Whispered, "More."

* * * * *

Hours later they were back in the blankets by the fire. Franco turned toward her, elbow on the ground, his head propped in his hand. "Why couldn't I sense you're a werewolf?" he asked.

She raised her eyebrows at him. "Because I'm not."

"I don't understand."

"Years ago, a wolf came to me in a dream and offered to share its life with me. I have an animal to call—a spirit guide or totem—that allows me to use its form. Technically I'm not a werewolf. I'm a shaman, able to call the wolf to heal or use it to fight or…well—to have sex." She blushed and buried her head until he pulled her out of the blankets. "The wolf lives in the spirit world unless I call her."

"Are you telling me you could try to summon the wolf and he wouldn't come?"

"*She*. My wolf is definitely female. But yes, Nadia lives in the spirit world. If she was busy in the spiritual plane or unhappy with something I'd done, I suppose she could refuse to come when I called."

Distracted by the thought of Tehya needing the wolf's strength and having her *not* show up, it took a moment for Franco to realize what she'd said.

"You named your wolf?" The concept was foreign to him. For all the mental gyrations he went through about his beast,

Franco was sure of one thing—the beast was him. He was the beast.

How very…Zen.

Tehya snorted. "I didn't name Nadia, she already had a name when she came to me. Doesn't your wolf have a name?"

Franco sighed. "No. I *am* the wolf. I don't really understand the difference." All of a sudden he thought about what they'd done earlier. "I wasn't making love to you—I was making love to Nadia?" He shifted uncomfortably as he tried to wrap his mind around the concept.

"We were both there. Relax. She liked it. A lot. In fact, she wants to do it again." She smiled invitingly.

Franco couldn't help the grin. He'd just have to make sure his wolf kept Nadia happy so she'd come whenever Tehya needed her.

Come? He was losing his mind if he'd resorted to double entendres.

"Franco, when you shifted from wolf to man, you had clothes on. Why do your clothes go with you? I have to strip naked. It would be much better if I could keep my clothes on."

"I don't really understand it, I just know when werecreatures shift, our clothes are absorbed into our bodies. I'm sure there are things you can do as a shaman that I can't."

She put her hand on the ground, willing the cave entrance to shrink then expand back to its normal shape.

"Like that! What the hell is that? You did that back in the cavern, made the earth move with just a touch."

Tehya looked past the fire, out into the starry night. "I seem to have a connection to Mother Earth."

Chapter Four
ᔕ

Coming awake in a near panic, Franco sensed people entering the cave where he and Tehya slept, and kept his eyes closed in feigned sleep. For one frantic beat of his heart he thought the evil presence from the mountain had discovered them.

No. He sensed no dark malevolence emanating from the visitors.

"I should kill you where you sleep, wolf," a deep voice growled in fury.

There was lots of anger, though.

Franco opened his eyes and met the livid gaze of a very large and deadly looking man. Gray braids hung over his shoulders, his copper skin just starting to show signs of aging. The man's dark brown eyes reminded him of Tehya's.

Movement behind the man caught Franco's gaze. A woman moved to stand beside the gray-haired man. If the man reminded him of his mate, the woman was like looking at a future picture of her.

Then his protective instincts rose. He shifted his body in front of Tehya's sleeping form when a dark Native American warrior-type moved to the other man's right. Franco bet Marine or Special Forces for this one. He had a look that said, "I know how to kill with my hands, don't fuck with me".

Franco sighed. Meeting Tehya's family while lying buck-naked beside his mate in a cave wasn't exactly what he had in mind when he'd thought of how this moment would play out.

He looked at the sunlight streaming through the mouth of the cave, deciding it must be early afternoon. They'd been asleep for about six hours.

He felt Tehya's hands on his back as she pushed him to the side.

"Daddy? Mom? Uncle Jason?"

Shit. It really was the nightmare he'd feared.

"What are you all doing here? Oh!" Tehya blushed when she remembered *where* they were and what she *wasn't* wearing.

"It's been nearly twenty-four hours since you sent the email," the deadly looking man — *Uncle Jason?* — said. His dark brown eyes were filled with mirth. Okay. Maybe Uncle Jason wouldn't try to strangle him with his bare hands today.

One glance at the father's eyes assured Franco his neck wasn't entirely out of danger.

What email? Franco wondered, shifting his gaze to Tehya. He couldn't help smiling. Her hair was a mess, her face burned by his whiskers. There were small love bites on her neck and upper chest where he'd sucked on her skin. On her neck, the red, raised marks of his wolf seemed to pulse in the light streaming into the cave. She had the look of a woman who'd been ravished long and often. Franco would be very lucky if "Daddy" didn't kill him.

"Twenty-four hours?" Tehya sounded amazed and Franco sighed. Yeah, they'd been in the cave for hours.

"I think it might be better to move this conversation to the cabin." Uncle Jason shifted his gaze to look outside. "Something's wrong. Tehya, did you check out the mountain?"

"I did, but you're right. This isn't the place for a lengthy conversation. You three go back to the cabin. Franco and I will meet you there in a sec."

"Franco." Tehya's father glared daggers at him. Her mother reached out to gently lead him from the cave — *after* looking at Franco with eyes that seemed to see all the way down to his toes. Shit! He had a feeling her mother would be the real threat.

"You know if you aren't five minutes behind us, Naomi and Jefferson will return," Jason said with a smile as he followed them.

"Great. I left the snowsuit behind. I'm going to have to go back to the cabin wrapped in one of these blankets," Tehya mumbled.

Franco looked at her and frowned. Waving his hand, he dressed her in jeans and a soft T-shirt covered by a down jacket. Then he handed her a brush. With a second flick of his wrist, he'd dressed himself. Cleared the cave of any evidence they'd been there.

Tehya blinked. "We never did find time to talk last night. I have lots of questions."

"As do I. Tehya? Is your family like you? I couldn't sense anything otherworldly about them, but I didn't about you, either."

Tehya sighed. "Yeah, but just how *otherworldly* they are, I'm not sure. I only know what I've been able to find out by eavesdropping and snooping. They haven't exactly shared their secrets with me. That's going to change," she said determinedly as she stalked out of the cave.

Franco would bet she hadn't shared her secrets with them, either. The next hour could prove to be very interesting.

Maybe if Tehya is ready to do battle over family secrets, her father will be distracted enough to forget he wants to kill me.

On the way to the cabin Franco remembered something. Her father had said, "I should kill you where you sleep, *wolf*". Somehow the man knew what he was. Or at least…some of what he was.

When he stepped into the cabin, Jason was the only one sitting down. Relaxed and at home in the overstuffed chair by the fire, he looked as if he were ready to be entertained. Tehya's father stood by the fireplace, her mother paced in front of the window. Before Franco could bite the bullet and move toward Tehya's father to introduce himself, her mother spoke.

"Something's wrong. I thought at first it might be him, but it's not."

"Something is very wrong. And no, it's not Franco. Family, I'd like you to meet —"

She stopped when Franco moved next to her, placing a hand on her arm. "We haven't talked about why I came back. I think before you introduce me to your family, we need to be clear on what I am to you. Your friend, your lover…or more?" Franco ignored the father's growl and his menacing step forward, focusing solely on his mate's beautiful eyes. "I came for you, Tehya. These last few months have been hell without you. I came back to ask you to marry me. To ask you to share your life with me, and thinking my secrets were best kept hidden. Last night proved I was wrong. Will you marry me, Tehya? Accept both beast and man, as I accept both you and Nadia?"

"Who the hell is Nadia?" her father asked heatedly.

"Shut up for a moment, Jefferson," her mother hissed.

"Oh, Franco. Yes!" Tehya exclaimed, throwing herself into his arms, wildly kissing his face. He took the opportunity to capture her lips with his own, to burn them both with passionate fire before stepping back and putting her at arms length. "Later," he promised. "I love you, Tehya. *Now* I'm ready to meet your family."

Tehya's mother was Naomi White Eagle, her father, Jefferson Standing Bear. Her uncle's full name was Jason Dark Eagle.

After introductions were done, Jason asked the first question. "Tehya, what did you find at the mountain?"

Tehya explained what she'd seen. Franco noticed she didn't say anything about how she got into the cavern, just told them there were cages with people inside them. Said she'd drawn a diagram, taken digital pictures and pulled files from the computer.

As she explained, she set her backpack on her lap. "I won't be excluded from this," she said seriously and looked around the table, meeting everyone's eyes.

"You've already taken enough chances, Tehya," Franco insisted, and was relieved to see Jefferson nod his head in agreement. "I don't know what's going on in that cavern. I saw enough to know it's dangerous. I don't want you *or* your family involved, you don't have any idea what to expect."

This time Jefferson didn't nod. He scowled. Jason laughed.

"Franco, I'm not sitting on the sidelines for this one." Tehya glared at him.

"Yes. You are. You're *mortal*, Tehya. You can be killed very easily. I won't risk your life." Franco ignored the narrowed eyes and questions on her family's faces.

"What? I can be killed and you can't? That's just stupid, Franco. If I can't go, *you* can't go. I refuse to let those poor souls suffer any more torture."

"You. Are. Not. Going. Into. That. Cavern." He bit out each word.

For a moment the silence in the room was thick. Then Tehya exploded. "How do you expect to get *into* the cave? Walk in the front door?"

"We'll take the passage you created with your magic!" he snapped, missing the look of surprise on her parents' faces.

"Hah! No you won't. When we left I touched the wall, thanking Mother Earth for sheltering us. I asked her to erase all traces of our passage. The earth reverted to what it had been before I showed up. The tunnels are gone."

"Then I'll take you back there, let you touch the damn dirt and you can get your wolf butt back here!"

This time it was Jefferson and Naomi who exploded.

"*What?!*"

"*Magic?*"

"*Wolf? Tehya, explain what he's saying!*"

Tehya's head dropped. She played with the backpack in her lap. Jason sat back in his chair with a smug look on his face and Naomi began circling the table. Everyone waited for Tehya to speak. Franco felt Naomi's hand on his shoulder as if in sympathy. Surprisingly, he felt a wonderful warmth and happiness seep into his bones. Everything would work out fine.

"Mother!" Tehya said sharply.

Franco returned to being upset when Naomi moved away. Before he had a chance to question what just happened, Jefferson broke the silence.

"Who is Nadia?"

Tehya didn't seem to be able to answer, so Franco asked a question of his own. "When you came into the cave, why did you say, 'I should kill you where you sleep, wolf'?"

"Daddy!" Tehya exclaimed in horror.

Franco reached out to cover her hands with his. "If we had a daughter and I found *her* the way he discovered *us*, I might be tempted to kill first and ask questions later, Tehya. I don't blame him."

Franco watched her eyes widen, her hands go to her stomach in a protective gesture, and fought to keep his expression from revealing his shock.

Shit! They hadn't used any protection last night, something impossible to do in wolf form anyway. Once they'd returned to their human forms they'd been so hungry for each other he'd never even considered slowing down long enough to put on a condom.

Not now. He'd deal with that later.

When he looked away from Tehya, he caught Naomi's eye and realized she knew *exactly* where his and Tehya's thoughts had gone. She raised one eyebrow and allowed a half smile to touch her lips.

Thank god and goddess Jefferson had no clue.

"I called you 'wolf' because, well..." Tehya's father looked at her, then back at Franco with a question blazing in his eyes. He didn't know if his daughter knew Franco's secret.

"You said 'wolf' because you somehow realized I carry one inside me." As Franco said the words, Jefferson watched his daughter for her reaction to the statement. He seemed puzzled when she didn't react.

"How is it you know of *my* wolf, but don't know about Tehya's?"

"*What?*" both Naomi and Jefferson exclaimed again. Franco noticed Jason didn't seem to be surprised.

Tehya sighed. "The wolf came to me as a spirit totem."

"Which is convenient, since my wolf has claimed her as his mate. And so have I."

"Are you telling us you have a wolf spirit totem too?" Naomi asked.

"Nah, I'm just your garden-variety werewolf," Franco replied.

Tehya rolled her eyes at his comment and turned her attention back to her family. "My spirit wolf is called Nadia." She didn't seem willing to add a lot of detail.

"How long?" Naomi asked.

"Since I was twelve."

"Why haven't you told us?" Naomi asked. Both she and Jefferson seemed hurt.

"You've excluded me from the family secrets! I only know what I've been able to piece together by listening at doors and snooping around." She waved her hand at her father. "Dad goes out into a field and makes lightning. I've seen him do it." Before her father could answer, she glared at her mother. "You touch souls—sensing goodness or evil. Did either of you bother telling me? No. I had to discover all this on my own. I still don't know why we even *have* magical powers."

Franco realized Naomi had been touching his soul when she'd put her hand on his shoulder. He squirmed uncomfortably in his seat. *What had she seen?*

Jason began to speak. "In a *normal* Native American family, animal totems act as guides throughout your life. They're used to help us get in touch with our feelings, to grow emotionally and spiritually. We can pray for a specific animal to guide us, or a certain animal may come to us *because* of our need. The wolf is a teacher and a pathfinder. His presence signifies a person needs help or guidance in his or her life. Fortunate enough to be visited by the wolf, you would go on to teach others many of life's lessons. He can also be helpful in building personal strength, teaching us to value our inner voice."

He paused for a moment to study Tehya. "As you've noticed, in this family, spirit totems are much more."

Tehya couldn't stop the snort of laughter.

"As to who we are...we're protective shamans. Our family made a pact with the Great Spirit at the beginning of time." He turned to Franco. "The short version is we believe man was created by Sinauf, a god who was half man, half wolf. His brothers were Coyote and Wolf. According to our legends, Sinauf was preparing for a long journey, so he made a bag. In this bag he placed special sticks—all the same size but different types of wood. The bag was magical, and when Sinauf put the sticks inside, they changed into people. As he put more and more sticks into the bag, the noise the people made aroused the curiosity of all the animals.

"After filling his magic bag, Sinauf closed it and went to prepare for his journey. His brother Coyote was curious. He made a little hole with his flint knife near the top of the bag and peeked in to see what his brother had.

"When Sinauf returned, he picked up the bag, threw it over his shoulder without realizing there was a hole at the top and headed for the *Una-u-quich*, the distant high mountains. Long story short…through Coyote's hole in the top of the bag, the people started jumping out. When Sinauf reached *Una-u-quich*, he found only a few people left in his bag. Our family was among those remaining. When the people jumped out of the bag, some of them fell into magical places and were transformed. As with all living creatures, some of the magical beings were good, some bad. Our family agreed to protect mankind from the evil created during this time. There's a catch. Not all of our family members are born with supernatural abilities. So we wait, sharing the heritage with those who show signs of power." Jason looked pointedly at Tehya.

Tehya looked around at her family. "Because I kept my powers secret, you assumed I didn't have any?"

"Well. I suspected something," Jason laughed.

Franco piped up. "This is all great and I really want to pursue a deeper understanding of shamanism and your family. But we need to get those people out of the cages. Something Tehya didn't tell you—I'm not even sure she realized it—all the captives were either a paranormal species or humans with magical abilities. There is some sort of magical siphoning spell inside the mountain. My shields didn't stop the process but shifting to my wolf helped slow the effect. Tehya didn't appear to be bothered by it."

She shook her head. "No. I was fine. Nadia felt something she didn't like. It was like running fingernails down a blackboard. Made my hair stand on end."

Tehya dug something out of her backpack. "That the people in the cages are supernatural explains something I read on one of their files. The comment followed notes indicating they terminated many of their earlier *experiments*." She looked down at a note she'd made and recited, "Duplication is easy, both subjects retain all powers and inherent strengths of the original creature. Unfortunately, if the primary subject morally rejects our training, the secondary creature cannot be swayed to embrace our ideals. Their usefulness is doubtful." Tehya looked thoughtful for a moment. "Sounds to me like they're trying to make supernatural subjects who embrace their agenda, whatever that is. Is anyone hearing preternatural army in the subtext...or is it just me?"

"Shit. I'm reading between the lines too, sweetheart. If they've already decided it isn't working, why are they still there?" Franco frowned.

Tehya grimaced. "The file was stamped with a big red 'Termination'. I believe, in this case, they literally shot the messenger for carrying bad news."

Franco got up and strode over to the phone resting on a side table in the living room. He picked up the cordless and started dialing while he paced. "I'm calling my family. They're trained for this. They have the added benefit of being almost impossible to kill."

At this point he started mumbling to himself, unaware of the shocked look on Tehya's face or the gleam of laughter in her family members' eyes. "Hell, I'm several thousand years old, for goddess sake, and if I die, my damn brother can just wave a wand over my freaking dust and bring me back to life. I will *not* allow my mate to put herself in danger. What the hell is the use of having an immortal family if you can't use them to keep your mate safe?"

Tehya spoke, her voice tight. "What do you mean, 'immortal family'? Shit! In just a few short years, I get to look like an old hag and *you* will still look just like..."

Seeing her fallen expression, Franco hung up the phone before the call went through, going to his mate's side. Naomi beat him to it. She wrapped her arms around her daughter in comfort. "Not quite, dear."

Jason smirked. "Naomi's right. When our family agreed to serve the Great Spirit, to round up the creatures that meant harm to his children, it was decided we would need an edge. How old do you think I am? Never mind. We don't have time for guessing games. I'm over four centuries old. We can be killed, but just like Franco's family, it's a pretty complicated process. Severed head is one of the few things that will work. Tehya, your life span should be many centuries long."

Naomi nodded her head. "Yes. And there's something else. In our family, if a shaman finds a true mate, the two souls will entwine." She smiled. "When I touch either of you, I can feel the other. Your souls have already started to connect. Besides extending Tehya's life, it may allow crossover between abilities." She smiled at Jason and Jefferson. "Don't be surprised if Tehya's wolf gets stronger or if Franco eventually hears a whisper or two from Mother Earth."

"Mind telling us about your family? How did you get to be immortal?" Jefferson asked.

Franco realized he might as well get his convoluted family history out in the open. "The De'Angel family name actually comes from a prehistoric description of our father. Michael—the angel of life."

"You're an angel?" Disbelief was evident in Tehya's voice.

"No. The De'Angels are Druid-mages."

"Druid-mages?" Now Jason's voice held skepticism.

"Druid is like a species name. Among Druid's, there are many levels of abilities, mage being the highest rank in power. In De'Angels, the magic runs strong. We're born Druid-mages, with the ability to reinvent ourselves in a variety of paranormal forms." Franco sighed, knowing the explanation would just raise more questions. "My parents live under the Atlantic Ocean, this period of their lives spent as mermen. My sister, Marissa, is currently a vampire. My older brother, Ricardo, very seldom chooses to be anything but a regular ol' Druid-mage. Right now he's honing his skills, studying magic and elementals of past history. In any supernatural form we can do magic, but our abilities are strongest when we're just our Druid-mage selves."

"You mean as a werewolf your magic isn't as powerful as it would be if you were in your original incarnation." Naomi wasn't asking a question, she was helping the rest of her family understand what he'd said.

"Exactly. No matter what form I'm in, Ricardo's magical abilities make mine look like I just picked up a *Magic for Dummies* book." He shook his head in exasperation. "To make everything just a little more complicated, Ricardo's wife, Jane, is a vampire hunter-turned-Druid-mage. Marissa's husband, Jack, is a were-dragon. He's not a Druid-mage, but a bitten shifter."

Franco realized Tehya and her family had gone quiet, with glazed looks in their eyes.

"Never mind. Let's just say my family dynamics are a little weird. The important thing is the entire group knows how to fight. Ricardo and Jane can be here in an instant, Marissa and Jack in less than an hour. They live in the Denver area. I'll call them in."

Jefferson raised his hand to stop him. "You said your powers were drained by a spell or something in the cavern. What if your family can't use their magic? Tehya didn't think she was affected, so let Jason go look at the mountain. He can get in and find out if his shamanism is sapped by the unholy magic. I'll go check out all the ways someone might get up to that mountain. With so much snow, they'd have to bring the people in on big Sno-Cats or some other type of machinery. I want to know how they might try and run from us when the time comes. After we've checked out a few things, we can get together and come up with a plan."

Jefferson stood and promptly left, content his wishes would prevail.

Franco recognized the trait. It was something his father would do. Naomi followed her mate out of the cabin.

Jason stood and started to leave, turning around to wink at Tehya. "I'd say you have a solid five hours alone. I'd tell you to get some rest...but I don't think you'd listen."

Chapter Five

❧

Franco needed to give Tehya's family plenty of time to get away from the cabin. He decided he'd better do something with his hands before he simply pinned Tehya beneath him on the rug in front of the fire.

"I don't know about you, but I need a drink." He walked over to the cupboard where the liquor was kept and considered his options. "Can I make you something?"

"Sounds great. I'll have a Hair of The Wolf That Bit You." She frowned, reconsidering. "Maybe not, it turns my lips and tongue blue."

"As long as I don't end up with blue balls…" He leered at her, making her laugh.

Twenty minutes later, Franco had Tehya spread naked on the sheepskin rug in front of the fireplace. He dipped his finger into his drink, spreading the cold, blue liquid over her nipples. He bent to lick the puckered nubs. "Ummm. This tastes wonderful."

Tehya giggled. "Are you sure you wouldn't like me to return the favor?"

"Later, sweetheart. Right now I want to savor my future wife."

Laying his body over hers, he bent to capture her mouth, using his knee to part her thighs before settling between them. The feel of all her lovely soft flesh against his body was heaven.

He slipped his erection between her slick folds, rubbing the sensitive tip over her slit. He enjoyed the sight of her beneath him, writhing on the rug in erotic agony.

"Please…oh, god. Franco!"

"Tell me what you want, Tehya. What do you need me to do?" Punctuating his question, he leaned down to tease her dark nipples with his tongue, laving the taut little berries. The musk coming from her skin served as an aphrodisiac to his senses.

"Fuck me!" she growled.

"Like this?" he murmured into her flesh. Using his hand to position his cock at her pussy, he pushed the crown in a scant few inches, slowly flexing his hips. Her body radiated fire and warmth and pure carnal lust. He planned to stoke that fire to a raging inferno.

Tehya thrashed her head from side to side. "Nooooo…" She tried pulling him into her, digging her hands into his hips while tilting her pelvis in an attempt to meet him more than halfway.

Franco wasn't through teasing her. He grabbed her hands and positioned them above her head, using one hand to anchor them in place, the other to skim the delightful curves of her body. He lingered over her amazing breasts, smiled as she arched her back into his touch, silently begging him for more. His thick fingers compressed a nipple, her dark areolas lifting with each panted breath, the warm weight of her breast pressing up into his palm.

He used his fingers to pinch harder, rolling the turgid flesh between them. He tugged rhythmically at her nipples while he continued the shallow thrusts of his hips.

Her cunt dripped with her juices, the heated liquid pouring over the head of his cock. His gaze drifted lower. The neatly trimmed, dark tuft of curls at her center looked like an arrow, guiding him to paradise. The sight of his blood-engorged cock disappearing into her flesh made him shudder.

His fingers slipped through those curls, rubbed around her swollen clit, the slick moisture feeling like liquid silk. He vibrated her hard button until she screamed through an orgasm. He felt her contracting muscles milk the tip of his shaft. She felt so good!

Tehya thought she might be losing her mind in the sensual haze. The sensation of Franco's hard cock just slipping inches inside her, with his fingers playing her clit until she exploded, was wonderful. It wasn't nearly enough.

"Fuck me! Hard!" she demanded, digging her heels into the floor.

This time he let her win. Shifting forward to bury his cock balls-deep in one wonderful plunge, he allowed his body to sink into her flesh.

"Yes!" she screamed. Momentarily stunned by the sensation of being so full, so overwhelmed, she wrapped her arms and legs around his body to hold on tight. Over and over he withdrew. Slammed back. The echo of their bodies slapping together bounced off the walls of the cabin. She gulped in air, smelling the rich, lush scent of their combined desire. It didn't take her long to fall hard over the edge into a second orgasm. This time he followed right behind her, shouting his satisfaction.

* * * * *

The beautiful golden eagle circled the sky above the clearing, diving down to the waiting group below. Just before it looked like the bird was going to hit the ground, the night air surrounding it sparkled with an effervescent glow. Jason's feet touched the ground. He shifted his shoulders where the eagle's wings had been only seconds before. Like Tehya, Jason's clothes were left behind when he shifted. He calmly pulled on jeans and a sweatshirt then led them all into the cabin to settle in front of the fireplace.

Franco saw Tehya blush. Knew she was thinking of the many carnal hours they'd just spent on the rug. Idly he wondered if Tehya's father could turn into a bear. Were all shamans able to shift to the creatures of their name, or were

Jason Dark Eagle and Tehya Running Wolf just coincidences? Somehow he didn't think so. He shook the musings off. There would be time to worry about this new world of magic. Later.

Jason didn't waste time. "The wizard who carved that atrocity isn't there. I did manage to find traces of his black magic in the cave. Enough to get a feel for his magic signature—and it is definitely a 'he'. There are six people in cages, twice as many guards and a couple doctor types. If we go in now to rescue the captives, we'll lose the chance of getting the wizard," Jason said in disgust.

Tehya spoke up. "If I can take one of the computers, I might get enough information to come up with a name or a place."

"Can you track the wizard from his scent?" Franco looked at Jason.

The man shook his head. "No. Not scent, but the feel of the magic. Preternatural creatures leave a distinct impression on the world around them. Or if I have a name, I can search the wind."

Now *that* was just a little too mystic-bullshit for Franco. "Well, I can track him by scent. Together we should be able to find him. Eventually."

"We can't wait for the wizard to return," Naomi interjected. "I got close enough to touch a sleeping guard. At least one of the captives is marked for death in the morning."

With that chilling pronouncement, they decided not to waste any time. Franco called Ricardo before they left the cabin. If something bad happened to all of them, Franco wanted him to know where to find the bodies. Ricardo wasn't happy to be excluded.

The looks on her family's faces when Tehya touched the cliff wall, making the earth shift to form a tunnel, were priceless. They all got into the cave without incident. Once inside, Tehya, along with her mother, went to grab at least one computer hard drive. Jefferson went along to disable any resistance they met on the way.

Franco had to believe Tehya would be safe with her parents while he and Jason freed the prisoners. Silently the two men made their way to the cavern floor through a tunnel Tehya provided for them. It was late. The large room lit by only a few security lights.

In wolf form Franco followed Jason. Growled a low warning when he caught the scent of two guards. Jason nodded. He'd seen them. Jason went right, while Franco went left. His target was standing over by one of the cages. Poking at the captive.

He never knew what hit him.

Franco leaped on his back, taking him to the ground. Sat on him with his jaws at the guard's neck until Jason joined him and handcuffed the man's hands behind his back with Zip Ties they'd taken from the cabin, then knocked him out. Two guards down, ten to go.

He watched as Jason unlocked the cages with the guard's keys. The captives shuffled out, some in better condition than others. One of them needed to be carried, but his twin was able to take care of him.

This was weird.

All the prisoners were twins. Three sets of twins.

Jason asked about the other guards. A pair of werewolf twins led the way to a room off the side of the cavern. The off-duty guards were sleeping inside.

Jason and Franco, along with the healthier prisoners, handcuffed the rest of the guards. Jefferson managed to subdue the few doctors. It was all too easy.

Not a drop of blood was spilled. *Pity.*

Naomi had located a refrigerator and, once outside, gave blood bags and raw steaks to the starving captives. Standing in the clearing, Franco shifted from wolf to man and turned to the prisoners. He recognized one of the vampires.

"Jonathon," he said, going to the man. Standing beside the centuries-old vamp was his twin. "I didn't know you had a twin."

The vampire shook his head. "I don't. Evidently you don't realize what's been going on in this hellhole. This is my genetic twin, but he's a clone. They've been magically duplicating paranormals. Trying to create some sort of army. Somehow this crazy wizard figured out how to make exact replicas of each of us, within about two weeks. They thought if *we* didn't cooperate, our clones would." He laughed bitterly. "Wrong. Each clone mirrors its genetic twin in every way — including mindset."

"What are we going to do with the guards and doctors?" Tehya asked as Franco hugged her to him.

Before she finished the sentence, a helicopter appeared in the clearing. "My brother notified the people I work for. CCOM will take care of them."

"CCOM?"

"Think CIA for paranormals. I'll explain later, sweetheart." Much later. Franco had a feeling Tehya wouldn't have a problem with his job — unless he refused to let her join. She would be the perfect recruit. Franco sighed.

Jonathon interrupted his thoughts. "You know this place isn't the only one. Davian has at least one other facility. I was transferred here only a few weeks ago. He'll keep trying."

"I don't think so." Jason's grin was full of determined satisfaction. "Now I have a name."

Franco hugged Tehya tighter. He figured he'd let Jason worry about Davian for now.

He was going to be busy.

Hair of the Wolf That Bit You

8 oz Boons Blue Apple Wine

1 oz Destinee Sapphire Liqueur

1 oz De Kuyper Island Blue Pucker Schnapps

1 oz Mancini Blue Vodka

4 oz Seltzer water

Put the ingredients into a cocktail shaker. Shake 'til mixed. Pour into a glass with 1/4 cup crushed ice.

Add a honeydew melon ball, garnish with shredded, toasted coconut, a sprig of Wolfs bane — if you're feeling adventurous. But DON'T eat it — and a few dog...er, *wolfie* hairs.

Enjoy a howling good time!

Also by Ravyn Wilde

ဆ

About the Author

ဆ

Ravyn Wilde was born in Oregon and has spent several years in New Guinea and Singapore. She is married, has 3 children and is currently living in Utah. Ravyn is happiest when she has a book in one hand and a drink in the other — preferably sprawled on a beach!

Ravyn welcomes comments from readers. You can find her website and email address on her author bio page at www.ellorascave.com.

Tell Us What You Think

We appreciate hearing reader opinions about our books. You can email us at Comments@EllorasCave.com.

GIFT WRAP OPTIONAL
TJ Michaels

ಐ

Trademarks Acknowledgement

ಐ

The author acknowledges the trademarked status and trademark owners of the following wordmarks mentioned in this work of fiction:

Frosty the Snowman: Time Warner Entertainment Company

Hershey: Hershey Chocolate & Confectionery Corporation

Hummer: General Motors Corporation

Old Bay Seasoning: Old Bay Company, Inc.

Rudolph the Red-Nosed Reindeer: Rudolph Company, L.P.

Prologue

&

The flames from the fireplace cast a warm glow over the writhing couple. Their bodies so close they seemed as one, as if the golden peachy hue of his skin spread decadently over her darker caramel tones like the dipping of sweet, ripe fruit into melted fondue. The dusting of baby-fine reddish-blond hair dusted across his hard, slabbed chest teased her sensitive breasts. The softness of the sheepskin rug underneath her backside paled in comparison to the exotic sensation of the downy sprinkle tickling and tormenting her diamond-hard nipples.

Gently, deliberately he took her mouth. How did he manage to make her feel both ravished and eased? How did he tease, coat and strip her of her senses all at once? His mouth tasted of mulled wine — all sweet honey, cloves and spice — and the sudden surge of heat where he nipped her bottom lip infused her blood with need.

The man was erotic perfection. There was only one problem — she was stark naked and he still wore his jeans. Boy did he ever look good in jeans, but right now she'd rather have him bare-assed naked. Besides, the deep burning in her womb was all his fault and he was damned well going to take care of it! The man had appeared and promised the Christmas gift of a lifetime. Surely fucking like bunnies after so much time apart fit the description of such a gift.

"Oh Michael! Please...please fuck me!" she cried shamelessly, grinding her hips in a hard circle as her bare thighs pressed tight against his denim-clad ones. Before her eyes, the fabric of his jeans shimmered like starlight reflecting off metallic blue sand before melting completely away from his glorious body. Finally, his muscular thighs and solid calves were naked and burning against her smooth skin. He lowered his head and firm, warm lips teased the spot just underneath her right ear. First a feather-soft kiss, followed by a

decadent open-mouthed lick, then pleasure-pain filled nips. Her whole body erupted in goose bumps.

"Mmm, Michael. Dear god," she whispered on a gasp when his teeth rasped over an extremely sensitive area between her neck and shoulder. The contact caused a shiver so strong her teeth chattered as if she stood out in the snow in her underwear. God, the sensation shot clear down to the little hairs on her baby toes. No one had ever found that spot. Until now. Until him.

Her voice was a quiet but earnest plea as she writhed, pinned underneath his perfect physique. Her creaming hot core ached to be filled with the hard length pressing against her moist folds while something else — something primal and wild — wished to be marked, physically marked, as his.

"Aaaah! Please...please bite me." Mmm, he was driving her wild, making her frantic, needy, hungry. "Baby, please..." she pleaded unabashedly as her strong fingers dug into his scalp, loving the soft silky slide of the thick waves covering his head. He kept right on nipping and sucking, driving her need until the air fairly crackled with it.

Then the scene shifted and she stood outside herself, watching her wanton actions as if through someone else's eyes. And what a decadent sight it was!

Michael raised his head away from her sensitized skin until his clear emerald green eyes held the gaze of her light honey brown ones. His expression, both tender and triumphant, gave him the look of a caring lover and primal predator.

"Michael?" she asked, wondering at the questioning look in his eyes. Didn't he know what she wanted? Didn't he understand how much she needed it?

"Mel, are you sure? If I do this, there's no turning back. You'll be mine. Forever."

His voice was firm, sure. The words echoed and resonated in her head, but with them came a strange sense of calm in the midst of the sensual storm he created around her.

"Yes, yes I'm sure. I need you to...I-I want it." She stood next to the fireplace looking down at her naked self, listened to the urgency *in her voice when she begged him to finish what he'd started. Watched the toned muscles of his back bunch and tense as he lowered his chest to hers. Felt the burn of her hip flexors as she spread her legs as far as they would go. Trembled at his deep growl when she turned her head, stretching her neck to give him more room to play.*

Baring his fangs, ecstasy written across his handsome features, the thick length of his steel-hard cock eased into her welcoming body. Her pussy spasmed when the gold, yellow and red flames blazing in the fireplace reflected off those beautiful white incisors. Unafraid, she itched with anticipation, reveled in the knowledge that he was finally going to fuck her and bite her! The fat head of his cock slid home and bumped against the opening to her womb at the same time the gentle prick of his teeth pierced her flesh.

He drew deeply. A strangled scream erupted from her throat as she came on the spot.

Melaniece shot up in the bed, her sweat-soaked camisole sticking to her back. Quaking uncontrollably, she tried to catch her breath as the remnants of the dream eased its grip. What a strange mix of…of what? Excitement? Fear of the unknown? Both? Hell, she had no idea. One hand instinctively went to the gentle throb on her neck—a spot that hadn't been the least bit tender when she'd gone to bed. The other gingerly eased down along her soaked folds and brushed against her throbbing clit. Well, one thing was for sure—that was one hell of a dream. Again.

Chapter One

ജ

Melaniece Matthews muttered to herself, carefully navigating the icy winding road leading up to the high country.

"Man, what a weird dream. Michael, a vampire?" The same strange dream plagued her at least twice a week for the past six months. They'd started immediately after she'd returned from a short trip home to California. It had been so good to see her friends and family after being away for eight years. And beyond lovely to see Michael Bannon again—the man she'd always loved. And, sigh, the man who'd seen her as just a great friend. Instead of marrying her, he'd hooked up with someone else, a woman named Janna. The end result? Six years of hell on earth for him. And now he haunted her in her sleep.

While Melaniece could admit she'd thoroughly enjoyed hanging out with him after so many years, she sure as hell wasn't going to admit he'd been on her mind ever since. Her dream crept around the edges of her mind. "What if he is a vampire?" she smirked to herself, a sarcastically evil grin plastered across her lips. "That would explain why he ripped my heart out by marrying Janna. There'd certainly been plenty of blood to go around."

Peering through the cold, clear windshield, Melaniece grimaced as her thoughts turned to her favorite holiday. Instead of the usual elation about Christmas, she was assailed with a mix of emotions she couldn't quite nail down. There was the thrill of spending time with her children after a whole year of separation, chased by a longing for intimate companionship so acute she found herself on the verge of tears. Then, right there at the back of her mind was an elusive sense of naughty anticipation. But for what? A good lay? Not likely. She had no prospects and no interest in hunting for any. Michael's handsome face popped into her head complete with fangs and a roguish grin, just like in her dream. Damn, she could practically feel the gorgeous, redheaded hunk making love with her as his incisors rasped over her skin. Yep, right there on the big sheepskin rug in front of the fireplace. Perfect spot.

"Hah, right!" she laughed with an unmistakable snort and waved the image away. But her breathing quickened in spite of a refusal to acknowledge the fine-assed man with fangs dancing around in her head. Give it a minute and her pulse would return to normal, right? Woo, she needed to turn off the heat. In spite of the freezing cold, the car was hot as hell. After a quick glance down at the console, she rolled her eyes up to the roof of the car. The damned heat wasn't even turned on!

"Good grief, I'm hopeless," she quietly grumbled. And it was all her dream man's fault. Key word—dream. First off, she'd long given up hope in that quarter. Second, there was no such thing as vampires. So Michael was single again. Big deal. They'd had a great time reuniting in California six months ago. Who cared? None of it meant he wanted her now any more than he had eight years before.

With the car packed full of wrapped packages and luggage, Melaniece focused on the upcoming holiday. A glimpse at the pile of boxes in the backseat brought a small smile as she reminded herself this was a season to give generously to those you loved…and those who loved you back. And boy was she prepared to do just that.

Her children had spent the past year in an exchange program teaching English in Japan. It was amazingly expensive to live on the exotic little island. With most of their meager salaries going toward rent, groceries and train fare, the two had gone without some conveniences. When they returned to Minato-ku, a suburb of Tokyo, they'd sure as hell take lots of top-of-the-line goodies with them. Nothing but the best for her kids.

Christmas Day was fast approaching. She looked into the rearview mirror and spoke sharply to the woman reflected in the narrow glass.

"Okay you," she said to herself. "No more goofy dreams, no more wasting time mooning over someone you can't have and no more vampire nonsense. It's Christmas and you're gonna accept whatever Santa decides to give you. Got it?"

Got it. She popped a classic holiday CD into the player and hummed along with "Santa Baby". With genuine laughter, Melaniece let Nat King Cole chase away her blues as she headed up the highway to her vacation home to meet her family. Up there among the snow-capped peaks, the long-toothed boogeyman was not allowed, no matter how yummy he looked in her sleep, damn it.

The sun had just dipped below the mountain peaks when Melaniece pulled into the garage. Snow had begun falling in fat, wet flakes and she was relieved to see a big, black SUV covered with a fresh dusting of the white stuff parked on the other side of the wide garage. She slammed her car into park thinking now was a good time to do a funky little happy dance—her children, Denise and Melvin, were already here.

The second she shut off the engine and popped the trunk, an excited and very loud female came hurtling out the door. A blur of what looked like a white sweatshirt covered with red Japanese kanji symbols and a pair of black pants practically tackled her before she'd cleared the car door.

"Hi, Mom!" Denise screeched.

Melaniece's heart melted and a big grin tipped up the sides of her mouth. Awww, it was so nice to be loved by one's children.

"Hi, sweet pea! It's so good to see you. Where's your brother?" Melaniece asked, trying to peek over her daughter's shoulder toward the open door leading into the house.

"I'm right here, Mom. How are you?" Melvin asked cheerfully. Long jean-clad legs carried him out to the garage and to Melaniece's side. Six-feet-two inches of slender muscular male wrapped his arms around both sister and mom, engulfing them in a warm group hug.

Melaniece stepped back and grinned widely at her "babies". At eighteen and twenty years old, they were mirror images of herself, with the exception of their dwarfing her modest five-feet-four inches. Long, dark locs covered their heads, apple pie cheeks sported dimples and they both flashed perfect, bright smiles. Their cocoa-colored skin and strong physiques were rounded out by stellar personalities. Beautiful and handsome described them to a tee.

Melaniece stepped back and shook her head in disbelief at Melvin. "Boy, are you ever gonna stop growing? I know you've grown at least a few good inches since I last saw you. And so good-looking, too! You know you get that from your mama, right?" she quipped. And there it was—the blush only a teasing mom could bring about in a grown son. It bloomed in his cheeks, turning his cocoa-colored skin a shade more reminiscent of a caramel-covered apple!

"And you should see all the girls that chase after him! And once I caught him and the neighbor…" Denise chimed in, ever the older sister.

"Mom!" Melvin implored.

"Okay, enough teasing your brother," Melaniece chuckled, feeling happier than she had in…well, since her trip home to Michael, er, California. But she wouldn't dwell on that. Or her goofy dream.

"Help me with my stuff?" Moving toward the already open trunk of her car, she turned to grab whatever was closest at hand and began to fill the arms of both Denise and Melvin with their Christmas gifts.

"Good lord, woman! What is all this?" Melvin asked, feigning a gasp under the weight of a particularly hefty box.

Melaniece didn't answer, just smiled and handed over package after package until both their arms were loaded. Before she could reach for another one, Melvin said, "Go on in and relax. We'll bring this stuff in. Dinner is already prepared."

Melaniece felt her stomach tighten and rumble. Gosh, with all the packing, the long drive up, and preoccupation with her dreams—not to mention the constant low-grade arousal because of them—she'd completely forgotten about breakfast and lunch. Well, her stomach made it clear it was feeling neglected and the loud rumble was heard by all.

An aroma hit her nose the second she stepped over the threshold into the house. Shrimp, tomatoes, garlic…Old Bay Seasoning?

"Wooo! I smell it," she cried happily. "Cajun food! Oh yeah! Uh-huh!" An awful rendition of the Electric Slide dance carried her on inside. She headed directly to the kitchen, not the least bit offended when her kids' chuckles followed her. Yep, this was going to be one heck of a Christmas!

* * * * *

With dinner done and dishes cleared, Denise and Melvin decorated the seven-and-a-half-foot real pine Christmas tree they'd picked up in town earlier. An overstuffed Melaniece slid onto the floor in front of the fireplace and watched them at play. Her fingers sank into the thick pile of the sheepskin rug as she lay on her back and moaned with a lopsided smile plastered on her face. Dinner had been fabulous. Denise had made Shrimp Creole with Dirty Rice and Melvin had whipped up a peach cobbler made with homemade butter crust. Oh god, she was so full, all she could do was lie there, soak in the warmth of the fire and hope she didn't explode. But hell, she'd die fat and happy.

When the doorbell sounded, she didn't move from her warm spot on the floor. Besides, she had a good idea who it was and secretly wished the cockeyed nosy neighbor would just leave her customary Christmas cookies on the porch and leave.

"Get that, will you Denny?" Melaniece drawled sleepily, eyes half-closed. The soft footfalls of her daughter's bare feet, the quiet click of the deadbolt and easy swish of the front door opening reached her ears. She waited to hear Denise's "thank you for the gift, Mrs. Orley". A few moments passed but the neighbor wasn't calling out her customary holiday greeting, nor was Denise giving her usual Merry Christmas to whoever was at the door.

She definitely knew something was going on when the little hairs on the back of her neck joined her stomach in an out-of-the-blue spastic butterfly dance. Melaniece cracked open one eye and looked toward the door.

Two large suitcases sat in the middle of her now snow-covered foyer floor and Denise, who was doing a fabulous job of completely ignoring her, thus avoiding her stare of doom, helped a bundled, but familiar-looking, form out of a thick parka.

Melaniece glanced over at her son and froze. If the boy wanted her to believe nothing was out of the ordinary, his ear-splitting grin pretty much gave him away. But whatever it was, he wasn't telling.

She watched layers of clothing fall away from the person. A jacket, sweater, snow pants and boots had been hiding a wide, solid-looking back, thick muscular thighs and an ass that couldn't possibly belong to a mere mortal. Successfully swallowing the lump growing in her throat, Melaniece sat up, both mouth and eyes wide. Oh, lord! Had the kids ordered her a stripper? Woo, what a hunk!

The hunk turned to face her and snatched a knit cap off his disheveled head to reveal tastefully cut auburn hair, startling green eyes and sinfully full lips.

"Holy. Shit," Melaniece whispered.

Michael Bannon walked into her living room, eyeing her like the cat who'd swallowed the canary...or in this case, the partridge in the pear tree.

* * * * *

Michael had never seen a black woman go pale before. It would have been comical if it hadn't been so important for Melaniece to be happy to see him. He kicked off his boots and strode into the living room. Though his steps were deliberately slow and easy, he was so eager to wrap the woman in his arms; it still felt like he was practically running.

"Michael? What the hell are you doing here?" Melaniece gasped, still sprawled on the floor in front of the fireplace. Damn she looked sexy. It was just like he'd imagined in his dreams — her lying in front of the fireplace waiting for him to ravish her lush, beautiful body.

Suddenly she sprang up from the floor with a wild-eyed expression like she'd been caught with her hand in the cookie jar. And she didn't look happy to be caught, at least not by him. But that was just too bad. He'd come all this way only for her, and he'd be damned if he wasn't going to have her.

"Hi, Mel," he deliberately crooned, knowing how much she loved his "deep" voice. "Aren't you glad to see me, babe?" he asked stretching out his arms to her. Arms that had become well acquainted with holding her during her last trip home. And there was nothing like cuddling with Melaniece Matthews. But this time, there no need to leave it at cuddling. No need for her to assure him he was more than ordinary in spite of his crumbled marriage. Self-confidence restored, he was all man standing in her house with outstretched arms. Hell, screw a cuddle, she looked so deliciously surprised standing there in her skintight tee and comfy sweats, her hair all over her head, nervously nibbling on her bottom lip. He wanted to strip her bare and lay it on her right here, right now.

So far she hadn't said a word. For now, her tongue seemed stuck to the roof of her mouth. But Michael, being his old self again, didn't wait for her to acclimate. Instead he pulled her into his arms and wrapped them around her until his nostrils were full of the scent of delicious, mouthwatering woman. And it was absolutely decadent.

"Mmmm, it feels so good to hold you again, Mel. Merry Christmas, beautiful."

"Uh, yeah, er, Merry, uh, to you, too," she mumbled like an idiot. It was all his fault. This was Christmas, a holiday she'd always spent with her children. And he just shows up out of the blue? So where was her mad? It must be out shopping or something because it certainly wasn't coming to her rescue by helping her regain any semblance of common sense. Aw who was she kidding? She couldn't even stay mad at him for breaking her heart eight years ago, having forgiven him long before he'd ever begged, literally begged, for forgiveness when last they'd seen each other. So, she certainly couldn't stay mad at him for crashing her Christmas, right?

Then his broad chest smashed against hers and a pair of the sexiest lips this side of creation nibbled at her temple.

"God, you feel so good in my arms. I'm really looking forward to spending this Christmas with you, Mel. I promise to make it special. Really special."

Yep, she was a goner. His arms tightened and the massive erection she hadn't noticed in her stupor now burned through her clothes, searing the skin just above her womb. Melaniece practically lost it on the spot. She went from shocked to sex-starved in ten seconds flat. Hell, she could think clearer if she had any blood flowing up to her brain. Right now, it was all circling her clit with a ferocity that practically buckled her knees. The shock of finding him in her house was swiftly replaced by a ridiculous urge to jump his bones and have him...bite her. What the hell?

Just then, her dream came rushing to the forefront of her mind. Ridiculous. There were no such things as vampires. But there was such a thing as a sexy as hell Michael Bannon standing in her living room, holding her tight, whispering in her ear.

"Uh-hem!" came a totally not-subtle clearing of throats from behind her. Melvin grinned from ear to ear as he stuck out his hand to Michael.

"My god, boy, look at you! I've known you since you were two years old and no more than two feet tall. What are you, over six feet now?"

"Yes, sir," Melvin said around a huge smile, holding his hand out. "It's nice to see you again." The two clasped hands like old friends. Well, they were old friends. "I think the last time we hung out, I was nine or ten and we laid out under the stars on the Fourth of July watching the fireworks."

"Hey, I remember that!" Denise chimed in, coming to stand next to her brother. "We were at Waterworld laying out in the grass while the sky lit up. That was so cool. It's great to see you again, Mike. Haven't change a bit."

"Well, you have," Michael said, eyes wide. "You've really grown up, and just as lovely as your mom."

"Well, can we show you to your room?" Denise asked, blushing prettily.

"Why don't you take him up, Denny? I'll pull his car into the garage," Melvin said, holding his hand out for the car keys. Seconds later, Melaniece stood in the middle of her cozy living room alone and in a daze while her daughter took Michael and his bags up to the guestroom and her son disappeared through the laundry room door and out to the garage. In less than five minutes, her world tilted a hard right leaving a giddy but confused Melaniece to run to catch up.

After a bit of small talk, complete with a yawning Michael, obviously tired from his long trip, Melaniece jumped on the excuse that he needed some rest. She flew to her bedroom and uncharacteristically locked the door. Even now her knees trembled, her pussy was doing some freaky humming thing and the sensitive spot where neck met shoulders tingled. She tried to get her mind to quiet down enough to actually sleep, but nooohohoho, her brain was off doing the nasty. It conjured images of Michael Bannon on his knees, licking and sucking her unhooded clit until she screamed. Michael bending her over the back of the loveseat, sliding a hard cock into her soaked pussy. Michael, dipping his lovely red head to suck hard on her aching nipples while he held her tight against his body and plowed home. And the beautiful contrast of her dark, Hershey skin rubbing and sliding against his fair freckled skin.

After hours of tossing and turning, she sighed tiredly and looked up to the ceiling.

"Dear lord, please help me get through this Christmas without doing something stupid...like screwing Michael Bannon's brains out."

Chapter Two

"Fuck me! Yes, give it to me," she wailed as Michael's thick, hard cock slammed into the moist depths of her aching cunt. It felt so good, his strokes so sure and strong she didn't think she could ever go without it again. Then it was time. Time for him to take her to a place only he could, and she couldn't wait a second longer to soar there.

"Mmm, yes," she hissed. "Bite me. Please bite me again..."

Now this is new, Melaniece grumbled to herself. She snapped awake only to find her hands firmly wrapped around her breasts, roughly kneading them through her soft silk nightshirt. Her thighs rubbed together as she tried to push the dream away. The dream she wasn't supposed to be having anymore, damn it.

Peeling her fingers away from her swollen breasts, she rolled over on her stomach, smashed a pillow over her head and tried harder to ignore the rolling heat that had her nipples diamond-hard and the soft skin between her legs moist.

And it was all his fault. Damned man, showing up out of the blue.

Throwing the pillow clear across the room, Melaniece sat up and listened, wondering if Michael was up yet. After a few moments, she wondered if anyone was up. She thought she caught the faint whiff of freshly brewed coffee, but heard nothing. Not a single sound. No one walking around upstairs. No water running. No one talking in the wide open space of the living room just on the other side of her main bedroom wall. And where was the Christmas music, or Denise and Melvin knocking on her door telling her it was time to get up to open the gifts? What the hell was going on? Well, other than her blasted horny state.

Muttering aloud while kicking her way clear of the bedsheets, she headed for a decidedly chilly shower before leaving her room.

She rounded the corner into the wide hall and came to an abrupt halt. Across the large living room was a bare-chested Michael Bannon slaving over a hot stove. And damn if he didn't look scrumptious while doing it. And she'd been right about smelling coffee, eyeing a crystal mug of the steaming dark liquid held by the strongest, most beautiful fingers she'd ever seen on a man.

Come on, girlfriend, the man doesn't bite. Or does he?

"Mel, your coffee is getting cold," he said, that silky voice rolling over her senses like so much melted chocolate. Oh god, this was just too much. How the hell was she going to handle staying in the same house with this man and not having her sensually wicked way with him? Okay, one step at a time. First, get your damned feet uprooted from the carpet.

"Come on, Mel. I don't bite you know," he said, grinning broadly. "Well, not unless you ask me to." Okay, he was smiling and she didn't see any fangs, but his words kicked up the heat in her blood. And if she thought any longer on them, she'd have to run back to her room and take care of the dull ache brewing between her thighs on her own. Instead, she playfully rolled her eyes at his naughty jest, managed to both chuckle and walk through the living room to grab a cup of coffee off the kitchen counter.

His back to her, Melaniece practically drooled at the play of muscle as he lifted a heavy cast-iron skillet from one burner to another, and worked a spatula like a pro.

"I believe you like crispy bacon," he called over his shoulder. "Home-style hash browns with green peppers and scrambled eggs. Scrambled light, not scorched, right?"

She mumbled an "uh-huh" and turned toward the living room. Perfect. A fire blazed in the huge fireplace. The shades were up, allowing a grand view down into the valley as the snow continued to fly. "Frosty The Snowman" played quietly on the large screen TV, and the Christmas tree lights twinkled gaily, lighting up the brightly wrapped gifts and... Whoa! Hold the door. She didn't recognize a good number of the presents piled on top of the ones she'd lovingly wrapped with her own hands. There were twice as many as there were when she'd gone to bed last night. And she still hadn't seen Denise or Melvin. What the hell was going on?

* * * * *

If the woman was determined to ignore him, she had another think coming. He hadn't come all this way to let her get away a second time. She'd been his best friend before he'd fallen for Janna only to discover everything he'd ever wanted in a woman was spelled in a single word—Melaniece. He'd realized too late that while he'd never chanced revealing who he really was to anyone, Melaniece was probably the only woman in the world who'd always been willing to take him as is. Flaws, fangs and all.

Before she rounded the corner and stopped dead across the room, he'd caught the scent of her arousal, of the creamy heat settling between her legs. Last night she'd been distant, her scent one of surprise and even a bit of unease. But not today. Today she wanted him. The knowledge caused a chain reaction through his entire being, from his mind, down to his heart, and on through his body to settle heavily into a throbbing erection he didn't bother trying to hide.

Thanks to Denise and Melvin, Michael had two plates piled high with all her favorite breakfast foods. There was nothing he loved better than the smell of hickory smoked bacon in the morning, but Melaniece's natural fragrance overrode everything else. It was as if the woman filled the room with herself. Then the scent changed, became dark grey and tainted until clawlike tendrils wrapped around his gut and pulled. Hard. Something was wrong. She was...what? Afraid? Nervous?

When he turned to see her staring at the gifts under the tree, he understood. Time to put his plan in action. He set the plates on the breakfast table and padded on silent feet to stand directly behind her.

"Mel," his voice soft and coaxing, not wanting to frighten her further. "Baby, come and have some breakfast with me."

She whirled around with fire in her eyes. Finely manicured brows snapped together to practically form a single wavy line across her forehead. He immediately knew he'd pegged her wrong. She wasn't afraid. She was pissed the hell off.

"What the hell is going on here, Michael?"

No more than a hairsbreadth from her, it took a whole lot of self-control to keep from simply sweeping her into his arms and taking her to the floor. But she was mad. And if he knew anything about this woman, she was like a dog with a bone when it came to getting to the bottom of anything.

Plastering on an innocent-as-a-newborn-babe expression he just stood and looked at her. Well, she wasn't buying.

Suddenly a hard finger stabbed him in the chest as she growled up at him.

"First off, it's way too quiet in here. Second, you're here, in my house! You just pop up out of the blue and I'm supposed to figure this is all normal? Puh-lease!"

"Popped up out of the blue? Mel, we've been talking once a week since we saw each other six months ago." It was almost comical to watch the emotions fly across her lovely face as she searched for a rebuttal. If she was at a loss for words, he knew it wouldn't last long.

"Well, fine!" she fumed. "But you didn't say anything about coming for the holidays, damn it. And who do all these gifts belong to? Better yet, where the hell are my kids?"

Slowly easing his hands toward her to rest them on her shoulders, he gently guided her toward the table in the breakfast nook. "Mel, they went out for awhile but don't worry. They'll be back. They just wanted to give us some time alone, that's all." Okay, he wasn't quite telling the truth. So sue him.

"Went out? In this weather? Are you crazy?" she questioned fiercely, gesturing toward the windows. Now he wished he hadn't bothered to open the blinds or pull the drapes back. The snow fell so thick you couldn't see anything past the panes of glass.

"Come eat, sweetheart," he said firmly, managing to get her all the way to the breakfast table but her butt was nowhere near a chair.

"But…"

"No buts, Mel. Sit down and eat with me."

"What idiot would go out in this kind of…"

Okay, there were two ways to get a determined woman to hush. And Michael had no problem pulling the first one out of the hat. If he had his way, he and his cock would get around to the second way later.

Wrapping both arms around her warm body, he went in for the steal. A kiss so blatantly hot and consuming it shook him down to the root of his soul. The second their mouths met he felt a fusion, a connection so profound there were no words to describe it. He felt a rumble begin in his chest and rise up to a low hum as he deepened the kiss, pressing through the seam of her lips to taste her sweetness. Mmmm, coffee and cream from a woman whose silky brown skin resembled what she tasted like. God, he had to have more. And she was willing to give it, to open to him, to let him take what he wanted. Yes, this was more than just a kiss. This felt more like…a gifting.

All on their own, his fingers found their way up to her naturally wavy hair to tangle there. When she moaned sensuously at the soft pressure on her scalp something anciently primal threatened to break forth. His gums tingled sharply.

Now her arms twined around his neck, pulling, seeking.

Her lips and tongue dueled, seeking, wanting. Then the taut nipples of her lush, full breasts stabbed into his bare chest through her thin, silk lounge shirt. Lust and longing replaced the blood in his veins and pumped through his body with every beat of his heart. The cock tenting his pants reached out for her warm body, throbbed against her belly, seeking a home.

She broke the kiss on a whisper.

"Michael." A small but strong hand slipped to his nape to pull him toward her neck as she tilted her head on a pleading gasp.

"Mmm, lick me. Bite me." Oh god, did the woman know what she was asking for? The incisors he kept hidden from the world threatened to slip free.

Oh shit, not yet, he yelled to himself, fighting for control. *Damn it, man, no teeth. No teeth!* The first pass of his lips over the pulse point calling his name was a close thing. He took a deep breath, commanded his dick to stop screaming and gave her the rasping lick she'd asked for. As for the bite, that would have to wait.

Glad several buttons at the top of her lounge shirt were undone, Michael dipped his head and let his tongue play from her collarbone up to her ear lobe. She shivered under his tongue and her scent went from intoxicating to bone-searing wet. Hot. And if the bullets he was sweating and her endless squirming were any indication, it wasn't nearly enough.

Her clean flavor burst over his tongue and lodged itself in his memory forever. She tasted spicy, exotic. Like...*his.*

What the hell was happening to him? Such strength of yearning wasn't anything familiar to him. Nothing he'd ever experienced with any other woman.

Is this why he'd shied away from her years ago? He'd felt inexorably drawn to her, even found himself in a fulfilling friendship with her that felt like more. Comfortable, yet wild. Untamed. Fucking scary. So he'd fled to a woman that didn't affect his self-control in such a way. But he knew better now. The unsettled dancing in his gut when Melaniece was around made perfect sense. He'd acknowledged it the moment it kicked in again at their reunion six months ago. And it made even more sense now after kissing her. She'd always been meant for him. His woman. His mate.

And he instinctively knew how to please her. Like a beacon in the night, a certain spot at the juncture of her neck and shoulder seemed to glow. And he knew, just *knew* exactly where to go next.

Skip the preliminaries. There was a driving need to mark her, mate her. A hard suck at that glowing spot on her neck had her moaning. He laved, nibbled and worked it until she clutched at his back, pressing so close he felt their molecules meld. A strong thigh lifted to bare her warm, hot center to his hard cock. Her calf wrapped around his ass and she ground her pussy against his aching shaft.

Hell, if he didn't land on the breakfast room floor on buckled knees, then he'd surely come in his pants. God, the woman was so sexy. So sensually uninhibited.

His hands touched everywhere, gliding, seeking from her firm rounded breasts, down over her trembling stomach. Then around her full delicious hips to cup her lovely round globes, grinding his cock into the hollow of her creaming cunt.

He loved the way his name sounded on her lips.

"Michael," she gasped after a particularly hard nip. "Please…"

Lifting her in his arms, he turned his back on the cooling food he'd so lovingly prepared. In the living room in front of the fireplace, he eased her onto her back on the plush sheepskin rug to deliver something else. Lovingly. Prepared.

Oh yes, this was it. Stripped bare and loving it, Melaniece spread her legs wide, inviting the man of her dreams to slide home. Enthralled by the flexing of his thick biceps as he supported his weight, she was caught off guard by the sudden urge to yank him down on top of her and take all his weight onto her own body. To wrap her legs around him and hold him tight.

Then those delicious lips eased over her again, slipping, sliding and tasting her until she was practically mindless. So aroused, the slick evidence of her desire spilled out and over her pussy to pool around the puckered hole of her ass. In this moment, Melaniece wanted this man more than anyone or anything. It was almost a consuming madness, this urgency to have him inside her.

"Guide me in, Mel," he said, his voice gruff, lips drawn tightly against his teeth. Her fingers wrapped around the warm pulsing rod that called her name with a need of its own. Soft silk wrapped around hardened steel, her thumb grazed the flared tip and spread his essence over the plump head just before settling him at her ready entrance.

She could feel her cunt pulse in anticipation. Her breasts tingled. Her lungs tightened. The hot mushroom tip of his cock burned at her entrance, easing slowly inside and...

Damn it. The phone rang.

Chapter Three

ဢ

Melaniece couldn't believe it. Maybe if she closed her eyes and clicked her bare heels three times this nightmare would be over. What the hell was Santa trying to do to her anyway? A loving that would have bordered on cataclysmic was interrupted by the telephone. Thinking the kids might be stuck in a ditch somewhere, she rushed to answer it. It was them on the phone and they'd ditched her all right, left her up here in the mountains to be bushwhacked by Michael. And now Mother Nature decided to keep her stuck here with the man.

"This is just not happening," she fumed as she strode uncaringly naked to the laundry room. Yanking open the door she stared out into the garage. No joke. The kids' SUV was gone, replaced by Michael's monster machine—a jet-black Hummer took up more than its fair share of the three car garage.

Michael's hands lovingly caressed her shoulders accompanied by the hot, hard length of his cock brushing up against her bare ass, a reminder of what they'd been up to when the phone rang. Bastard.

"Mel, it's not as bad as it looks, I promise."

"How can you say such a jacked up thing to me, Michael? I've never spent the Christmas holidays without my children. Ever!" Every spot on her now tense shoulders and neck grew warm. Such talented fingers. Oooh, the easy massage was working. *Come on girl, get it together. You're supposed to be mad, remember?*

"I'm going home to Denver to join them. You can stay here if you like until the roads are clear enough for you to drive home." Damn it was cold. The backs of her legs were nicely warmed by an obviously heat efficient Michael along with the warmth streaming from the laundry room, but the front of her body was so chilled her poor nipples felt like little fudgesicles. Tempted to step back and lean against the spinning clothes dryer, she yanked away from Michael's gentle touch instead.

Mad? Absolutely. Stupid? Hell no, and there was no way she was going to chill her toes by stepping into the garage. Holding onto the doorjamb she leaned out and stretched for the door opener mounted on the wall.

"Mel, don't you dare open that garage door while you're standing here naked," Michael warned. Oh, so now he was going to tell her what to do? Not bloody likely. He had some nerve and how dare he growl at her like that. She would have told him so if her eyes hadn't been pasted to the sight revealed by the open garage door.

"I repeat, this is just not happening," she whispered. "Oh come on, Santa, work with me here."

"What was that, Mel?"

"N-Nothing. Never mind." All she could do was stare at the six-foot wall of snow standing between her car and the driveway outside.

At least the kids left last night, otherwise they might not have made it to Denver at all in this mess. And it was still coming down in big, wet flakes. Instinctively she turned to the huge vehicle parked next to hers, but could only shake her head. Even Michael's Hummer wasn't big or bad enough to get out of the garage. They were well and truly snowed in. And before she could make it out of the laundry room, the dryer began to spin slower and slower until it stopped altogether…just before the lights flickered off. Along with everything else in the house. Damn, damn, DAMN!

With some growling of her own, Melaniece turned on her heel, elbowed past Michael and stomped straight to her room. Now where had she put the battery-powered weather radio

Melvin gave her a couple of years ago? Yanking an oversized T-shirt off the shelf, she pulled it on quickly and bent to the task of digging through the plastic storage boxes. Blast it all, she could barely see in the dim light filtering into the closet from the window across the room. Relieved when her hand closed around the small square metal and plastic box she snatched it out and turned it on.

Sitting on the edge of her bed, she turned the tuning knob until she found a clear channel. She didn't need to look up to know a concerned Michael Bannon's eyes were plastered to her face. She felt him, knew he was worried about her. The knowledge made her want to reach out to him, stroke the soft waves on his head with one hand while easing eager fingers over the planes and ridges of his beautifully defined chest and stomach. A still very naked chest and stomach.

"The National Weather Service predicts this blizzard will blow out in the next forty-eight hours. The worst of the snow started falling early this morning around three a.m. If you had somewhere to go, we hope you got there last night."

Her hopes plummeted.

"Smart-assed weather man," she grumbled quietly to herself, massaging her temples. Just great, now her head hurt.

Perhaps if you stop grinding your teeth you wouldn't have a headache.

Aw shut up! she sneered to the conscience she didn't want to have right now.

"Interstate 70 is closed on both sides of the Eisenhower Tunnel. Eastbound lanes are closed clear down to Denver with a break just East of the airport, then closed from Bennett clear to the state line and on into Kansas. Highway 6 is closed north of 70 and Highway 285 West of…"

Fabulous. Just great.

Melaniece clicked off the radio, set it on the nightstand and rolled up in a ball on the bed. Everything was out of her hands, all beyond her control. She felt so helpless and inept.

Clutching a pillow to her face, she did something she hadn't done in what felt like ages. She cried.

* * * * *

It felt as if someone had wrapped their fingers around his heart and squeezed when Melaniece's sobs reached his ears through her pillow. This was supposed to be a happy reunion, not a miserable holiday. He'd rather have someone rip his guts out than see his woman like this.

"Baby, please don't cry," he cooed softly, easing onto the bed with her to gently pull her into his arms. "I can't stand it, Mel. Don't cry, sweetheart."

She just cried harder, her body shaking as the heartrending sobs tore him apart. But at least she'd given up stuffing her face into her pillow and held onto him instead.

"It was supposed to be a nice surprise, but if it'll make you feel better, I'll tell you everything, all right?"

She nodded her head with a sniffle and relaxed against him. Stroking her thick, black curls, Michael looked down to where he'd deliberately entangled his legs with hers. Such a beautiful contrast. Her skin was silky-soft and the color of toffee against his fair tones. His mind conjured an image of French vanilla and cocoa swirled ice cream. And he'd like nothing more than to have her melt all over him. But first, he needed to soothe her. The need to let his mate-to-be know how much she was loved overrode all other desire.

"Mel, baby, I've been communicating with your children for the past six months." She looked up at him with an expression he couldn't quite pin down—some strange mix between astonishment and tenderness. At that moment, the woman looked so sweet and vulnerable he knew he would protect and keep her for the rest of their long lives together.

"Once you gave me your permission to contact them in Japan, we kept it up. Thankfully they remembered me from our times together when they were little. I, uh…" he pulled in a deep breath knowing he had to push forward. Had to reveal everything, no matter how hard, no matter how stupid he made himself look. After all, he had indeed been a total numbskull where Mel was concerned.

"Go on," she nudged, one of her fingers gouging him in the ribs. It tickled.

"I apologized to them, Mel."

"What? What for?"

"Because I was wrong. Wrong for getting so close to them only to completely disappear from their lives after I married Janna. Your kids should have been mine. Even if I'm not their biological father, I loved them and still love them like they're mine. I should have been there to care for them, to help you raise them. And they forgave me."

"Hmmm," she said sleepily, settling more comfortably into his arms. Sigh, this felt really good. He could really get used to lying with her like this.

"So, I told them that I'd made a mistake by not asking you to marry me, Mel. I was wrong. And scared."

He felt her tense up, the comfort of cuddling with him forgotten. "Scared? Now that doesn't make any sense. You weren't scared of marrying Janna," she gritted through clenched teeth, voice laced with a little bit of anger and a lot of pain.

"You're right, I wasn't afraid to marry her. I was afraid to marry you."

"Wha…!"

"Mel, when I'm with you all I want is to be closer, so close I can smell the air you breathe, hear the thoughts you think. I want you, need you with something so fierce and primal I can't explain it. I've never felt this way about anyone."

"News to me," she snorted. A deep chuckle escaped before he could catch it. The woman was a treasure.

"Well, it's not news. It's not even new. It's something I've felt since the day I met you. And it scared me, baby."

Upon one elbow now, she watched him closely as if she were searching for something or trying to figure out the missing piece to the puzzle.

"If it scared you before, then why are you here now? And how did you pull this off without me knowing?"

"First, Denise and Melvin arranged for the post office to hold all the packages. All I had to do was address them all to Melvin. Denise made sure I knew how to get up here. In case you hadn't noticed, I drove. It took me two days."

She turned her head toward the window and grimaced. "Yeah, looks like you made it just in time. Okay, that explains the gifts under the tree and why I don't recognize half of them. But you still haven't explained why you've done all this and why they're in Denver while you're here with me."

"I'm getting there, just hold your horses."

Another finger jab to the ribs had him chuckling again.

"After explaining to the kids that I wanted another chance with you, they gave me their blessing. Denise and Melvin ducked out as their Christmas gift to you. You see, they seem to be under the impression that you still love me. And hopefully you'll have me, because baby I sure need you."

The way her tongue danced across her lower lip made the little hairs on the back of his knuckles stand on end. He wanted to run a single finger over her luscious cherry mouth while he wondered how his cock would look nestled there. Enough talking.

With a squeak, she was on her back looking up at him. God he was so glad she was naked under that damned T-shirt. It rode up around her glorious backside leaving her open to him. Her beautiful honey brown eyes slid closed when he nudged her legs apart and settled his nakedness between her thighs. Damn, she smelled so good. The scent of warm, welcoming pussy wafted up between them and he felt his gums tingle again as her tender folds embraced him. Only this time he wasn't sure he could keep them hidden, and even less sure he wanted to.

"Have me, Mel?" Nuzzling her ear, he licked a path down to the gloriously sweet pulse point just below. "Please?"

Her response was a sensual hiss and a roll of her hips so he continued to taste, touch and purposefully torment. If someone held a gun to his head on the condition that he leave her now, he'd just be one seriously wounded vampire. Her body moved with a belly dancer's hypnotic rhythm, calling him, welcoming him. But he needed more. He needed the words. Close to losing the ability to think beyond her lush body, he spoke quickly.

Drawing a breath into too-tight lungs, he forced his mouth to speak and braced himself for her answer. If she refused him, he would have to find the strength to let her go. Oh god, please let her say yes.

"Mel, I have to know, baby. Will you have me?" He knew he wasn't playing fair by teasing the puckered points of her lush breasts while he asked the question. To hell with playing fair.

Her back arched up off the soft comforter. "Oh god, Michael."

"I can't hold off much longer, Mel. I want to be inside you so bad I'm practically shaking with it."

"Michael…please."

"Not good enough, baby," he hissed, all of his nerve endings firing in anticipation of finally joining himself to her. "Will. You. Have. Me?"

"Yes! I'll have you, all of you. Please."

That's all he needed to hear. Angling his pulsing cock at the entrance to heaven, there was no resisting the urge to slide it up and down her creaming slit until he was coated with her essence. Her strong thighs fell completely open and he eased inside. All the air was sucked from his body when her tight sheath spasmed wildly around him, milking, pulling.

"Oh baby, fuck me. Hard. Deep," she gasped.

"Mmm, and how about long and slow," he gritted out around his incisors and sank all the way inside her gripping, dripping channel. Okay, slow was definitely out of the question.

"Fast, rough," she panted as he ripped the T-shirt from her bountiful body. God he loved her curves.

"How 'bout all morning? Maybe, all day?"

"Oh yes," she whispered. "All day."

Melaniece felt her body stretch and open to accommodate his girth. Until today she'd had no idea he was so huge. The man's cock was a woman's dream. Wide from base to tip, but his length was perfect, not too short, not too long. The mottled, almost purple head wept for her and she found herself wondering what he tasted like. The thought was wiped from her mind when he parted her swollen lips and eased inside. God, she was so full of him, stretched so tight the friction was exquisite.

Then he began to move and her world tilted far right. This wasn't sex. This was beyond anything she'd ever experienced with a man. Now perhaps she understood what he meant when he said he felt such a strong need for her it was scary. The second he pushed inside, the love and care she'd always felt for him exploded in her breast, so overwhelming it was almost a spiritual experience.

Reaching up to bury her fingers in his soft, wavy hair, she pulled him to her lips and kissed him wildly, frantically. She could have sworn he spoke to her, gently called her…but his mouth was fused to hers.

"Easy, sweetheart, easy. It's okay, I feel it too," his words were like a balm, soothing the flaming heat engulfing her mind, body and soul. But she didn't want to be soothed. She wanted to be fucked. Melaniece looked up at the man who made her fly.

She opened her mouth to tell him to fly faster. The words froze in her throat.

Teeth. Very long teeth. Oh my god, he really was a vampire!

"Stay with me, Mel," he said around his fangs and sunk deep, tapping the entrance to her womb.

"Oh god!"

Another deep, soul-stirring lunge. Followed by another and another.

"Yes," she heard him growl. "Come for me, Mel. Come on, baby." And her body rushed to comply.

He took her with a ferocity that shook her down to her very toes, whispering how much he loved her, how good she felt wrapped around his hard cock. Suddenly she didn't care what Michael might be. Only that he give her more. Make her scream.

Full force, her dreams flooded her memory featuring Michael and his too-long teeth. Still, she wasn't the least bit afraid. Instead, the yearning in her bones increased tenfold until she wanted so badly to be one with him she was willing to do anything, everything. As he lowered his head and sucked the sensitive spot between neck and shoulder, her whole body spasmed. The spring of her desire tightened around the nerves in her lower back and squeezed. The tickle-ache fluttered down the back of her thighs, and at the same time streaked up through her belly to spread like liquid ice-fire through her chest. Oh god, she was going to explode.

She came apart in his arms, her womb pulsing, eager for his cream. And still he moved inside of her, rode her through it, only to throw her into another round of soul-rending orgasm. But she needed more.

"Aaah! Michael, come for me...bite me," she pleaded.

"Not this time, baby. But soon."

She almost cried at his answer, but she was too busy screaming as she came again.

Chapter Four

ɞ

Melaniece woke with a yawn. A good stretch revealed deliciously sore muscles that wouldn't mind another workout. She rolled over expecting to make contact with a solid chest and warm male flesh, but her fingers met nothing but cooling rumpled sheets. Sheets that smelled of hot sex and scrumptious male.

Wow, he'd put a serious loving down on her! She couldn't recall ever wanting to be taken so desperately. Nor had she ever been so stuffed full of hard throbbing cock only to want to be filled some more. Just the thought of that wild romp brought all the wonderful emotions rolling back up to the forefront of her mind. And her body eagerly responded. Good god, this was crazy.

And where was Michael?

She tried to click on a lamp. Damn, still no power. One glance at the portable clock on the nightstand made her wish for a battery operated coffee maker. Her stomach immediately reminded her that the man she'd spent the morning loving had cooked her breakfast earlier. They'd just never gotten around to eating it.

Quickly showered and back in her lounge suit, Melaniece strode into the front rooms. Damn it, there he was again in her kitchen with nothing but a pair of dark blue lounge pants. What was he thinking by showing all that delicious cream-colored skin and those fabulous piles of muscle? How the hell was she supposed to form a coherent sentence with his biceps flexing with such simple tasks as spreading peanut butter on a piece of bread, or his back muscles bunching as he pulled the refrigerator door open to retrieve the jam?

Good god, she was turning into a total nympho.

Before she could open her mouth, he turned and she practically drooled as his left pec danced before her eyes when he set a plate on the counter in front of her.

"Mel, you all right?"

"Uh, yeah, sure. Great. Food."

He chuckled, following her line of sight to the rippling abs marching down his torso. "You like?" he asked, striking a Herculean pose.

"Oh, yeah," she whispered. "I definitely like." But she made no move to touch her food. He smiled. It lit up the room.

"Mel?"

"Huh?" Oh, god, she sounded like a halfwit. Who cared? Intelligence was overrated anyway.

"Breakfast, sweetheart. Late, but definitely worth it."

"Uh-huh."

"Come on, woman," he sighed hopelessly, a thick erection beginning to rise to greet her. "You keep looking at me like that and you won't eat again until dinner."

Neither of them spoke during their meal. After eating the best peanut butter and jam sandwich she'd ever had, fresh-cut apples sprinkled with cinnamon and a small glass of cold milk, Melaniece rose from the breakfast table, took both their plates to the kitchen and placed them in the sink. Making a beeline for the spacious living room, she stretched out in her favorite spot on the rug in front of the fireplace, glad Michael had thought to stoke the flames earlier. She tossed a couple of heavy oak pieces into the flames and lay back with a contented sigh. Her stomach was blessedly full but her mind flew a mile a minute. Where were his fangs? Did they just kind of come and go? How had she known him for so long and not have a clue? And why the hell did she trust him so implicitly?

Michael's voice cut into the chaos of her thoughts.

"Do you want to talk about what's on your mind?" He was too perceptive by half. And now as he sat down on the floor next to her, he was way too close. The insides of her thighs pulsed.

"And just what is on my mind, exactly," she huffed, pushing her arousal away.

"You want to know about vampires," he stated matter-of-factly.

"No, I want to know why the hell I've been dreaming of vampires only to have one walk into my house. Then I want to know why I'm not scared shitless."

"Well, doesn't that all fall under the *I-want-to-know-about-vampires* category?" Smart assed, gorgeous, green-eyed hunk. She rolled her eyes and didn't say another word as he began his explanation.

"You understand the workings of DNA, right?"

She deliberately looked at him as if he were nuts. He knew what she did for a living. What good biogeneticist didn't understand DNA?

"Here's the quick explanation. You already know I'm not human. My blood and semen have regenerative properties to non-vampires. That's why I didn't come earlier, I wanted you to know how it will affect you first. Over time my DNA will enhance yours. You'll get sick less and less until you don't get sick at all. Your strength will increase, your senses will heighten and your metabolism will behave differently so you won't age as quickly as other humans."

Her eyeballs started to cross as he read off the laundry list of bodily changes resulting from sex with him. The so-called "quick version" was a lot to take in but, thankfully, she understood it all. But when he was finished she still had questions.

"What about blood? I won't, uh, will I…"

"No, you won't need blood but you may crave mine occasionally. However, I require it. Unfortunately, vampires aren't perfect. My blood can't sustain sufficient levels of hemoglobin so I have to ingest some blood. And I still have to eat lots of protein to keep my muscle going. Can't get away from the need for calories."

"But what about garlic, silver? And I've seen you walking around in the daylight for as long as I've known you."

"Baby, if you mate with me, we have all the time we need to get into all this. My need for you is beyond biological instinct, Mel. Just trust me. I won't ever do anything to hurt you. And contrary to popular myth, you can't be turned. Even if you could, I would never do such a thing if you didn't want it, okay? I want you to be my mate. Now and forever."

"Do vampires actually live forever?" she wondered aloud.

"No, just long lived and we'll have plenty of years together. Think about it, but later. Right now, I have a gift for you to open."

"But it's not Christmas yet," she squeaked as he hauled her up off the floor with so little effort it amazed her. Guess those muscles weren't just for show after all.

Settled in his lap in front of the huge gaily decorated tree, Melaniece held, with trembling fingers, a gold parchment envelope with a gold foil bow. She jumped when, suddenly, the tree lights flickered then lit up the envelope in her hands as the power surged on.

"Go on, open it," he encouraged, his emerald eyes twinkling with mischief. Carefully opening the glued flap so as not to tear the beautiful envelope, she eased the contents out and gawked at the document that had been tucked inside. It was a contract. A realtor's contract. Oh my god, the man had put his house in California up for sale! What the…?

Before she could form the thought, her question was answered. Out of his back pocket he removed another envelope she hadn't noticed before. This one he opened himself and handed her the papers inside.

"Oh dear lord! Michael, what have you done?" she gasped in disbelief, the papers shaking in her trembling fingers.

"When I came here, Mel, I came prepared to do whatever was necessary to have you. I've spent the last eight years without you. I can't go another day, sweetheart." Her eyes went so wide she could feel the corners give when he unfolded the official document and confirmed her suspicions—a deed. To a house in her neighborhood.

"And if you refused me this holiday then I was just going to have to hang around a while. Aww, sweetheart, please don't cry. You know what it does to me."

The tears ran unchecked down her cheeks and she couldn't do a thing about it. Her emotions were simply too raw, her nerves too exposed. A man she'd never expected to have had done all this for her?

Easing her back in his arms, he kissed the top of her head and insisted they watch something lighthearted and just enjoy the rest of the day together. He clicked the remote and the disk in the DVD player whirred. The first scenes of her favorite holiday movie appeared and a tremulous smile spread across her face. But even Rudolph The Red-Nosed Reindeer couldn't completely dissolve the lump in her throat nor the humble acknowledgement that this man did indeed seem ready to do anything for her.

* * * * *

In her bed alone, Melaniece's thoughts flew around her head like the balls in a pinball machine. He'd sent her to bed ahead of him then hadn't joined her. Why? Was he trying to give her time to think about mating with him? Was he having second thoughts? Men, she would never figure them out.

After falling into a fitful sleep, she rolled over and checked the time. The dim blue sticks and lines of the digital clock read twelve-twenty-two. At least a couple of hours since she'd settled under the thick fluffy comforters alone. She thought about Michael. An urgent yearning bloomed in her belly and she practically leapt from the bed. Every muscle in her body burned for action, itched to jump up and move. Her knees felt like little ants were running around underneath the caps, breath hitched in her throat and the inside of her thighs began to tremble.

Michael. She just had to be with him, had to touch him. Needed him with an urgency that bordered on…what? Is this what he meant when he said he'd never felt such a need for a woman? If so, she was beginning to understand. After a few more seconds, she kicked out of the covers and paced back and forth in front of the huge bed. What to do? Go look for him? Stay put? Hell!

Decision made, she left the bedroom and headed upstairs to the guestroom. Peeking her head inside, the wind was knocked out of her sails. He wasn't there. Where had he gone? Then, out of the corner of her eye, she spotted a slight movement. Easing quietly to the second floor railing, she looked down on the kitchen, the breakfast area and the huge living room. The lights on the Christmas tree blinked on and off and the fire in the fireplace had burned down to a pile of red-hot coals. And Michael stood just outside the sliding glass doors on the porch looking down into the snow-covered valley.

Her feet were moving before she could form another thought. Bright moonlight reflected off the snow, twinkling like diamonds embedded in the blanket of white covering the land. His skin looked aglow, almost pearlescent. In only a pair of weathered jeans, he leaned forward, perched his elbows on the railing and lifted his head to the sky. The man was masculine perfection. Her womb went white-hot.

Easing the glass door open, the moisture of her breath formed little puffs of steam as she spoke.

"Michael? What are you doing out here?" She took a step back at the haunted look in the eyes of the man she loved. Gently reaching out to stroke his chilled arms, she whispered, "You okay?"

"Not yet, Mel. There's something I need. Badly."

And she intuitively knew what it was, and it wasn't sex. Her heart sped up until it practically beat out of her chest. *This is it, take the plunge, woman. It's now or never.* Lowering her lashes, she sucked in a deep breath, then looked up at him with what she hoped were come-hither eyes. Firmly, she took his hand in hers, urged him back inside and slid the door closed behind them.

"Come on, sweetie, let's go to bed," she cooed with a sultry smile.

Michael picked her up and the cold skin on his arms warmed instantly under her backside. His words only made her hotter.

"Better yet, let's not." With that, he stalked to the thick sheepskin rug in front of the fireplace, eased her down and tossed a fresh log into the fireplace just before he stripped her bare.

* * * * *

Oh goodness, it was just like in her dream!

The flames from the fireplace cast a warm glow over the writhing couple. Their bodies so close they seemed as one, as if the golden peachy hue of his skin spread decadently over her darker caramel tones like the dipping of sweet ripe fruit into melted fondue. The dusting of baby-fine reddish-blond hair dusted across his hard slabbed chest teased her sensitive breasts. The softness of the sheepskin rug underneath her backside paled in comparison to the exotic sensation of the downy sprinkle tickling and tormenting her diamond-hard nipples.

Gently, deliberately, he took her mouth. How did he manage to make her feel both ravished and eased? How did he tease, coat and strip her of her senses all at once? His mouth tasted of mulled wine, all sweet honey, cloves and spice and the sudden surge of heat where he nipped her bottom lip infused her blood with need.

The man was erotic perfection. There was only one problem — she was stark naked and he still wore his jeans. Boy did he ever look good in jeans, but right now she'd rather have him bare-assed naked.

Only he was real, in the flesh and driving her wild.

"Michael, please," she panted, clutching at him to get him closer. "I-I want you to mate with me. Right now."

Michael raised his head away from her sensitized skin until his clear green eyes held the gaze of her light honey brown ones. His expression, both tender and triumphant, gave him the look of caring lover and primal predator. She didn't care. She needed this. Needed him.

"Mel, are you sure? If we do this, there's no turning back. You'll be mine. Period." His voice was firm, sure. The words echoed and resonated in her head, but with them came an enveloping sense of calm in the midst of the sensual storm he created around her.

"Yes, yes I'm sure. I need you to...Oh god, I want it." Squirming desperately underneath him, Melaniece spread her legs as far as they would go. Trembled at his deep growl when she turned her head and stretched her neck to give him more room to play.

The sight of his incisors lengthening made her pussy spasm so hard she would have swooned if she hadn't already been lying down. Then came the sensual scrape of his fangs against her tender flesh. Her whole body shook like the last leaf on a bare October limb.

Michael relished every shiver and tremor snaking through her body as he prepared her for his loving. He knew she was aroused to the point of trying to flip him onto his back and have her wicked way with him. But he took his time. The need to make this special for her overrode all else.

His cock bobbed with the beat of his heart when she stroked the extra sensitive spot between her neck and shoulder and pleaded, "Bite me, Michael. Please, bite me right here."

But he didn't bite her neck. Instead he bowed his body, settled his swollen cock at her soaked entrance and dipped his head to her breasts. Swirling his tongue around and around the puckering tips, he teased her until he sensed she was approaching frustration. When Melaniece opened her mouth to demand he fuck her already, he sank his sharp fangs into the sensitive skin just above her nipples. At the same time, his cock pushed into the tight channel of her pussy. Her demand came out a strangled scream of pure pleasure as she came on the spot. Incisors gently eased out of the little wounds and his mouth wrapped around her diamond-hard nipple and suckled her fiercely, drawing the sweet red elixir into his eager mouth with the same rhythm he stroked his steel-hard cock in and out of her gripping heat.

He released her luscious breast from his mouth with a soft pop. Michael sat back on his heels, pulling her fabulous body with him. Every soft moan, every sensual plea wrapped around his rod and stripped what little self-control he had. Completely uninhibited, she rode him hard until the thick natural waves of her hair became a beautiful tangle around her shoulders. The smell of her skin mixed with the heady fragrance of her sopping cunt was an aphrodisiac. He could feel her sheath fluttering from her first orgasm and knew it wouldn't take much to throw her into another.

Reaching down, he eased his thumb into the tight puckered hole of her anus. Melaniece arched wildly and yelled to the high ceilings.

"Oh dear god! Fuck me!"

Michael lost it. Pumping into her like a wild man, her hips and ass bouncing on his thighs, he rode her into oblivion. Rode her until her inner body gripped him like a vise, demanding he release his seed.

"Oh yeah, baby," he breathed raggedly. "Ride me, Mel. Ride my cock." There was no holding back from this woman. With a final thrust, he was planted at the entrance to her womb and exploded, splashing his thick cum against her greedy womb.

It was the most satisfying bout of hot, sweaty sex he'd ever experienced in his life. The woman was a treasure, a sinfully rich, unique treasure. And all his.

Heart hammering in his chest, a breathless groan erupted from his throat as he slid out of her tight cunt. His cock slapped heavily against his thigh, still hard.

"Wow," she breathed, trying desperately to catch her breath.

"Wow is right, baby. How 'bout some more wow?" Without giving her a chance to answer, he scooped her up into his arms and headed for her bedroom.

Melaniece found herself tossed unceremoniously to the middle of the bed. She lay there, watching Michael stalk her. The man walked back and forth around the bed as his eyes drank in her sweat-slick, overheated body. Suddenly she felt the urge to tease, seduce, yes, maybe even challenge him.

His eyes glinted in the dim light given off by a stream of moonlight that snuck in through a small opening in the drapes to fall across her naked torso. Knowing the light cream of the duvet underneath her would show off her body to advantage, she began. Never taking her eyes off him, she let her knees fall open so he could see his thick cream overflowing her pussy and disappearing down between her cheeks to wet the linens.

Parting her lips, her tongue came out to play and traced a wet path across her upper lip. Dipping her head, Melaniece watched him through her lashes as she made her next move. His mouth fell open, incisors peeking at her as her hand spread her dark labial lips to expose the pink juicy flesh inside.

"Don't push me, Mel. You have no idea what you're doing, woman."

She ignored the warning. Tightening the muscles of her vaginal floor Michael's deep breathing gave way to a shiver-inducing animalistic growl as he watched her pussy flex at him.

"I'm warning you, baby. Not a good idea."

Flipping over on her stomach, Melaniece pushed up on her knees and dropped her chest to the bed. Reaching back she spread her cheeks, looked back at him and wiggled her ass.

Moving faster than she could see, Michael was on her, burying his face in her sopping core. When he couldn't get close enough his fingers dug into her hips and raised her clean off the bed until only her elbows remained on the comforter. Damn! He was eating her upside down! Feasting, maddened, he ate her pussy like a starving lion let loose in the middle of a plump herd of gazelle. She tried to resist the havoc he wreaked on her senses, tried to pull into herself and maintain control. But it was impossible. He clamped onto the little hood of her clit and suctioned the overloaded bundle of nerves into his mouth.

Oh yes, she was definitely going to die of pleasure. But at least she would die fucking happy!

She tasted like vanilla and cream, savory and smooth mixed together in a irresistible syrup that teased his tongue. The more he lapped at her delicious pussy, the hungrier he became until his whole face was into the task. Her moans of ecstasy, wildly flailing legs and gasps of pleasure made him just want to gobble her up. His mind barely registered that the woman he devoured was yelling, begging. For him to stop? Was she crazy? He couldn't stop. He wasn't full yet.

"Michael! Oh dear god, please stop! I can't take any more. Please…" Finally her words began to register. The grip of her tight sheath on his tongue told the rest of the story. She had completely come apart. Had come so hard her stomach muscles clenched and she trembled from head to toe as her pussy gushed.

Still holding her suspended above the bed, he started to ease her down but couldn't resist one last lick. The length of his tongue dragged from the entrance of her slit to her sensitive clit. Her whole body convulsed then went completely limp, breathing harshly. He'd completely lost himself in the taste of his woman. How long had he been eating her? How many times had she come? If the soaked condition of his face was an indication, the answers were long and many.

But he was far from done.

Arranging her boneless body up on her knees, Michael held her by her wide, firm hips and plunged home. The sensation so intense, his shaft tingled and his balls ached. He wasn't going to last long. But then, neither was she.

"Michael, I can't take it. It just feels too good," she whimpered.

"But you will take it, Mel. Every. Inch." How the hell was he finding the mental bandwidth to sound halfway reasonable?

Driving into her heat, her mouth formed the words he wanted to hear. His name tumbled end over end from her lips. She coated him with her thick juices. Michael's cock swelled even further until the skin of his cock seemed stretched so tight he thought he would burst. A low humming sensation zipped from his balls up to the tip of his cock and back. He exploded inside her, filling her perfect cunt with his thick cum.

Long moments passed and he still felt his cock spurt with even the faintest flutter of her cunt. When he finally slid from her body, she was fast approaching blessed oblivion. But Melaniece had one more request before sleep claimed them both.

Rolling slowly over to her back to cuddle against his side, she whispered, "Michael, sweetie?"

"Yes, baby?" His words sounded lazy even to his own ears, but his heart was so full of happy contentment the feeling was beyond heady. It was indescribable. Mel was truly his in every way. A woman who had no reason to trust him now gave him far more than he could have ever dreamed possible. He felt whole and complete. Mated.

"Bite me, again?" she asked quietly.

"Mel, I shouldn't."

"Just one more time, sweetie, please?"

"Baby, I don't want to take too much."

"But you said I would never have to ask you twice," she cooed.

The woman was incorrigible. With a half-smile, he sighed, "I did say that, didn't I?"

She nodded, one hand stroking the sensitive spot on her neck, the other teasing the spot above her nipple where he'd bitten her earlier.

"Well, a man is only as good as his word," he said, lowering his mouth. Just one more time.

Chapter Five

ɛɔ

"Good morning, beautiful." The gentle nuzzling at her ear tickled. Melaniece hunched her shoulder to dislodge the offending lips with a giggle. Boy, she could really get used to waking up this way. Sweet kisses on down her neck. Strong but easy fingers traipsing over her bare shoulders. And lots of hard, hunky man spooning behind her. She rolled over with a contented sigh, inhaling his masculine scent. "Merry Christmas, handsome."

He dropped a quick kiss on her brow and whispered, "Merry Christmas, Mel." Wow, the man didn't even have bad breath. Maybe there was something to this vampire stuff.

The soft slide of the blankets moving down her body caused a shiver of anticipation. This insatiable lover had taken her during every waking moment of the night. If it hadn't been for the need for sleep, she knew he'd have made his home inside her sore but already tingling pussy.

The blankets down around her stomach, the exquisite rasp of his neatly trimmed nails scraping over her puckering nipples sent a yummy zing of streaking for her cunt.

She'd been awake for, what, almost three whole minutes and her body was already creaming for him? This was ri-goddamned-diculous. A chuckle escaped before she could stop it.

"What's funny? Does the thought of having a vampire on your ass amuse you?"

"No, the thought of my ass wanting to have a vampire on it is a little bit funny, yes," she said with a big grin. But just as quickly as her smile appeared, she felt a frown take its place as a sudden sadness enveloped her. She missed her kids.

"What's wrong, baby," Michael asked, his body unnaturally still next to hers, as if he'd suddenly been transformed into a marble statue or some other equally difficult-to-move object. Strange, she could actually *feel* the concern roll off him in waves the second her expression reflected sadness. But this was supposed to be a happy time. There was no way she would wreck a Christmas he and her children worked so hard to orchestrate by dwelling on her own selfish, though natural desires.

Tell me, I'll do anything to make you happy. Whoa, how'd he do that? It was as if he'd spoken right into her head.

There are some advantages to being mated to a vampire, Mel.

He'd done it again! And she could tell his words were meant with humor because she could...well, she could just tell. But how?

Can you hear me, too? she asked, thinking the words rather than speaking them.

Yes, but you don't have to close your eyes and scrunch up your face in order for me to hear you.

He was laughing at her! Bastard.

Yes, but it seems I'm your *bastard.*

Okay, all this mind talking was giving her a headache. Time to use words now.

"Actually, it's the face scrunching that's causing the headache, baby."

Chuckling at herself all the while, she delivered a smile-laced scowl. "Stop laughing at me and explain what just happened, damn it."

"Remember I explained bonding, and how my blood and semen will enhance you? This is one of the benefits."

"But I thought you said..."

"You won't and can't be turned, Mel, but my bodily fluids will affect you, baby. You'll heal faster and your senses will heighten, including some of the typically dormant ones."

"Like empathic and telepathic abilities?"

"Exactly," he crooned into her ear, his tongue sending a shiver up into her scalp. Obviously, he'd rather be doing something other than talking, but he continued anyway. "But you'll only be able to hear and speak to me telepathically, no one else. And I promise to give you privacy, sweetheart. I won't ever pluck thoughts from your head without permission."

"Can I read *your* mind if you're not speaking to me?" she asked eagerly.

"No, thank god! Not unless you'd possessed the ability already." Her mouth dropped open in dismay but he soon had her laughing again when he said, "Don't tell me that you, a biogeneticist, believed everything you've seen on TV?"

She couldn't help giving him a playful punch to the gut for the little sarcastic remark because she had indeed thought Bram Stoker's Dracula was paranormal gospel.

Reaching up to wrap her arms around his neck, she said, "Since I'm learning about your kind, tell me how I can get some of that good-smelling vampire morning breath."

"Kiss me," was his answer. And by the time he finished taking her mouth like he needed to draw his last breath from it, Melaniece was gasping. The craving erupted so rapidly along her nerve endings from just a gentle meeting of the mouths. It was the most decadent thing she'd ever experienced.

Now he eased up on his knees and planted himself squarely between her wide-spread thighs, leaned forward and licked the spot on her breast he'd bitten the night before. Warmth, no, *sizzling* heat spread outward from that spot just above her right nipple until it engulfed her entire upper body. She squirmed and writhed, grabbing two fists full of his hair to pull him closer.

"Michael, that feels so good. Will I ever get used to this insane reaction to you?"

"God, I sure hope not," he said, a satisfied smirk firmly in place. "Because now that I have you I'll never get enough of you, Mel."

Wrapping her legs around his waist, she was eager to get at what she really wanted — some Christmas cock. And since he was already gloriously naked, she didn't even have to unwrap his package.

"Well, stop talking and ease inside for a little good morning coochie. And while you're at it, bite me again."

"You won't ever have to ask me twice, baby. Never."

"Oooooh," was her only response as he sunk balls-deep and tenderly rocked her to completion.

Showered and wrapped in a soft, thick terry robe, Melaniece opened her bedroom door and was greeted by a welcome sound — noise, lots of it. There was the loud ripping of paper, laughing, talking. And very loud Christmas jazz spilling out of the surround sound speakers in the living room.

And cinnamon rolls! She'd recognize that smell anywhere. And there was only one person who could tickle her taste buds like this. Denise! Aw, just wishful thinking. The blizzard of the century had just blown out last night. There was no way the roads were clear enough...sigh. Oh well.

She took her time making her way down the hall and to the living room. Michael had obviously made a trip out to the garage as a good supply of wood was stacked next to the fireplace. The air was nicely warmed from the flames in the wide hearth. He held out a steaming mug of what looked like hot chocolate. Her eyes met his, the vivid green reminded her of precious gemstones. A devilish twinkle had her tilting her head in question when he winked and motioned his head toward the overstuffed loveseats while speaking privately along their newly forming bond.

Merry Christmas, Mel. I love you, baby.

"Merry Christmas, Mom!" two very familiar voices

chimed in unison. How in the world? Her mouth fell open at the exact moment two tall bodies exploded off the loveseat and practically tackled her and her mug of chocolate.

She looked back and forth between Michael Bannon and her children.

"How did you pull this off? How did you guys get back here?"

"They managed to get the roads cleared early this morning," Denise said, unwrapping her arms from around her mother and heading back to a basket of sweet rolls on the coffee table.

"So, here we are," Melvin said in his smooth tenor voice, leading her to the loveseat and handing her the first gift to open. The second she was seated, Michael eased his big body down next to hers and reached for another box and placed it in her lap. Soon she had more gifts to open than she had hands to open them.

Melaniece just couldn't believe it. At one point, she'd expected to have neither lover nor children here to share such a special holiday. And here she was with both.

Talk about a dream come true!

Also by TJ Michaels

∞

Egyptian Voyage
Jaguar's Rule
Primed to Pounce
Spirit of the Pryde

About the Author

ဆ

Born into a musically eclectic family, TJ's first love is music. She sings, even outside of the shower. She also loves to read. You'll find her with her head buried in a book every day of the week, whether it's her own creation or something snagged at the bookstore.

So, where does this writing stuff come from? Working for a pretty interesting organization allows her to interact with even more interesting customers. With an imagination expanded beyond belief after the birth of her two (now teenaged) children, spinning life's experiences into tales is a blast! And now that books have caught up to technology, TJ's eBook reader is shown no mercy, forced to entertain her at all hours of the day or night. Even in the dark!

Her favorite compositions are multicultural romances in various genres, some naughty, none nice. With several works in the wings, TJ loves to spin, create, and explore whatever world her mind decides to conjure. She currently lives in Colorado with her two children, and enjoys working as a technical resource with a company that provides analytic solutions to large pharmaceutical manufacturers.

TJ welcomes comments from readers. You can find her website and email address on her author bio page at www.ellorascave.com.

Tell Us What You Think

We appreciate hearing reader opinions about our books. You can email us at Comments@EllorasCave.com.

WITCH'S CURSE
Myla Jackson

 හ

Trademarks Acknowledgement

ᔕᔉ

Chapter One

ஐ

"Don't forget to check on her every day. She needs people, even if she says she doesn't. Trust me on this." Catherine moved through the eighteenth-floor studio apartment in the Hell's Kitchen district of New York City, straightening paintings, fluffing the bright pillows she'd added to the couch and watering the plants she'd grown from clippings off Dolly's huge collection of houseplants and herbs. Basically, she was delaying her descent to the building lobby for the annual tenants' New Year's Eve party.

I don't need a babysitter. Kindra's thought made her jump. So often lately, Kindra remained silent, preferring Catherine to handle everything in their shared existence.

"I'll check on her." Dolly stood by the door, a determined smile on her freckled face, although tears welled in her bright green eyes. "I can't believe you won't be here after tonight. I mean you will, but you won't. Ah hell. I'll miss you."

"You promised me you wouldn't get all mushy, so don't go there." Catherine spun away, refusing to give in to tears. Instead, she marched into the kitchen and yanked the refrigerator door open, snatching the bottle of Merlot from the sparkling clean shelves lined with healthy foods. All the groceries and cheerful decorations throughout the apartment would be her only legacy to Kindra to encourage her to maintain the healthy body Catherine had worked so hard to establish over the past year.

"I can't believe it's been a year since I met you." Dolly took the bottle from Catherine and tucked it under her arm. "I still have a vivid memory of Kindra standing on the ledge outside that window as the clock struck midnight." She nodded toward the tall window overlooking the bright lights of New York City. "If you hadn't landed in her body at that exact minute, she'd be dead."

You should have let me go. I only wanted peace.

"Peace my Aunt Fanny. You were sacrificing a perfectly good life and a boatload of talent. Think of all you've accomplished this year."

I didn't do it. You did. You're the strong one.

"And you're the one with all the talent. I can't paint my way out of a shoebox."

It's not enough.

Dolly's brows rose into the burnished copper curls brushing across her forehead. "You're doing it again."

Catherine's gaze moved to Dolly and she took a moment to remember Dolly was physically the only other person in the room. "Sorry. Kindra and I were having a little discussion about talent and wasting it."

Dolly stared at the paintings covering every free space on the walls of the apartment and some standing against the walls. "These are so beautiful. Why doesn't she put them in a gallery and sell them?"

No! They're not good enough!

"Kindra thinks they aren't good enough." Catherine shook her head. "Tell her, Dolly."

"I'm glad I know about your little secret, otherwise I'd think you had that multiple personality disorder." Dolly stared straight at Catherine and plunked her fist on one hip. "Kindra, get over it. These paintings are so stunning and full of emotion, they bring me to tears. The galleries will go wild over them. I have a buddy who works at a gallery down the street. I bet I can get them in there."

Catherine shook with the force of Kindra's fear. "Okay, okay. So you won't take the paintings to the gallery. It's okay.

Dolly won't make you do it." She shrugged at Dolly. "You can't force her."

Dolly fingered the silver pentacle amulet around her neck, the sign of Wicca. "How do you do that? How can you stand to have two people in one mind?"

"I'm the guest. Kindra owns the body and soul. At midnight, I move on and Kindra is on her own again." Though her words were flat and matter-of-fact, the closer she'd gotten to the midnight deadline, the more worried she'd been about Kindra. Could the young artist manage on her own? Would she try to commit suicide again?

"I think I would go nuts moving from body to body every year. How disconcerting to wake up in someone else's life. You must have really pissed off the powers that be."

Catherine's jaw tightened. "Just heed my warning. Don't use your powers for selfish reasons. Follow the Threefold Law to the letter."

Dolly snorted. "Like I have powers."

"We each have powers within us, we only have to learn to tap into them."

"I'm only a play witch, you're the real deal."

"Was." Ninety-nine years ago, she'd broken the Threefold Law of Wicca and used her magical powers to come between a man she *thought* she loved and the woman he *truly* loved. The cost for breaking the law was losing her powers and being cursed. And the curse couldn't have been a simple wart on her nose. No. The Witches Council had to come up with something more elaborate and fitting the crime.

They cursed her to an endless existence of living each year in a different woman's life. New Year's Eve a hundred years ago, when the clock struck twelve, her body died and her soul drifted into the body of another woman. For an entire year, she lived in that woman's life, in that woman's body, sharing all her hopes, fears, trials and desires. At midnight on

New Year's Eve, she moved to another and so it had been for ninety-nine years.

As midnight approached, Catherine knew her time in this body had reached an end. Kindra Marshall, her current host, wouldn't remember her when she'd gone, but she'd remember everything else from the past year and hopefully continue on where Catherine had left off.

From the moment she'd leaped into Kindra's body, Catherine knew she could help the woman. First thing was to get her down off the ledge and back on track in her life. She'd done all she could to bolster Kindra's spirit and boost her self-confidence. Her work showed it. Her talent for magnificent painting had grown in beauty and skill over the past year and she was ready to stand on her own.

Then why did Catherine have the feeling she was abandoning her?

"Any chance of you jumping into my head?" Dolly hooked her arm through Catherine's and walked with her to the door. "I'd sure like to know all the spells you know."

"I don't get to choose. I get what they give me." Catherine turned to her. "Do you remember the healing spell I taught you yesterday?"

"Yeah. I've never had such a quick recovery from a migraine. Thanks."

"See? You have powers. All you have to do is believe in yourself."

"I could say the same for you."

Catherine shook her head. "I screwed up. I'm locked into this deal until the council sees fit to free me."

"Well then, tell Kindra to take a break and let you have one night out."

"She doesn't mind and she's so quiet, I barely know she's there."

"Good." Dolly's lips turned up in a wicked grin. "'Cause tonight, we're going to get you laid."

"Remember, this isn't my body."

"Like you said, Kindra won't mind. She might even enjoy it." Dolly punched the down button on the elevator. "Call it your last night in town. We're going to party!"

* * * * *

"BJ, I don't feel much like celebrating. I think I'll just hang out here and watch a game on television." Sam Cade dropped his keys on the counter in the kitchen and pulled a six-pack of beer out of the fridge. He yanked a can out of the plastic rings and tossed it to his friend, BJ Drake.

"Oh no you don't." He popped the top and downed a long swig of the stuff before continuing. "You're going out with me even if I have to drag you. What are friends for if they can't be there when you get dumped?"

Sam glared at BJ. "Thanks for rubbing it in."

"Hey, you were the one who'd told me you saw it coming."

"Yeah, but somehow I didn't think it would be on New Year's Eve."

"I think Ashley was looking forward to the diamond earrings you gave her for Christmas." BJ grinned. "Didn't give them back, did she?"

"Not a chance." He should have broken it off earlier instead of waiting for Ashley to do the dumping. Six hundred dollars was a lot of money on a cop's salary. "I'll count it as an expensive lesson."

"To hell with the lesson, I'd ask her to give them back."

"Let's not talk about it anymore. I just want to move on." Sam headed for the couch, scooping the television remote up in one hand. "Who's playing tonight?"

BJ swiped the remote and stuffed it between the leather couch cushions. "I told you I wasn't letting you off light. I'm without a date, and you're without a date. It's New Year's Eve and we're going out."

Sam chuckled. "Sorry, I don't date guys."

BJ heaved a huge sigh. "A million starving comedians and I get stuck with you. Come on, at least let's see if there's any action at the party downstairs. I hear your building has one of the best New Year's Eve parties in the area."

"No, I'm not in the mood."

"Forget it, you're coming. I'll pick a woman for you, and you can pick one for me. Maybe we'll have more luck if we don't pick our own."

"There's a thought." Despite his desire to stay in and forgo the partying, he owed his friend for standing by him. "Okay, but only for an hour. If it's lame, I'm opting for the game on TV."

"Deal."

"And I get to pick the woman for you?" He rubbed his chin. "Let's see, should we be able to weigh her in pounds or tons?"

"Watch it, buddy, I can always return the favor."

Downstairs, the lobby was decorated in shiny gold streamers, silver balloons and enough sparkling lights to light all of Hell's Kitchen. Sam checked his watch. He owed BJ fifty-five more minutes.

The disc jockey played a soft, sultry tune. Sam was a practical guy who rarely hit the dance floor, but something about this song called out to him. The song was ripe for couples to do some serious belly-rubbin' and a dozen or more couples headed for the dance floor and to the music.

Damn. New Year's Eve and alone.

"Hey, I got one for you." BJ handed him a glass of champagne and pointed across the floor at a woman with long, golden blonde hair and a shimmering silver dress that hugged every curve of her body. He glanced around. "Where's mine?"

Sam missed BJ's question, his gaze captivated by the woman standing with a glass of champagne, a sad smile playing around her lips. Something about her pale blue eyes and the way she stared with longing at the couples dancing amid soft blinking lights called out to him. Despite his words to the contrary, Sam wanted to meet the woman. His feet shifted and he stepped out.

BJ's hand smacked him in the arm. "Did I do right by you, buddy?"

Boy, did he. No use letting him in on the news. BJ would just get a big head, besides, Sam wasn't sure he should move on his instincts to go meet the woman. "I guess she's all right."

"Now, where's mine? I'm anxious to meet the future Mrs. Drake."

Sam gave his friend an exasperated look. "Aren't you getting ahead of yourself?"

"I never date a woman I'm not willing to marry." BJ stared around the room. "So where is she?"

A woman with a shock of bright red curls joined the blonde. Sam squelched the chuckle rising in his chest. Perfect. "She's next to the blonde. Say hello to the future Mrs. Drake."

"Hey, I gave you a sex goddess and you give me Little Orphan Annie?"

"BJ Drake, I've never known you to pass on a challenge. Are you telling me you aren't going to give my choice for you a chance?"

BJ scowled. "Some friend you are." He grabbed another glass of champagne from a passing caterer. "Come on, let's go meet our futures."

Now that he was headed across the floor to meet the blonde, Sam wasn't so sure it was a good idea. What would he say? He'd been out of the dating scene for the most part, having been in a steady relationship for the past year and a half. His gut clenched and butterflies invaded. Storming a crack house wasn't nearly as nerve-racking as chatting up a strange woman who looked like a supermodel.

Since this was BJ's idea, Sam couldn't back out now. Not with BJ headed the same way. Tamping down his nerves, he attacked the task as if he were about to face a crime boss head-on.

When Sam and BJ were only halfway across the floor, two other men approached the women. They shook hands and then the men led them out onto the dance floor.

"Damn." BJ shook his head. "Guess if you snooze you lose. I was getting used to the idea of a redhead. I've never been with a redhead before."

"Songs only run for three minutes," Sam pointed out. Not that he cared. Or so he told himself, although the sense of relief he felt came out of nowhere when he realized the music had changed to a lively rock beat. The thought of the silvery blonde in another man's arms did bad things to his insides. Was it possible to be jealous even when you hadn't met the woman?

BJ glanced around the lobby. "I could use a beer."

"What, had enough champagne?" Sam's gaze followed the woman around the floor.

"Not particularly. Wanna hit the bar?"

"You go ahead. I'm fine for now." BJ could have stayed or gone, Sam wouldn't have known. He only had eyes for her. Was she a tenant in the apartment complex? Had he ridden the elevator with her a hundred times and never seen her? Was he becoming obsessed in only a few short minutes?

Impossible.

By the time the song ended, his hands were clenched in his pockets. A sultry rhythm took the place of the rock song and the man the blonde had been dancing with grabbed her hand when she would have walked away.

No way. All his cop instincts kicked in and Sam charged onto the dance floor like a bull moose in full rut.

The woman was shaking her head and tugging against the man's grip.

"Hi, sweetheart. I see you found a dance partner while I was away." Sam turned to the man whose hand was gripping the blonde's wrist. "Thank you for entertaining my wife while I ran up to check on the babysitter."

"Huh?" The man's grip loosened, and he dropped the woman's arm. "Excuse me." Then he ran like a scalded cat.

"You'd think I had the plague the way that guy took off." She rubbed at the red mark on her wrist from the guy's bruising fingers. "Thanks." Then she turned the full force of her smile on him.

The music swirled around them, weaving a tantalizing spell on Sam. Now that he'd done the cop thing, he should turn around and leave. He'd just been dumped by one woman—he didn't need the complications of another woman in his life so soon. He'd only be on the rebound. Wouldn't he? "Would you like to dance?"

"I suppose it's only right, after all we're married and have children together." She moved into his arms and laid her fingertips against his chest, her body straight, despite the music's intimate rhythm. "One problem…"

"If it's a bad guy, I'll shoot him." He tried to pull her closer, but she pushed against him. "Really, I'm a cop, no thug is too tough." Where was he getting this corny talk? Sam resisted the urge to slap his own forehead.

"Slow down, Lone Ranger. I don't need rescuing." She laughed, the sound better than the music and twice as intoxicating as the best champagne. Make that rum and coke. "I just want to know the name of my husband."

Her scent wrapped around him, the soft aroma of honeysuckle and moonlight. He should leave, now. "Sam. My name's Sam Cade." He leaned back. "And your name?"

"Cath—Kindra."

Why had she stumbled over her name? Was she afraid he was a tom cat on the prowl? "Kindra, huh?" He stared hard into her pale blue eyes. "You don't look like a Kindra."

Her smile faded and she looked away. "Well, that's who I am." *Take it or leave it* were the unspoken words on the end of her sentence.

The sad look had returned and Sam found himself wanting to erase it. Must be the cop in him always trying to rescue the damsel in distress. "Now that we know each other's name, maybe we can dance." Just one dance and he'd leave her and go back to his room to drink beer and watch a game on television.

She melted into his arms and together they moved around the dance floor, or rather swayed in place, all the right body parts rubbing. The rubbing turned into an intoxicating friction that had his cock hardening against her soft belly. He shifted to ease a little distance between them. She'd run screaming if she knew what he wanted to do to her here on the dance floor.

When they turned, she moved closer, her head falling back, exposing the length of her slender white neck. Had he been a vampire, he'd have drunk her in. As a mere mortal, he pressed his lips to the pulse beating erratically beneath pale, silky skin. The moment his lips touched her, he knew he was a goner. He wanted to bury himself deep in this woman's body and claim her for his own. His knee pushed between her legs and he pulled her hips close. To hell with keeping his distance. He wanted to feel her sliding against him, skin to skin, cock to pussy.

Her arms tightened around his neck and she trailed kisses along his jaw line until her lips met his.

As his mouth plundered hers, he forgot where they were, all his earlier troubles, everything but the taste of this woman who'd bewitched him from the moment he saw her across the room.

His tongue dueled with hers, his hands slipping lower to rest on the curve of her buttocks. When he came up for air, the room slowly materialized until he realized they'd been going at it in the middle of an empty dance floor. The DJ had taken a break and he and Kindra were the only people left standing.

Heat rose up his neck and into his cheeks.

Kindra blinked and looked around at the people staring at them. Her pale skin turned a delicate pink and she pushed away from him. "I'd say everyone would be convinced we're married now. If you'll excuse me..." She turned and slipped away, disappearing into the mass of people lining the makeshift dance floor.

Sam took two steps after her and stopped. Did he really want to follow a woman who made him completely forget where he was? A woman who made him forget he'd had a steady girlfriend until just a few hours ago?

His body throbbed, *Hell yes!*

All the more reason to go back to his room and take a cold shower.

"Sam. I didn't know you had it in you." BJ handed him a beer, his gaze following Kindra's movement toward the elevator.

"Had what in me?" Sam couldn't take his eyes off her, despite his determination to give her up.

"That dirty dancing thing you were doing out there. I didn't even know you could dance." He nudged Sam in the side. "By the way, thanks."

"For what?"

"Dolly."

"Dolly?" Sam's brain wasn't engaged in his friend's conversation.

The redhead had caught up with Kindra and stopped her before she could push the elevator button.

"The woman you picked for me. The redhead? Hellooo." BJ smiled and waved at her. "She invited me up to her place. I'm bringing the drinks." He held up a bottle of Chardonnay and two wineglasses.

Dolly was saying something to Kindra. The blonde shook her head and then glanced back toward him, that sad look shadowing her pale face. Dolly left her and crossed the room toward Sam and BJ, her frown turning upward the closer she got to BJ.

Kindra stood for a moment, her shoulders slumped, staring at the elevator. Then, as if she'd made a decision, she threw her shoulders back and punched the button.

Knowing that elevator door would open and Kindra would get inside and disappear galvanized Sam's feet into action. Why was he holding himself back from exploring the possibilities with this woman? Something told him that if he let her get away tonight, he might never have a chance to talk to her again.

As foolish as the thought was, the air couldn't move freely through his lungs until he caught up with her.

When Sam reached the elevator, Kindra had stepped inside and the doors had closed. Damn! He watched the digital readout of the floor numbers as she ascended into the building. Seventeen…eighteen…nineteen…

With only twenty-five floors, she had to stop soon. Unless…

Twenty-five.

The elevator stopped on the top floor. The floor leading to the rooftop.

Sam poked the up button and tapped his foot impatiently as the second elevator made its descent from the twelfth floor. *Hurry up!*

She had to be on the roof. If not, he'd pound on every door on the twenty-fifth floor until he found her. He had to see her again.

Once inside the elevator, he leaned against the railing and stared at his reflection in the shiny stainless steel wall in front of him. Was that man with the crazed look in his eyes really Sam Cade, the cool, professional cop? His short dark hair stood straight up as if even his hair was tense. He ran a hand across his head, hoping to smooth his hair and his nerves.

He'd never been this anxious to see anyone, much less a woman who was practically a stranger. For a moment he considered stopping on another floor and getting off. This was crazy. He was crazy.

Then the door opened on the twenty-fifth floor. Across the hallway were the steps leading up to the roof and her.

Chapter Two

ဢ

Catherine stood at the railing near the edge of the building fingering the small silver pentacle Dolly had given her as a gift on her last birthday. She wished she'd brought a wrap. Though the air was warmer than usual, it was still in the fifties, too cold to stay out for long.

After leaving the lobby, she couldn't go back to Kindra's empty apartment. With the full moon rising over the city, she had to get out for some air. This was her last night sharing Kindra's body. At the stroke of midnight, she'd start her new life in another woman's world.

Who would it be? A housewife, a businesswoman? A college student? A grandmother? For the past year, she'd inhabited the body of a young artist. An artist with serious emotional problems. Had Catherine not come to help her, she'd have been dead at the age of twenty-seven. Her fear for the girl was real. She didn't know how Kindra would hold up on her own.

"Hello, Catherine." A male voice drifted toward her as if on a breeze.

When she turned to see who'd called out her name, a violent shiver shook her from the back of her neck to the base of her spine. The night air was cool, but the trembling had nothing to do with the air temperature.

A man with shocking white hair and eyes such a pale blue they could be mistaken for ice stood three feet away from her. He wore a black trench coat and black trousers and had the hollow-eyed look of one who lived without the benefit of the sun for too long.

"Michael," she gasped, backing up a step until her bare back hit the cool metal of the rail.

"I've come to collect Kindra."

She frowned, her body stiffening. "No!" She held her hand out as if that would stop the Angel of Death from taking what he wanted. "I won't let you."

Michael shook his head, his lips twisting into a sad smile. "You can't protect her this time. When you're gone, she's mine."

It's okay, Catherine. Really.

"I won't let you die, Kindra. I won't let him take you." What she wouldn't give to have her magic back to toss a fireball at the Angel of Death. So what if it got her another ninety-nine years cursed. She'd do it for Kindra.

I want to go. I'm tired. I don't want to fight my demons.

"You're talented, beautiful and a gentle person. You deserve to live and share your talents with the world."

It's too hard.

The door leading to the stairs rattled. Someone was coming up to the roof.

Michael gave Catherine one last steady stare. "I'll be waiting." Then he was gone, as if he'd never even been there.

Kindra retreated to her silent place, leaving Catherine alone on the rooftop, the cold seeping into her skin.

Her knees buckled and she sank to the floor, her eyes dry, her heart aching for the young woman inside her. How could she stop the inevitable? She'd cheated death from claiming his prize a year ago, but she had no choice this time. A sob rose in her throat and she swallowed it down, burying her face in her hands.

"Kindra?" A deep male voice called out to her.

Gentle hands gripped her shoulders and lifted her to her feet. Then she was pulled against a solid wall of muscles and engulfed in a warm embrace. "What's wrong?" Sam Cade tipped her chin up and stared down in her eyes.

What could she say? By morning Kindra would be dead and Catherine would be somewhere else? A mirthless laugh escaped her lips, followed by a trickle of tears trailing down her cheeks.

Sam's thumb brushed a tear away, a frown creasing his forehead. "How can I help if you don't let me know what's bothering you?"

"You couldn't fix the problem if you tried. Even I can't."

"At least let me try."

She shook her head and pressed her cheek to his chest, listening to the sound of his heart beating against her ear. "Just hold me." She needed to feel him, touch him. He was so alive. Catherine wanted to feel alive again.

"You're freezing. Why don't you let me take you back to your apartment?"

"No!" Not yet. Not until midnight. Then she could let Kindra go back to her apartment and go to bed. Maybe she'd wake up just fine. Maybe Michael would give the girl a reprieve from death.

Maybe pigs flew in Manhattan.

"Then come back to my apartment. I have coffee and hot cocoa." He hooked his arm around her shoulder and led her away from the rails and through the doorway into the stairwell.

Numb and shivering now, Catherine's teeth rattled against each other. She let Sam take over. For so long, she'd had to be the strong one in every life she'd inhabited. Tonight she faced the knowledge her host would die. Suddenly the will to live welled up inside, filling her with a sense of urgency.

She turned to Sam. "Make love to me, Sam."

His eyes widened and he paused on the head of the steps leading down to the elevator. "Here? Now?"

"Yes. Here and now." She had to show Kindra how wonderful it was to live, how beautiful making love could be. Catherine wanted all those things herself. A chance to live with one man for the rest of her life. Kindra had to see how precious was her gift of a healthy body with nerves, sensations and emotions to feed the soul. Catherine slipped the straps off her shoulders and shivered. "Make this a night we'll both remember."

* * * * *

Sam's nostrils flared and his cock shot to attention. "I can't say I don't want this because, dammit, I do. But this isn't the place. I barely know you. You're cold and will catch your death."

"Excuses. Don't give them to me. I don't have time." She shook her hair back, her eyes flashing. All the sadness had disappeared, replaced by quiet determination. "Do you know what it's like to live like every day might be your last?" She unzipped the back of her dress. And let it slide to the floor. In nothing but her lacy white string bikini panties and high heels, she reached for the buttons on his shirt. "Make love to me, Sam Cade. Please. I need to feel alive."

He reached out to push her away, only his hands didn't cooperate. Instead of pushing her away, they slid over the smooth white skin of her shoulders and down to the gentle rise of her breasts. His thumb rubbed the peaked tips, enjoying the way she quivered beneath his touch.

She worked the buttons loose one at a time until she reached his waistband. With a surprising amount of strength, she yanked the shirt from his pants and whipped the top button open on his trousers. Before she unzipped, she cupped his cock and balls, her fingers curling over them, squeezing gently through the fabric. A moan rose from her throat and she pushed his shirt open, pressing her breasts against his chest. Her calf slid up the back of his leg and brought him closer until her crotch rubbed the top of his thigh. "I'm on fire. Fuck me, Sam. Here in the stairwell."

"What if someone comes up here?"

"Let them watch. I'm alive and I want it all."

Ashley hadn't responded to his caresses with this much passion since their first date. No. She'd never responded to him with a free flow of passion, the dirty words or the roving hands. Hands that were now digging between his skin and the fabric of his boxers to fondle his cock.

Then she was tugging the zipper down and pushing his trousers to the floor, her hands skimming over his buttocks, cupping them in her palms and pulling him against her.

Sam was taken aback by her aggressiveness but too turned on to back down now. He leaned forward, captured the rosy tip of her breast between his teeth and sucked it into his mouth, laving it until it pebbled into a firm knot. Skimming the valley of her cleavage, he rose to the other breast and nibbled and licked it until it matched the previous one.

Kindra's fingers dug into his scalp and pressed him to her, a moan rumbling in her chest. "More."

Sam dropped to one knee on the cold tiled landing and trailed a line of kisses over her torso and down her flat belly to the indention of her bellybutton. His fingers dipped further south to cup the mound of light-colored fur covering her pussy. The curly hairs were soft as spun silk and parted easily. With the tips of his fingers, he delved between her folds and found the hard little nub of her clit. Gently at first, he stroked her, dipping into her pussy for cream to lubricate his efforts. She was warm and wet there. He wanted to taste her nectar, swallow her juices and fuck her with his tongue.

As if she read his mind, the hands in his hair pushed his face lower.

His fingers smoothed a line between her cunt and her clit and he looked up at her as he lowered his lips to take her in his mouth, sucking her pussy. Her sweet cream wet his lips and tempted his taste buds and he dug his tongue inside, flicking and thrusting in the motion his cock longed to replicate.

His dick filled and straightened, taut with need. If he followed his cock, he'd slam into her and fuck her against the wall. But he wanted her to find pleasure first and her moans and the way her pelvis rocked to the rhythm of his tongue thrusts provided more stimuli to prolong his desire and build his craving to be inside her.

With his thumb strumming her clit, he moved it to the opening of her pussy and poked it in. He licked his way up to her clit and flicked and teased her until her fingers pulled on his hair so hard, surely it would come out. Then she cried out and her hips jerked with her release. Sam didn't let up. He persisted until she dragged him up by the hair.

When he stood to his full height, he cupped her butt cheeks in his palms and raised her up his body to wrap her thighs around his waist. Then he pushed her against the wall, both of her hands trapped in one of his over her head.

"Fuck me, Sam." She leaned close and flicked her tongue over his lips still coated with her essence. "Fuck me like there's no tomorrow."

He needed no more encouragement. With her pinned to the wall, he slid his rock-hard cock into her until he filled her completely. Her warmth and wetness ignited him and he slammed into her, thrusting in and out. The force of his strokes made slapping, slurping noises that echoed off the bare walls of the stairwell.

Kindra's head moved side to side as she gasped and grunted with the effort to match his pace. "Oh God, that feels so good. I've never felt so alive, so full. Harder!"

He thrust again and again until he burst over the edge, a cataclysm of sensations exploding in his body. As he returned to earth, he let go of her wrists and gathered her against him, his knees shaking.

The sound of the elevator bell rang in the hallway below, followed by shouts and giggling.

"Someone's coming." Sam lifted her off his cock and stood her on the landing. As she stood in dazed silence, he slipped her dress over her shoulders, feeling like a heel. He had his pants up and almost zipped when a crowd of party-goers filled the stairwell below.

"Whoa!" A young man shouted, grabbed for the railing and missed. "Looks like someone beat us to it."

The men shouted with laughter and the women giggled.

Anger shot through Sam. Not at the people below, but at himself for making love with a beautiful woman in such a public place. She deserved better.

"Did you save some for me?" another man shouted.

The dazed look disappeared from Kindra's face and she smiled. "Sorry, all fucked out. Guess you'll have to find your own." With that, she pranced down the steps and through the mob, her dress hanging open in the back, the crack of her ass showing. When she got to the bottom, she looked back at him and quirked an eyebrow. "Are you coming? The night's not over until midnight."

Sam grabbed his shirt and took the stairs downward, two at a time, surrounded by wolf calls and slaps on the back.

When Sam joined Kindra, he zipped her dress up to shut off the view to the others.

A man shouted from the top. "Hey, you forgot something." In his hand, he twirled the lacy white panties Kindra had worn.

Sam would have run up the stairs and punched the man, taken the panties and come back down.

Kindra stopped him.

"You keep them for good luck." Then she hooked her arm through Sam's and led him to the elevator.

The thought that she wasn't wearing underwear made his cock throb anew. Was the incident in the stairwell a once-only event? Would she want to go at it again? Was he crazy to think he could do it again so soon after the last mind-blowing fuck?

Once the elevator doors closed, Sam punched the button for his floor.

When Kindra didn't reach for her own floor, Sam almost whooped aloud. He assumed she was going to come with him to his place where they could finish what they'd started.

When he tried to slip into the shirt he held, a slim white hand yanked it from his fingers and tossed it in the corner.

"Uh-uh." She shook her head and ran her fingers over his chest and downward. When she got to his pants, she made quick work of unzipping his fly and letting his cock spring free.

She stepped away from him, gathered the hem of her dress and lifted it above her waist. "I've always wanted to do it in an elevator." Then she propped one high-heeled shoe on the railing, exposing her glistening pussy to him.

Sam's mouth watered. "Aren't you afraid the doors will open?"

"That's the fun of it. The danger, the uncertainty. Isn't that what life is all about? Living each moment, in the moment?" She ran her hand over her soft blonde curls and dipped a finger into her pussy. "Hurry, before we get to your floor."

Sam didn't need any more of an invitation. He wrapped her legs around him and slid deep inside her warm, wet cunt, his cock filling and swelling the deeper he went.

She braced her palms on his face and made him look her in the eye. "I want you to know, I don't do this with perfect strangers. It's just tonight being New Year's Eve and well...you. You're just what this body needs." Then she pressed her lips to his, her tongue sweeping along the seam until he opened his mouth enough to let her inside.

What did she mean by *just what this body needs*? Though the thought puzzled him, it didn't worry him as much as the elevator opening and revealing them to the public. How would that look if the cop got arrested for indecent exposure?

The fear of getting caught spiked his adrenaline and he pumped all the faster. When the elevator bell dinged he jumped.

Kindra laughed out loud, a breathless sound, her eyes alight with mischief. "You should see your face."

The door slid open and he glanced over his shoulder, fully expecting to see Old Lady Benton with her little white Malti-poo mutt on a leash to go outside. Anticipating her outraged expression, Sam released the breath he'd held. The hallway was blessedly empty.

Grabbing her beneath the legs, without breaking their intimate connection, he half-ran, half limped down the hallway to his apartment. There he fumbled in his pants pocket for the key.

"Damn!" If he could only get inside before someone saw them so that he could finish what they'd started in the elevator.

Kindra's laughter filled the hallway, the sound contagious.

By the time he unlocked his door and fell inside, he was laughing right along with her and almost dropped her on the hardwood floor.

By the time they made it to the bedroom, his cock had slipped from inside her and gone soft. He set her on her feet and cupped her face in his hands. "I love your laughter and your smile."

The sad look returned, darkening Kindra's pale blue eyes to a rain-cloud gray. She tossed his shirt across a chair, her hands burning a path from his shoulders, down his arms and to his hips. "I've never had as much fun making love and probably never will again."

"Never say never." He wanted to make her laugh again, to bring out the smile he was quickly learning to love. "We always have tomorrow."

Her forehead wrinkled into a frown and she stared up into his eyes. "Sam, promise me something?"

"Anything." He slid the straps of her gown from her shoulders, following their descent with his lips. A kiss across her collarbone, one on the tip of her shoulder, another in the crook of her elbow. Her gown slipped down to her hips.

"If I'm not the same tomorrow, be gentle. Be patient."

He looked up, confused by her statement. "Are you telling me you had too much to drink tonight?"

She shrugged, the act making the gown slither to the floor. Naked except for her high heels, she was glorious. "Something like that."

"I promise I'll be patient." He pulled her against him, his cock swelling and nudging against her belly. "But for now, I'm anything but patient. I want to be inside you, filling you, fucking you." Then he kissed her, his hands sliding over her ass, his knees nudging her legs apart. If he didn't take her in the next few minutes, he'd explode. Then when he was a little more in control, he'd ask her what the hell she meant by not being the same tomorrow.

* * * * *

Catherine bounced from desolation and despair to joy and laughter and back to desolation. How the hell did she expect Kindra to react to all the stimuli she was subjecting her to?

As she backed toward the bed, her pulse pounding against her ears, her body on fire with desire, she sent a silent entreaty to her borrowed soul. *Kindra, this is the kind of thing you'd be missing if you give it all up.*

Kindra shivered, not in fear but in anticipation. *I could never do this on my own. You are my strength.*

When the backs of her legs bumped against the mattress, Catherine caught her breath. The hallway was exhilarating, the elevator exciting, but this...in a bed, like real lovers, was dangerous. Yet she couldn't slow the momentum, didn't want to. *Come along for the ride, Kindra.*

Gladly. I live through you, Catherine.

Her body an inferno of need, Catherine couldn't stop now, but she wanted Kindra to know this could be hers. *Let me show you what making love with a real lover feels like.*

I'm with you. Kindra's spirit lifted as if giving Catherine permission to show her the magic of making love.

Catherine scooted her ass up onto the bed, her legs still dangling over the side. She pushed aside the inner voice and let herself be in the moment with Sam.

He shucked his shoes and dropped his pants to the floor, his gaze locked with hers. "You're beautiful, Kindra."

Catherine couldn't help sharing one more comment with Kindra. *See? He thinks you're beautiful.* She pushed aside her own stab of envy for this woman whose perfect body wasn't hers. At one time she'd had her own vessel. She'd been blonde and blue-eyed, considered a beauty in her own right. But she'd squandered her looks and powers. Surely she could convince Kindra not to squander hers.

As Sam approached her, Kindra remained silent, a touch of fear edging its way past Catherine's desire.

Then Catherine was alone in her head, appreciating the jutting evidence of Sam's lust. His cock thrust out straight and thick.

With her pussy creaming, Catherine licked her lips, anxious to taste him.

Before he could reach the bed, she slid off and dropped to her knees, gathering his length in her hands. "You are magnificent."

Sam's chuckle cut off in a strangled sound when her lips wrapped around the tip of his cock.

Catherine glanced up.

His head was tipped back, his eyes closed. "Can't say anyone's ever called me magnificent. Sexy or handsome, maybe, but not magnificent." His words, an attempt at humor, were forced through clenched teeth.

Catherine ran the tip of her tongue across the velvety tip of his cock, dipping into the hole at the top. "How can you be so hard when your skin is so soft?" She didn't give him a chance to answer. Didn't want an answer, just wanted to experience every sensation. Her fingers feathered downward. Cupping his balls, she squeezed gently while she took him into her mouth.

Strong hands laced through her hair, pulling her closer until his penis touched the back of her throat. When she pulled back, he hissed, his hands clenching.

She settled into a steady rhythm, drawing him in and out of her mouth. Her hands grasped his hips, rocking him in and out to her strokes.

The tension built in the muscles of his ass, the thrusts growing faster and more uncontrolled. Suddenly, he stopped, his body going rigid, then he tried to push her away.

Despite the grip he had on her hair, Catherine held his hips in place and sucked his cock, coaxing him to come inside her mouth.

Warm liquid squirted into her throat and filled her mouth. She swallowed and teased the base of his cock with her tongue. He tasted of salt and musk, a heady combination that made her body burn for him.

When his cock quit throbbing, Sam pulled Catherine to her feet and lay her down over the edge of the bed.

Before she could protest, not that she would, he dropped to his knees, spreading her legs wide. One at a time, he draped her thighs over his shoulders, pressing kisses to the sensitive skin. He plunged his index finger into her pussy and twirled it around, scraping the inner lining of her cunt, teasing and flicking. When he removed the finger, he traced a slick path up to her clit and rubbed the nub, soaking it in her own juices. His tongue followed his finger, dipping into her cunt then licking a line up to her clit where he settled in to wreak havoc on her.

Lapping, nibbling and flicking raised her to a heightened sense of desire so great she felt as if she'd spontaneously combust. Was he a wizard capable of magic? Catherine couldn't believe a mere mortal could elicit wave upon wave of lust from her body.

As she crested and road the waves, his fingers dug into her cunt, filling and stretching the walls, pumping in and out in the same rhythm as his thrusting tongue. His thumb probed the tight ring around her ass, pressing against the entrance without going in.

Catherine's fingers clenched in his hair, her moans growing louder and more frequent. When she hit the top, she screamed out his name.

Sam's thumb pushed through her anus and his fingers shoved into her cunt as hard and deep as he could. All the while he flicked at her clit in a frantic pace meant to blow her mind.

And it did.

A kaleidoscope of sensations tumbled through Kindra's body, the force so great it rocked Catherine's world too. Never in nearly one hundred years had she felt such intensity, nor would she in another hundred years.

As she fell back to the earth, another ache built within. She wanted Sam inside her, filling the emptiness, warming her in places no one had touched in so long. So what if this wasn't her body, so what if after tonight she'd never see him again. Tonight was her chance at a little happiness. To hell with tomorrow.

Sam rose from the floor and flipped her over to where her tummy lay across the bed, her ass bumping against his hard cock. He pressed the tip of his penis to the lips of her cunt hovering on the edge. His large, calloused hands gripped her hips and he eased into her.

This is different. Kindra's voice popped into Catherine's lust-muddled brain.

"Do you like that?" Catherine spoke aloud, for a moment forgetting Kindra's voice was inside.

"You have to ask?" Sam thrust again, his hard cock speaking of his satisfaction.

Harder. It feels so good.

"Harder, Sam. Fuck me harder." She pushed up on her hands, rocking back against him, meeting each of his thrusts. The sound of his thighs slapping against her ass grew louder each time he plunged inside her.

Sam reached forward and palmed her breasts, massaging and pinching the tips as he fucked her like a dog.

The position was animalistic, it was an incredible turn-on and Catherine climbed that ragged peak to orgasm. Then she caught a glimpse of them in the mirror over the dresser. His muscular body riding her pale, sleek one. Catherine rocketed to the top, her body jerking with the force of her release.

She collapsed on the bed, her arms shaking so much she couldn't hold herself up. Sam collapsed over her, still inside her, still throbbing his own release. When his cock stopped spasming, he rolled to the side and pulled them both up to the pillows.

Once Catherine rested in the crook of his arm, her face pressed to his chest, he let out a shaky breath. "You're incredible."

"Same to you." She ran her fingers over the coarse hairs sprinkled across his chest and moved a thigh over one of his legs until her cunt pressed against his skin. She could go at it again and again all night long. If only she had all night.

Her head shot up. "What time is it?" Holy crap. She'd forgotten about the time. She couldn't leave Kindra in Sam's arms. She'd be completely freaked out when Catherine left her body.

Sam twisted his head around and fumbled with the alarm on the nightstand. "It's eleven-fifty-three. Why? Did you want to ring the New Year in?" He pressed a kiss to her hair and sucked the lobe of her ear between his teeth. "I can think of better ways to welcome in the New Year."

Panic rose up inside her, threatening to choke off her air. "I can't. I have to go."

"Why?" The arm around her tightened.

She leaned into him and pressed a kiss to his chest then moved up until her lips hovered over his. "I have to."

"When can I see you again?"

As if a knife cut into her, Catherine sucked in her breath, reminding herself that in five minutes she'd be God knew where in someone else's body, starting all over. Swallowing hard on the lump in her throat, she sent the silent question to Kindra, *Do you want to see him again?*

Fear racked her, making her entire body shake. *I can't.*

Catherine dropped a kiss to his lips, delving deep, knowing this would be their last. "I can't see you anymore." A tear slipped from her eye dropping to his cheek. Before he could form a response, she leaped off the bed. "I have to go."

She scooped her dress from the floor and stepped into it, zipping it the best she could as she scrambled for her heels.

"What the hell?"

"I can't explain. I can't see you again." She couldn't face him, couldn't witness the look of betrayal in his eyes.

"Are you married?"

"No." When she spotted her shoes, she grabbed them and ran for the door. With only minutes to spare, she had to get out. But she couldn't resist one last look.

Sam had climbed from the bed and was reaching for his trousers. His muscular, naked body was beautiful in the lamplight. She'd really miss him.

He was stepping into one trouser leg when Catherine jerked the door open. She had to get to the elevator before he did. If she left Kindra's body before she got away, Kindra would go nuts. Catherine punched the button on the elevator, holding her heels looped over one finger in her other hand. "Hurry! Hurry!"

As the doors slid open, Sam emerged from his apartment. "Kindra, wait!"

Catherine dove into the elevator and hit the button that closed the doors. Her fingers punched the lobby button. She didn't want to get off on her floor in case Sam followed her to Kindra's apartment. As the elevator descended, she counted the seconds. It must be midnight by now. When would her soul float free and Kindra be on her own?

When she reached the lobby level, she could hear the happy shouts of the party-goers ringing in the New Year. This was it.

"Take care, Kindra. I love you and please give your life a chance."

I love you too, Catherine. Don't worry about me. I'll be all right.

As she stepped into the crowded lobby, Dolly descended on her. "Catherine or Kindra?"

"Both." Catherine grabbed Dolly's hand and held on, not wanting to go but knowing she had to.

"The clock is striking midnight as we speak." Dolly hugged her. "I'll always be here for you. You know that."

"I know." Catherine kissed her cheek. "Be happy, Dolly. And watch out for Kindra."

"I will." Dolly's eyes glistened with unshed tears.

Myla Jackson

A tingling sensation started in her toes and worked its way up her legs into her torso. "Goodbye, Dolly. Blessed be."

Though Dolly's tears fell in earnest now, Catherine couldn't reach out and comfort her friend. She'd risen above the gathering, weightless and disembodied from Kindra's mortal being.

There in the middle of the dance floor stood Michael, dressed in black, his shock of white-blond hair a striking contrast to the somberness of his clothing. Invisible to all those around him, his gaze was locked with Kindra's.

"No!" Catherine could see all that was going on, but she was powerless to do anything about it.

Kindra moved toward Michael, her steps slow yet steady.

"Kindra? Are you all right?" Dolly held onto Kindra's arm and walked alongside her.

"I'm fine," she answered in a monotone voice, her gaze fixed in front of her.

"Shouldn't we go back to your room, sweetheart?" Dolly tugged the woman's arm to no avail.

"No, I think I'd like some fresh air." By this time, they'd reached the lobby doors exiting out onto the busy streets of Hell's Kitchen.

Dolly held tight to Kindra's arm. "No, you can't go out there."

Kindra turned to Dolly, her face set and strangely at peace. "Let me go, Dolly. It's what I want."

"No. Catherine made me promise."

"Go back to the party, Dolly." She peeled Dolly's hands off her arm and pushed through the door.

Catherine moved to follow, knowing she could breeze through the entrance as if glass, brick and mortar meant nothing.

Behind her, she heard a male voice call out, "Kindra!"

Sam pushed his way through the crowd, a frantic frown creasing his forehead.

Kindra didn't stop. She followed Michael out onto the street.

Catherine burst through the walls of the building just as Kindra reached the curb to the busy street. "Michael, don't do this."

"It's her time, Catherine. I've come to collect a soul, and I won't leave without it." Michael held out his hand to Kindra. "Come."

If she had a body, she'd throw it in front of Kindra to stop her, but Catherine was nothing more than a lifeless soul. "Please, Michael. If you want a soul, take mine. Kindra's young and has so much talent. She deserves to live. Spare her and take me."

Michael's brows rose on his forehead. "Take you? You stole her from me a year ago today. Why should I take you?"

"I don't know. Just do it. Kindra is a gentle soul who wouldn't hurt a fly. She deserves to live more than I do. I'm mean and nasty. That's why the council cursed me. I deserve to die. Please, Michael. Don't take Kindra."

Michael rubbed his chin for a moment and then looked up to where Catherine's soul hovered. "No." Then he stuck out his hand.

Powerless, Catherine watched in horror as Kindra stepped off the curb in front of a speeding car. The car hit her in the side, flinging her back to the curb like a rag doll.

At that exact moment, Sam spilled from the doorway onto the sidewalk. "Fuck!" He grabbed the closest person to him. "Call 911. Now!" Then he flung the man to the side and dove to the pavement where Kindra lay as still as death.

Sam felt for a pulse. "Kindra! Talk to me. Please talk to me. Oh God. No pulse." He breathed into her mouth and leaned his palms into the middle of her chest in the rhythm of one trained in CPR. "Someone please call 911." Sam breathed into her mouth again.

Catherine watched, her heart breaking at Sam's desperation. Then she felt a presence beside her, a warmth like a hand being placed on her shoulder. "Kindra?"

"Yes, Catherine. It's me." Kindra's voice sounded in her mind.

"Why did you do it?"

"I wasn't meant for this life. I wish you'd understand."

"But what about Sam? Now he has no one." And neither did she. The thought of going into another woman's body weighed on her like a pall of incredible sadness.

"He loves you, not me." Her voice faded as if swallowed in the depths of a cave.

"You don't know that for sure!" Catherine shouted, angry at the senseless death of a beautiful, talented woman. "It's selfish to take your own life. Don't you know what a gift it is to live in your own body?"

"Then accept my gift." The warmth of Kindra's spirit drifted away, her words resonating in Catherine's soul.

Her anger ran off like rain in a gutter until her thoughts grew numb. "Will you be happy, Kindra?" Catherine called out.

"I'm at peace."

What about Sam? Would he blame himself for Kindra's death? The tingling began again, a harbinger of her transition into another person's body and borrowed soul. Would she ever know what happened to Sam?

Her view blurred and distilled into blackness.

Chapter Three
ೋ

The body she landed in hurt all over, like being born again, only worse. And there was a heavy pressure pushing against her chest in a steady rhythm. Then someone's lips descended onto hers and breathed into her lungs.

The touch of those lips felt so familiar, so beautiful. The scent of mint and leather filled her nostrils. He smelled like...Sam.

Catherine lifted her arms and wrapped them around the person's neck and kissed him like there was no tomorrow and he kissed her back.

His hands ran through her hair and across her body. "Kindra! Please tell me you're all right."

"Sam?" she whispered. When she opened her eyes, she was no longer a disembodied spirit watching the scene of Kindra's suicide from above, she was in Kindra's body lying on the pavement with Sam leaning over her.

His brows were drawn together, his eyes suspiciously bright. "Can you hear me?"

"Of course," she replied, her voice sounding more normal. She tried to sit up, but his hand on her chest held her down. "What happened?" Why had she ended up back in Kindra's body?

"You were in an accident. Can you move? Are you hurting anywhere?"

She experimented with each body part, moving her arms, then her toes and when she got to her legs, pain shot through her left hip. "My hip. It hurts."

"Lie still. The ambulance will be here in just a minute." He leaped to his feet, his gaze panning the busy street to the left and the right. "Damn, where's that ambulance?"

"Kindra?" Dolly knelt down beside her and lifted her hand. "Are you okay, honey? Are you feeling yourself?" She stared down into Catherine's eyes as if searching.

"I'm here, Dolly."

The redhead leaned close and kissed her cheek, whispering into her ear, "Is it you, Catherine?" She leaned back to study her.

Catherine nodded.

Dolly's eyes welled with moisture and she mouthed the word, *Kindra?*

"Gone," Catherine said quietly.

"How? Why?" Dolly asked in a quiet tone.

"I don't know why." Catherine's body tingled, a wave of heat radiating throughout as if her spirit revived as well as the body she inhabited. It began at her center and spread throughout her being until she felt as if heat and light radiated from her fingertips.

"What the hell?" Dolly stood back, her eyes widening.

"What?" Catherine asked. Of all the others gathered around, gawking, no one was staring at her like Dolly as if she'd grown a horn in the middle of her forehead.

Dolly pressed a hand to her mouth and scanned the faces of people to her left and her right before she dropped to her knees and said in a hushed, reverent tone, "You're glowing."

Catherine lifted a hand. Just as Dolly said, her skin glowed an eerie yellow light. The same light she'd witnessed when she'd come of age as a witch.

She flexed her fingers and little bolts of electricity arced through the air.

"They're back!"

"Who's back?" Dolly's forehead creased in confusion.

"Not who, my powers are back!" Catherine grabbed her friend's hand and squeezed so tightly the woman grimaced. Joy filled every corner of her heart and for a moment she felt like shouting out loud.

Then she reminded herself of the cost of her regained life and powers. Kindra had given her the gift of her body. Catherine wouldn't be here without the young woman's determination to move on. Catherine attempted to sit up.

Sam immediately dropped to his haunches. "Sweetheart, you need to lie still until you can see a doctor. We don't know what kind of damage you received until they do X-rays."

"I'm okay, Sam. Really." She shifted to sit up and pain knifed through her hip. Despite her determination to hide her pain, she couldn't help grimacing.

The sound of sirens echoed off the buildings, moved closer.

Catherine cast a desperate glance at her friend. "Dolly, do you remember that poem I taught you last night?"

Sam stared from Catherine to Dolly and back. "Poem? You've been hit by a car and you want to recite poetry?"

Dolly nudged Sam aside. "What poem?" Her eyes widened and a smile lifted the corners of her lips. "Oh that poem!"

"Please hold my hand." Catherine reached out to her friend and in quiet voices they recited the words.

"Invoke the goddess of the moon

Invoke the god of the sun

Collect thy body and spirit

Combine their powers as one

Thy flesh, thy bone,

Thy heart and thy soul

Melded together

Shall heal as a whole.

So mote it be."

Catherine nodded and, together, she and Dolly closed their eyes, drawing from within and without on the strength of the earth.

"Kindra?" Sam's voice called to her, his hand cupping her face. "The ambulance is here."

She opened her eyes and smiled up at him, loving the way his brows dipped downward when he was concerned. "I don't need an ambulance." To prove it, she pushed to her feet and stretched. Her body was whole again. No pain, no bruises.

Her body.

How strange to think this vessel of flesh and bone would now be hers. After ninety-nine years of the curse, she'd resigned herself to sharing. Hollowness existed where Kindra's soul had been. Catherine mourned her loss, yet somehow she knew Kindra was where she wanted to be and her tortured soul was at peace.

"I still think you should let a doctor see you," Sam insisted.

"I'm perfectly fine. I don't need a doctor." She threw her arms around Sam and hugged him, the joy of the New Year filling her to full. She winked over her shoulder at Dolly. Dropping her voice to a low, seductive level, she whispered into Sam's ear. "I'll let you count all my ribs and search for bruises if it'll make you feel better. I know it'll make me feel better. What do you say?"

He pushed her to arm's length, scowling at her. "You need to see a doctor. You were out, your heart stopped, the works. I insist."

"And waste the rest of the night? Please, Sam. Let me show you how well I am."

Emergency medical personnel piled out of the ambulance and rushed forward.

Sam glanced from the medical crew to her and back. "At least let the EMTs look you over."

"Deal." She turned to the first man dressed in the navy blue uniform of the New York City Emergency Medical Services and grinned. "I'm feeling better."

After the man ran through her vital signs and shone lights in her eyes, he shrugged. "You appear to be fine. I recommend you go to the hospital for observation in case you have a concussion. But it's your call."

"Thanks." She hooked her arm through Dolly's and Sam's. "I think I'll stay here with my friends. We have some celebrating to do."

After the ambulance left without an additional passenger, Dolly pulled her arm free of Catherine's. "I have some serious dancing to do with a cop inside. If you'll excuse me."

"By all means, dance." When Dolly had disappeared inside, Catherine felt shy standing alone with Sam, which was foolish after the intimacies they'd shared a few minutes before. "So, Sam, what do you want to do with the rest of the evening?" She didn't look up at him, afraid he'd tell her to get her whacky self out of his life. What must he think after she'd run from his apartment and out into the street like a maniac?

"I don't know." He pushed a hand through his hair, making it stand on end. He stood in his untucked, wrinkled shirt and shoes without socks, looking sexier than any man had a right to. "It's been a crazy night."

She laughed. "You're telling me. I can't begin to explain it all, but I bet I can make it up to you." With a smile, she held out her hand. *Please, take it.* With all her heart she wished he'd take her back to bed and make love to her and only her.

For a moment, he stared down at her hand. "I've been a cop for eight years and this whole situation just doesn't seem right. My instincts have never been wrong." His gaze met hers.

"Do your instincts tell you that I'm bad news?" She held her breath, waiting for his answer. He might decide she was a flake and not worth the trouble. Catherine wanted him so badly her body ached, a delicious sensuous ache.

After a moment's hesitation, his lips curled upward in a smile and he shrugged. "No." A twinkle glinted in his eyes when he gave her a mock frown. "But I'm watching you." He took her hand and pulled her into his arms.

Her heart bursting with happiness, Catherine leaned up on her toes. "I'm counting on it." She kissed him on the lips and pressed her body close to his. "I'd much rather you were watching me in the nude though."

"Despite my better judgment, I have to agree." He returned her kiss and pressed one to the tip of her nose. "I've only known you for less than a day, but I think you've bewitched me."

Catherine straightened, her face going serious. "No, sir. I swear. I wouldn't bewitch you or anyone else. Promise." She held her hand up as if taking an oath.

He laughed and nibbled her ear. "I believe there's an elevator with our name on it."

"You're on."

They ran through the crowded lobby and into an empty elevator. Once the door closed behind them, Sam lifted her skirt, Catherine unzipped his trousers and they were making love before they hit the fourth floor.

As Sam drove his hard, thick cock into her pussy, Catherine wrapped her legs around his waist, threw her head back and shouted, "Blessed be."

Also by Myla Jackson

Ellora's Cavemen: Dreams of the Oasis I (*anthology*)
Jacq's Warlord *with Delilah Devlin*
Sex, Lies & Vampire Hunters
Shewolf
Trouble with Harry
Trouble with Will

About the Author

∞

I've written for Ellora's Cave since September of 2006 when my first release Trouble with Harry came out. Since then, I've expanded from reluctant genies to werewolves, chameleons, vampires and witches. For me, reading and writing gives me the freedom to explore strange new worlds and write the characters and creatures clamoring to escape my mind. I like writing everything from romantic comedy to dark and sexy suspense. Mostly I like to escape into other worlds whether grounded in reality or complete fantasy. Come...escape with me!

Myla welcomes comments from readers. You can find her website and email address on her author bio page at www.ellorascave.com.

Tell Us What You Think

We appreciate hearing reader opinions about our books. You can email us at Comments@EllorasCave.com.

Why an electronic book?

We live in the Information Age—an exciting time in the history of human civilization, in which technology rules supreme and continues to progress in leaps and bounds every minute of every day. For a multitude of reasons, more and more avid literary fans are opting to purchase e-books instead of paper books. The question from those not yet initiated into the world of electronic reading is simply: *Why?*

1. *Price.* An electronic title at Ellora's Cave Publishing and Cerridwen Press runs anywhere from 40% to 75% less than the cover price of the exact same title in paperback format. Why? Basic mathematics and cost. It is less expensive to publish an e-book (no paper and printing, no warehousing and shipping) than it is to publish a paperback, so the savings are passed along to the consumer.

2. *Space.* Running out of room in your house for your books? That is one worry you will never have with electronic books. For a low one-time cost, you can purchase a handheld device specifically designed for e-reading. Many e-readers have large, convenient screens for viewing. Better yet, hundreds of titles can be stored within your new library—on a single microchip. There are a variety of e-readers from different manufacturers. You can also read e-books on your PC or laptop computer. (Please note that

Ellora's Cave does not endorse any specific brands. You can check our websites at www.ellorascave.com or www.cerridwenpress.com for information we make available to new consumers.)

3. *Mobility.* Because your new e-library consists of only a microchip within a small, easily transportable e-reader, your entire cache of books can be taken with you wherever you go.

4. *Personal Viewing Preferences.* Are the words you are currently reading too small? Too large? Too... ANNOYING? Paperback books cannot be modified according to personal preferences, but e-books can.

5. *Instant Gratification.* Is it the middle of the night and all the bookstores near you are closed? Are you tired of waiting days, sometimes weeks, for bookstores to ship the novels you bought? Ellora's Cave Publishing sells instantaneous downloads twenty-four hours a day, seven days a week, every day of the year. Our webstore is never closed. Our e-book delivery system is 100% automated, meaning your order is filled as soon as you pay for it.

Those are a few of the top reasons why electronic books are replacing paperbacks for many avid readers.

As always, Ellora's Cave and Cerridwen Press welcome your questions and comments. We invite you to email us at Comments@ellorascave.com or write to us directly at Ellora's Cave Publishing Inc., 1056 Home Avenue, Akron, OH 44310-3502.

erridwen, the Celtic Goddess of wisdom, was the muse who brought inspiration to story-tellers and those in the creative arts. Cerridwen Press encompasses the best and most innovative stories in all genres of today's fiction. Visit our site and discover the newest titles by talented authors who still get inspired - much like the ancient storytellers did, once upon a time.

Cerridwen Press

www.cerridwenpress.com